MW01146486

Not They Who Soar

Books by Amanda Flower

The Katharine Wright Mysteries

To Slip the Bonds of Earth
Not They Who Soar

The Amish Candy Shop Mysteries

Assaulted Caramel
Lethal Licorice
Premeditated Peppermint
Criminally Cocoa (ebook novella)
Toxic Toffee
Botched Butterscotch (ebook novella)
Marshmallow Malice
Candy Cane Crime (ebook novella)
Lemon Drop Dead
Peanut Butter Panic
Blueberry Blunder
Gingerbread Danger

The Amish Matchmaker Mystery series

Matchmaking Can Be Murder
Courting Can Be Killer
Marriage Can Be Mischief
Honeymoons Can Be Hazardous
Dating Can Be Deadly

Not They Who Soar

AMANDA FLOWER

KENSINGTON
PUBLISHING CORP.

kensingtonbooks.com

This book is a work of fiction. Names, characters, businesses, organizations, places, events, and incidents either are the product of the author's imagination or are used fictitiously. Any resemblance to actual persons, living or dead, events, or locales is entirely coincidental.

To the extent that the image or images on the cover of this book depict a person or persons, such person or persons are merely models, and are not intended to portray any character or characters featured in the book.

KENSINGTON BOOKS are published by

Kensington Publishing Corp.
900 Third Ave.
New York, NY 10022

Copyright © 2025 by Amanda Flower

All rights reserved. No part of this book may be reproduced in any form or by any means without the prior written consent of the Publisher, excepting brief quotes used in reviews.

All Kensington titles, imprints, and distributed lines are available at special quantity discounts for bulk purchases for sales promotion, premiums, fund-raising, educational, or institutional use. Special book excerpts or customized printings can also be created to fit specific needs. For details, write or phone the office of the Kensington Special Sales Manager: Attn. Special Sales Department. Kensington Publishing Corp., 900 Third Ave., New York, NY 10022. Phone: 1-800-221-2647.

KENSINGTON and the K with book logo Reg. US Pat. & TM Off.

Library of Congress Control Number: 2025930439

ISBN: 978-1-4967-4768-6
First Kensington Hardcover Edition: June 2025

ISBN: 978-1-4967-4769-3 (ebook)

10 9 8 7 6 5 4 3 2 1

Printed in the United States of America

The authorized representative in the EU for product safety and compliance is eucomply OU, Parnu mnt 139b-14, Apt 123
Tallinn, Berlin 11317, hello@eucompliancepartner.com

For Willa Dickinson Flower-Seymour
and
in memory of her four little ones

Acknowledgments

The more that I have learned about Katharine Wright and her family, the more I have come to admire them. In particular, I admire Katharine, who was a strong independent woman in a time when that would have been, if not frowned upon, at least questioned. I have to thank her first for this novel and series; without her life for inspiration, they would not exist.

I also have to thank my wonderful agent Nicole Resciniti, who knows how much I love writing historical mysteries about real women. She works tirelessly to put me in a position to write for a living and write what I love. It is a rare gift.

I also thank the wonderful team at Kensington who I have been writing for, for well over a decade now. I'm so grateful to have a "home" in publishing, and I would like to give special thanks to my editors Liz May, Sarah Selim, and Elizabeth Trout and my publicist Larissa Ackerman.

I give a very special thanks to the archives department at the Missouri History Museum in St. Louis, Missouri, in particular Associate Archivist Dennis Northcott, who was able to give me detailed information about the attack on Alberto Santos-Dumont's airship at that fair.

I also thank my reader, Kimra Bell for her watchful eye, and Cari Dubiel and the Twinsburg Public Library and Kate Schlademan at the Learned Owl Book Shop for a wonderful launch party for the beginning of this series.

Thanks too to my husband, David Seymour, for his unwavering support of my career and me. I am so blessed to call him my husband and best friend.

Finally, I thank God for allowing my dreams to come true.

Acknowledgments

Not they who soar, but they who plod
Their rugged way, unhelped, to God
Are heroes; they who higher fare,
And, flying, fan the upper air,
Miss all the toil that hugs the sod.
'Tis they whose backs have felt the rod,
Whose feet have pressed the path unshod,
May smile upon defeated care,
Not they who soar.
High up there are no thorns to prod,
Nor boulders lurking 'neath the clod
To turn the keenness of the share,
For flight is ever free and rare;
But heroes they the soil who've trod,
Not they who soar!

—Paul Laurence Dunbar

CHAPTER 1

"Welcome to St. Louis!" the slim train conductor shouted at the top of his voice as I stepped out of the passenger car.

Puffs of white steam blew in my face and people of all ages and from all places dashed here and there as they greeted friends and collected their belongings. I had never witnessed such a scene in all my life. Nor had I ever seen such a crowded platform as hundreds of people awaited the next train.

I placed a protective hand on my new hat. It was the first purchase I'd made for myself in six years. My teaching salary was modest, and my income was folded into that of our household. The hat was bleached white straw with a wide brim decorated with pink, white, and yellow roses. Pink ribbons fell from the back of the brim to finish the look. I typically would not spend so much money on such frivolity, but my brother Orville, who was the snappiest dresser in the family, insisted I buy it before leaving for St. Louis. As he said, if I was going to the world's fair, I needed to look the part.

I also didn't want to disappoint my very dear friend Margaret, who invited me to the fair.

I adjusted my spectacles on my nose and scanned the crowd but could not spot her. Had I known that the station would be this bustling, I would have asked Margaret to meet me at the ticketing booth. I had no idea how she was going to discover where I was in this utter chaos.

Margaret Goodwin Meacham was my dearest friend in the world. We met as first year students at Oberlin College and were in the same graduating class of 1898. We both had excelled in our studies, and while I was a master of Latin and Greek, she was a student of literature and the star scholar of the Literature Department. I always thought it was fortunate that we had different courses of study. Had we not, we would have been in direct competition with each other, and that would be detrimental to our friendship as neither Margaret nor I liked to lose.

As much as I had wanted to see the fair, I had worried about leaving my father and brothers for such a long period. However, in Margaret's last letter asking me to join her, I sensed a bit of unease as she had wrote me, "I need my friend during this time." What time she referred to, I didn't know. In any case, I knew I had to be there for my friend in her time of need, just as I knew that she would be there for me.

Furthermore, I felt more secure knowing that our young maid Carrie Kayler was there for the day-to-day routine of running the house, and I asked her to make sure that the boys eat at least two meals. That can be a tricky task as they become absorbed in their work. It's a trait that the whole family carries.

I walked to the end of the train where there was more space in the crowd so that I would find my bearings and hopefully find the Meachams. In the very worst case, I did have the address of their flat in the city and could take a taxi there. However, I knew Margaret would be here looking for me, and I didn't want to cause my friend any undue worries when she was already dealing with so much.

I removed my glasses and cleaned the train soot from the lenses with a handkerchief.

As I was still cleaning them, I heard a shout. "Stop! Grab her!"

I didn't put my glasses on in time to see exactly what was happening, but I saw a blurry woman running toward me.

"Grab her!" another shout came.

Was she a thief?

I shoved the glasses on my nose and saw her face. She was young. No more than twenty-two if I had to guess. She had flowing dark curly hair and dark eyes, and in that moment those eyes were filled with abject terror.

"Stop her!"

I reached out my hand and grabbed her by the arm.

She looked into my eyes. "Help me. I need help."

I gasped. "What is your name?"

"Stop her!" The shouting men pushed their way through the crowd.

She looked over her shoulder and yanked her arm from me before running away. Her abrupt movement caused me to lose my balance, and I would have fallen into the track if someone had not reached out and grabbed my hand just before I tumbled into the trench.

I might have been rescued, but my new hat lay on the tracks.

"Katharine, are you quite all right?" Henry Haskell asked.

I blinked at him. "Harry?" He was looking quite handsome in a freshly brushed brown suit, his dark hair parted smartly down the middle and his mustache neatly combed. I had always thought him to be good-looking in his studious way and manners, but he had never been anything more than a good friend.

As it was, he was married to Isabella Haskell, a woman just a year my junior that he knew from his hometown in Lorain, Ohio.

"Harry, what the blue blazes are you doing here?" I shouted.

He chuckled. He still held my hand, his other hand under my elbow as if he wanted to make sure that I wouldn't leap onto the track of my own accord.

I pursed my lips together and looked at his hands.

He dropped his hands and blushed. "Katharine, leave it to you to get straight to the point. I'm here for the same reason that you are, I gather: the fair. I'm covering the aeronautics competition for the *Kansas City Star*. I was surprised to see that your brothers did not enter."

I sniffed. "The parameters of the competition do not make it feasible for success. How can it be fair for balloons to go up against flyers like that of my brothers'? The cards were stacked against them. Their work is far too important to put their flying machine at risk for an impossible task. Mark my words, as my brothers have not entered the fray, no one will be able to win that one-hundred-thousand-dollar pot."

"Then you came here alone?" Harry asked. He didn't even attempt to hide the concern in his voice.

"I'm meeting Margaret here. She and Meacham invited me. The only problem is, I can't find them in this crush of people."

"The platform should clear out soon with the whistle that signals the departure, then it will be much easier to see them," he said. "How did you lose your balance? I remember you being more sure-footed than that."

"A woman was being chased, and I stopped her. She pulled away from me when her pursuers were near. Surely, you got a good look at her as you were just at my elbow before I would have plummeted to my death."

The corners of Harry's mustache twitched as if he was trying his very best to control laughter that was bubbling deep in his gut.

"I don't know how you can view this as amusing." I folded my arms.

The mirth disappeared from his face. "I don't find it amusing that you could have been injured, and I am very glad that I was close enough to assist you. However, it did tickle my funny bone to remember how dramatic you can be. You wouldn't have died if you had fallen onto the track. You might have been bruised and sprained your ankle, but nothing more than that."

"How do you know that? A train could have come through just then and smashed me to bits, and furthermore, do you not see the sad state of my hat down there on the tracks?"

He shook his head. "As for the woman, I didn't see her. I was concentrating on you," he said. "I saw you from across the platform, and I knew by the look on your face that you were quite concerned. I hoped to offer my assistance. I had not known I was about to save your life."

"The platform was quite crowded, and I suppose it's possible that you didn't see the woman," I grumbled. "I don't know who she was, but I heard running footsteps and someone was shouting over and over again to stop her. I reached out to try to do as instructed and she asked me for help. Before I could offer assistance, she was gone again."

Harry held up his hands. "I believe you. You taught me at Oberlin, even though that was many years ago, that you are trustworthy. Had it not been for you, I would have failed Greek altogether, and you never told a soul that you tutored me. You kept my confidence, and I am indebted to you for that."

I lifted my chin. "And I will take it to the grave. However, everyone knew that you were tutoring me in math. It never bothered me that it was well-known."

"You do not have a man's embarrassment on such matters."

A tall, blond porter hopped down onto the tracks and retrieved my hat. He set it on the side and climbed out of the deep trench as if it was level with the ground. Had I jumped into the trench, I would have had to be lifted out, which would have been terribly embarrassing.

He handed the hat to me. "Yours, miss?" he asked with a bow.

"It is." I accepted the hat from his hand. "Thank you kindly for saving my hat." I examined it. Some of the flowers had been mussed and there was a bit of soot on the back of the brim, but overall, it was no worse for wear.

I thanked him profusely and reached into my pocket to hand him a coin to express my thanks, but to my shock, Harry handed him a five-dollar bill. The young porter's eyes gleamed.

I secured my hat on my head the very best I could. My hat pin was bent from the fall. I knew the hat would look crooked, but it just didn't seem right to forego wearing one. Every lady at the station wore a hat.

The young porter—who wasn't a day older than my high school students back at Steele High School, where I taught Latin when not running the household for my father and two bachelor brothers, Wilbur and Orville—turned to go. "Young man, did you see a woman running along the platform and someone shouting for her to be stopped?"

His Adam's apple bobbed up and down. "No, miss."

He wouldn't look me in the eye. I could hold my own with teenagers and I knew when they were lying to me. This one most certainly was, but I saw no reason to press him at that moment with Harry looking on.

Even so, I asked, "What is your name?"

"My name, miss?"

"So that I can tell your supervisor of the fine job that you did by saving my hat."

"Oh," he said and looked away again. "John Smith."

That was a lie too.

CHAPTER 2

After the boy who was not named John Smith left us, I turned to Harry. "I know you consider Orville a good friend. When you write to him, do not tell him about this incident. If my father and brothers learn of it, they will never let me leave the house again."

"I would never tell tales on you, Katharine," he said with that gleam in his eye again.

I narrowed my eyes at him.

"Katharine! Katharine!" Margaret called from the clearing platform. Using her parasol as a prod, she made her way through the crowd. When she finally reached me, she said, "Oh, my dear! There you are. Meacham and I have been looking for you all this time. I was so fearful that you missed the train. I was just heartbroken at the thought of that. I have been worried sick that something awful had happened to you."

I hugged her closely. "As you can see, sweet Margaret, I am perfectly fine. My hat could use tending to, but everything else is in order."

She looked quite pretty in a periwinkle dress and matching hat and shoes. Her dark hair was tucked under her hat with just a handful of purposeful wisps breaking free around her pale, lightly freckled face. Her eyes shone brightly, and as I stared at Margaret's infectious smile, one word flitted in my head: *happy*. After college graduation, while I became a school-teacher, she married a fine man by the name of W. C. Meacham, who we always called by his surname alone. Meacham was a good man and an executive at a bank in Chicago, and whisked her away from Ohio to the Windy City. It seemed to me that life in Chicago had done good things for my friend. She flourished as a wife.

"I'm so glad." She blinked when she saw Harry Haskell standing with me.

Margaret was the only person in the world who knew how I really felt about Harry. "Harry?" She looked back and forth between us. "What are you doing here?"

"It seemed that I was saving Katharine's life," he said in a deadpan voice.

I scowled at him and went on to tell my friend a shortened version of my little mishap.

"You just arrived, and you have already had quite the adventure," Margaret said.

I slipped my arm through hers. "I'm nothing if not exciting, my friend."

I thanked Harry again for his assistance and then said, "We should not keep Meacham waiting a moment longer than we already have."

Harry nodded. "I am sure I will see you both around the fair."

I nodded and said good-bye. It was a pleasure to see Harry again but disconcerting too. I knew I wouldn't be able to completely avoid him the next several weeks in St. Louis, but I was going to try my hardest to do just that.

Margaret looped her arm through mine and tilted her head toward me. "I was quite shocked to see you there with Harry

Haskell. He always did fancy you." She let the words hang in the air between us.

I gave my friend a withering look. "Nonsense. We are just friends, and I have no interest in anything more with him—or anyone else, for that matter. He's a very happily married man with a beautiful family, and I'm a very happy spinster. My students are like my children, and I care for them deeply."

"I know," Margaret said. "You are the most dedicated teacher. I should not tease you so."

"I had my chance once, Margaret, to marry my college sweetheart, and I rejected it. I am happy with the life I have chosen just as you are happy with yours."

She smiled at me. "I know, Kate, and your old college sweetheart wasn't nearly good enough for you. I have a mind that no one is."

I laughed. "Spoken like a true friend," I said as we stepped out of the station.

Just outside the entrance, Meacham stood next to a shiny new motorcar.

I hugged my friend's husband, who had become a friend to me as well. In the time they had been married, Meacham had been so kind to me and respectful of my close friendship with his wife. In fact, he encouraged Margaret to continue all of her female friendships after marriage. I believed that friendship and time with women she was close to had been a balm for my friend, as she desperately wanted to be a mother but had had no luck as of yet conceiving. I knew from her letters how much it pained her to be unable to give Meacham a child.

However, I liked to remind her that without consulting with a physician there was no real way to know who truly was to blame for the difficulties, and it could just be timing. Even then, I had my doubts in the medical practice that they really knew what led to infertility. It was early days in that medical study. I also knew that male doctors were far more inclined to avoid bruising a rich man's ego than blaming a woman.

"The porters will deliver your luggage to our flat. I thought we would travel home in style," Meacham said.

He was a slight man with a full dark beard and very serious face, as if he was always doing complicated mathematics equations and investments in his mind, which was possible.

Margaret removed a silk scarf from her satchel. "You will want to tie this around your hair."

"My hat is already in shambles. I wouldn't want the same to become of my hair. The scarf will only mangle it more." I waved away the scarf.

"If you want to keep the hat on your head and not flying into the wind, you will use it."

Begrudgingly, I took the scarf from her hand and tied it around my poor hat.

The engine roared to life. I knew that such noise had been known to startle some, but it didn't bother me in the least. Back home in Dayton, the roar of engines and machinery was a constant in my life as my brothers tried their very best to perfect their flyer. The back room of their bicycle shop always smelled of oil and burnt rubber.

Between the noise and the smell, I tried to go back there as little as possible, but the boys thrived in that environment. I tolerated it, as I knew that they were making history in the back room of the shop. Few people in this world even attempted a fraction of the things that my brothers had accomplished.

Meacham looked over his shoulder at me and shouted over the deafening sound of the engine. "Your brothers should have focused their genius on motorcars. They are the way of the future. It will be a hundred years before anyone travels by air. I read that in the *New York Times* about a year ago."

I held fast to the scarf's knot below my chin. The fabric tickled my face, and the wind was strong enough I didn't believe that even the scarf could hold my hat onto the top of my head.

"Wilbur finds automobiles to be loud and bothersome," I said. "No one in my family owns an auto as of yet, but I know that it is just a matter of time. Orville, in particular, likes to jump onto the latest trends. Besides," I went on, "they want to create something new. Not something that already exists."

Meacham laughed. "I only mentioned it because I know there is a lot of money to be made in automobiles."

"And my brothers believe that there is money to be made in the air," I said.

Meacham shrugged. "To each his own, as I always say. It takes all kinds to make the world go round. That is no more apparent than it is right here at the fair. You are going to be astounded when you see the displays, Katharine. I promise you that."

"He's right," Margaret agreed, smiling at her husband from the passenger seat. "I have only seen a few displays because I wanted you and I to experience the majority of them together, and I have been flabbergasted at everything I have seen so far."

As she said this, we drove around a traffic circle, and when we spun out the other side, the world's fair was before me. I gasped as my eyes took it all in. I inhaled deeply as if the sight caused me to forget how to breathe. It was stunning. All around us were vast green lawns, and buildings that were constructed to mimic Greek Revival architecture, and they shone so white, they gleamed in the afternoon sun. The Ferris wheel stood off in the distance and churned slowly through the air.

It was the largest collection of massive buildings I had ever seen in one place.

Margaret turned to face me. She held on to her scarf as well. Her eyes shone. "It's awe-inspiring, isn't it?"

"It is," I murmured. "Truly, these buildings will have put St. Louis on par with New York or even Paris. They are so lovely and well planned. I am shocked by the ornate carvings, sculptures, and columns on each and every one of them."

Meacham shook his head and was stopped from crossing by a police officer in a crisp uniform and a bobby hat in the style of the British police. "It's all a ruse."

"Ruse? What do you mean by that?" I grabbed on to the back of the front seat and leaned forward so I could hear him more clearly.

"Save for a few, the buildings are constructed from mud, water, and hemp. A stiff gust of wind could topple them from their weak foundations. When the fair ends, they will be leveled and a way will be made for a new St. Louis."

I wrinkled my nose at this. "Why would they do that? Doesn't the city want to use all these structures after the fair? They are all very beautiful."

"It was a cost-saving measure. The one building that will be here long after we are all gone is the Palace of Fine Arts. We will be attending a reception there this evening. If you are impressed with the outside of these buildings, wait until you see what they hold within."

Margaret looked over her shoulder. "I have briefly been inside of the Palace of Fine Arts, only the grand hall, and I have to tell you that I have never seen a thing like it. Gorgeous, priceless pieces from all over the world right here in St. Louis. It is mind-boggling to believe that so many countries and museums would lend their treasured pieces to the fair for all these months. If I owned something which held so much value, I would be terrified to let it out of my sight for a single second."

"I'm glad that we will be going to this building first. As you know, I have a great interest in the classics and am looking forward especially to seeing pieces from ancient Greece and Rome. I'd love to see anything that I can share with my Latin students when the fall term begins."

"Then you are in for a treat because there are plenty of both," Meacham said.

He drove the car down by the Plaza of St. Louis and the statue of the man for which the city had been named. Beyond that I caught a glimpse of the Grand Basin, which was a man-made lake dotted with small boats and gondolas, surrounded on all sides by perfectly manicured hedges and trees. Festival Hall, the centerpiece of the fair, was an ornately carved circular building with columns all the way around and an impressive dome on top. Every sight was grander than the last, and if Meacham spoke the truth, then what was inside of these buildings promised to be even more wonderful. I could hardly wait to take it all in. I had never seen something so grand in all my life.

I was relieved that Margaret had not suggested that we stay in that night so I could rest from my travels. My friend knew me well, and that would never do. My time at the fair was limited to just a few short weeks before I would have to climb back on the train and return to my duties as daughter, sister, bicycle shop manager, and teacher. It was so nice to leave those cares and worries behind in Ohio, even if it was just for a brief time.

When I first told my father that I had been invited to the fair, he had been against the idea of my going. He didn't know how he would manage without me. I reminded him that we have help in young Carrie Kayler, who over the last several months has become as much a part of the family as the rest of us. She was more than capable of caring for the lot of them, and I was even paying her extra for while I was away, because I had asked her to sleep in my bedroom until I returned home.

Typically, Carrie went to her own home with her parents and siblings every night. She seemed as happy with the idea as I did. Perhaps she needed as much of a recess from her family as I did.

And it wasn't like Carrie was the only help my father had. Wilbur and Orville were home this summer, and although my eldest brother Reuchlin and his wife and children lived in Kansas, my second eldest brother, Lorian, and his sweet wife and children were just a few blocks away from our family home in Dayton. My father had plenty of people to look after him, but he preferred for me to take to care of things. I was the youngest of his children and his only daughter. He and the rest of them had started relying on me the moment my mother died when I was only fifteen. It was my duty as the girl to take on the mantle as homemaker, but at times the responsibility of it grew heavy. I believed this trip would be good for me, and I would go home refreshed and with a renewed dedication and appreciation for my duties.

"Here we are," Meacham announced as he parked the car in a narrow spot on the street just in front of a plain brown building with potted ferns on either side of the door. It was the only bit of green in the place as the building was just two steps from the street.

"I know that it doesn't look like much," Meacham said. "But it was the best place that we could afford. So many residents of St. Louis are wise to the fact that there would be an influx of visitors looking for lodging to see the fair. The hotels near the fair are all filled up, and that is especially true this time of year. The committee expects that numbers will peak during the summer when children are out of school and the weather is good for travel."

"It's certainly why I came at this time," I said. I wished that I could attend at some time when the fair would be much less crowded, but a teacher's life did not make it easy to do anything in the months when school was open. In fact, taking time off anytime that class was in session was frowned upon.

Meacham leapt out of the car and ran around the front in order to open the passenger side door for his wife. When she was safely settled on the sidewalk, he came to open my door as well, only to find me on the sidewalk looking up at the three-story building.

He made a tsking sound. "As a gentleman, it is my job to open the door for a lady, and whenever you are around, Katharine, you don't give me that chance."

"I'm perfectly able to open doors for myself, but I do appreciate the sentiment. What time do we leave for the reception? I do hope that my trunk arrives before then, so I can change into something a little more suitable for such an illustrious event. I wouldn't want to embarrass either of you by attending in my travel clothes."

"The porters at the station work like a well-oiled machine," Meacham said, "so I expect your trunk to arrive within the hour."

"And if it doesn't," Margaret interjected, "I'm sure that I have something that you can wear. We remain close to the same size."

I nodded. Margaret had impeccable taste—and her husband's wallet—when it came to purchasing clothing. I knew whatever she offered me to wear would be far grander than anything that I packed.

The Meachams' flat was on the third floor of the building, and I was happy to see that the front windows were large and gave a clear view of the street and beyond. I could even see the turrets and peaks of the fair buildings and the edge of the Ferris wheel from where I stood.

The rooms were plain but comfortable. There wasn't much in the way of decorations on the walls, but I could see bare spots on the wallpaper that clearly indicated that a framed piece had once hung there. I guessed that the owner tucked away anything that they saw as valuable while their home was being rented, but I was disappointed by that. I very much would have liked to see some type of portrait or even a photograph of a member of the family. I was nosy in that way and could not resist learning all that I could about my whereabouts.

My brothers used to tease me when we were all small because I always asked so many questions of friends and neighbors when they came by. Wilbur and Orville would only show interest in a new person if they believed they could learn something from him, especially when it came to history or engineering. I believed that I could learn something from every person. That's where the difference lay between my brothers and me.

"Kate, your room is right through here," Margaret said.

I pulled myself away from the window and walked down the short hallway with her to a white room with blue curtains and a matching coverlet on the bed. There was a vase of daisies and lilies on the bedside table. I knew that finishing touch had to have been made by my friend.

"This is lovely and will suit me just fine." I removed my hat and set it on the bed.

She smiled. "I had hoped it would. But then, I had expected that it would." When I arched a brow at her, Margaret explained, "You're easy to please, Katharine. You have never been picky about such things."

I nodded. "All I need is a clean set of sheets and a pillow for my head and I will be just fine. It's from a life of living with boys, I am sure."

"Well, I am glad that we can offer you more than that here. Please make yourself comfortable, and I will find you something to wear for this evening. I'm not nearly as confident as my husband that your trunk will be delivered in a prompt manner. So many trains came in today, now that we have officially entered summer. It will be a great challenge for the porters to keep up. We have a few hours before we have to leave, and that will give you time to rest."

She left the room and closed the door behind her. As much as I was happy to be with my friends in St. Louis, I couldn't help but wonder what my brothers were up to. I knew they would be working on their flying machine all summer, but would they have any luck at all?

My brothers had spoken with a local Dayton farmer and asked him if they could use a portion of his fields for their experiments. Mr. Huffman readily agreed. The boys called the field Huffman Prairie.

While Wilbur and Orville were occupied, that left their engine man Charlie Taylor to his own devices when it came to running the bicycle shop. I didn't like the sound of that in the least. My brothers had unwavering faith in Charlie. I didn't care for how he spoke or the fact that he smoked like a chimney. I always knew when Charlie arrived at the shop because I could smell the tobacco on his clothing before I even saw him.

I grimaced when my thoughts turned to Charlie as I inspected the rest of the room.

There was a small writing desk in the corner of the room with fresh paper, ink, and a pen stacked on top of it. Margaret thought of everything. I was happy to see it as I was eager to pen my first letters home. Father, for one, needed reassurance that I made it to St. Louis in one piece.

I had very much wanted to see the boys fly and was torn over the idea of missing their first flights over the prairie because of the fair. However, I was confident that my brothers would be flying forever, and the Louisiana Purchase Exposition was once in a lifetime. Walking over to the window that faced the street and the fair beyond that, I realized how blessed I was to be there. It was going to be a memorable trip. What I didn't know, then, was that it was going to be a very deadly one as well.

CHAPTER 3

As it turned out, Margaret was right; my trunk was not delivered before it was time to dress for the reception. However, the dress that she provided me was far finer than anything I owned or packed for the trip. It was a pink, pin-striped gown with puffy shoulders and matching white kid gloves. The gloves were far too hot to wear on the balmy summer evening, but Margaret insisted that I keep them on to complete the ensemble. I decided to humor her and shove them in my wrist satchel at first opportunity.

The dress went perfectly with my hat. I was happy that I had been able to save it so I could wear it to the reception. Some of the flowers were crushed, but one would have to look very closely to see that. I was also able to remove the soot stain from the brim with a little borax and elbow grease. It wasn't worse for the wear. I planned to be more careful with it on the remainder of the trip.

While I looked like a young teacher on summer recess playing dress-up, which I in fact was, Margaret looked like an elegant lady in her lavender chiffon dress. The garment had petal-shaped cap sleeves, so she wore matching silk gloves that went all the way over her elbows. She had a matching lavender hat with baby's breath and dried roses in the front and a large satin bow in the back that completed the look.

Meacham, who met us at his automobile, looked equally dignified in a dark suit that I guessed was new, as his trousers pleats were so sharp they could cut paper.

On the ride to the Palace of Fine Arts, we spoke very little. Instead, I took everything in. Every direction I looked, there was so much to see. If not the buildings and attractions themselves, the people-watching was phenomenal. There were people from all over the globe in every style of dress, from the most formal to the most eccentric.

Meacham managed to find a parking spot nearly thirty yards from the palace. "I'm sorry that I can't get any closer, but everything beyond this is for pedestrians."

"That's quite all right. I have spent most of the last two days sitting on a train. It would do me well to walk. I am not used to sitting still for so long. You can even ask my students: I pace all over the classroom while I lecture," I said.

"You will get in plenty of walking while you're here," Margaret said. "When Meacham isn't with us, we will have to walk to the fair each day."

"It's less than a mile, and I don't mind that in the least. I'm quite fond of walking."

Margaret slipped her arm through mine as we made our way to the palace. I looked up and into the intricately carved marble facade. Every marble figure chiseled in the front of the building was perfectly put together. It made me wonder how long it took the craftsmen to make just one, not to mention the dozen or so figures on the building's face.

Ladies and gentlemen in fine clothing strode up the marble stairs. At the top of the stairs, I pulled my arm away from Margaret and looked back out over the fair. In front of me, I could see Festival Hall and, beyond that, the Grand Basin. I could just make out gondolas with men dressed in berets and red-striped shirts as they pushed their guests around the small lake. Large white swans also floated in the lake.

When I turned back, I found that Margaret and Meacham were at the head of the line to enter the palace.

"Pardon me. Pardon me. Pardon me," I said as I made my way to the front of the line. "My party is up there."

A man scowled at me. "Who do you think you are to push to the front of the line?"

He had a Latin accent and was a thin, short man in a pin-striped suit. He had a narrow chin and thin face. His thick mustache twitched while he spoke.

"I'm sorry. I'm with the Meachams. I need to get to them because they have my ticket to go inside."

His nostrils flared like a bull in a bull fight. "The Meachams. Are they not friends with the Wrights?"

"Very good friends. I know this because I am a Wright." I lifted my chin. I did not like this man's tone one little bit when speaking of my family.

"You are one of their wives, I take it."

I wrinkled my nose at the very idea. "Neither Wilbur nor Orville is married, nor do I seriously think they would even consider it. I assume those are the two of my four brothers you are thinking of. I am their sister, Katharine."

"Hmmm, a sister. They did not mention a sister when I visited with them a few weeks ago. I suppose you know very little about what your brothers have been up to. I wouldn't imagine they would share with you, as it would be far too complicated for you to understand."

I put my hands on my hips and glared at him. "I beg your pardon."

"Women don't have interest in mechanics." He paused. "At least, no respectable woman does. Their focus should be on the home and on children."

I never so badly wanted to pop someone in the mouth as I

did in that moment. Perhaps my personal interests were in languages and the arts, but that didn't mean I could not follow a conversation with my brothers about their flying machine.

"You claim to have met with my brothers."

He nodded. "I did. Their theories are intriguing, but I don't see how they can have long-term success in flying without an inflatable carrying them up into the air. If they continue on the same path, I am certain that they will crash to the earth and be severely injured, if not killed."

"Do you know much at all about flying machines?" I asked.

He scowled. "I am Alberto Santos-Dumont of Brazil, although I have lived in Paris for many years. I have come to the world's fair to enter the aeronautics competition, which everyone says I am certain to win."

As soon as he said his name, I realized who he was. Alberto was a man who was in pursuit of flight like my brothers, but while my brothers used power and wings and a heavier-than-air flyer, he relied on balloons. In my mind, that was cheating, and it was the very reason that Wilbur and Orville had no interest in joining a competition. It was not fair for a flyer to go up against a dirigible or some other balloon.

"Are your brothers here?" he asked.

"No, they are back home. They have much work to do."

"Or so they claim." He shook his head. "They are cowards for not entering the competition. Although I cannot blame them. If I was in their place and knew that my prized and successful flying machine had also entered, I would steer clear of the exposition as well."

I scowled at him and was about to tell him just what I thought of him and his balloon contraption, when Margaret appeared at my side. "Oh, Katharine, there you are. It's time to go in. Meacham is waiting at the door. Please hurry, the steward at the entrance is quite perturbed that we are holding the line up."

Alberto held on to his lapels. "I see you need to go with friends. I am happy to make your acquaintance. If you want to see what a real flying machine is like, I invite you to come to my hangar behind the aeronautic concourse tomorrow morning. I will be preparing for my memorable flight that will occur in a week's time. I would be honored to have one of the Wrights there to witness it. If you are present, you might be able to report back to your brothers that their wings will never be as successful as a balloon. Balloons will travel across the world in a matter of years."

I was tempted to see his flying machine in order to report back to my brothers. I was not nearly as gifted with taking photographs as my brothers, but I did wish that I had brought their camera with me to St. Louis. A photograph was truly worth a thousand words. The photographs that my brothers took at Kitty Hawk, North Carolina, were how they were about to prove, over and over again, that they flew for the first time last December. Without those pictures, I wasn't sure they would be believed.

Instead, I would have to rely on my memory and the description with my pen. Even if Mr. Santos-Dumont's flight was successful, he was nowhere as talented my brothers. No one was going to make me believe otherwise.

Margaret grabbed me by the wrist. "Kate, please come."

I nodded to Alberto. "Thank you for the invitation. I will consider it." I followed my friend into the palace. I was so irritated by Alberto that I was unprepared for the grandeur I saw before me when we entered the palace.

The ceiling had to be forty feet up, and everything around me—the walls, ceiling, and floor—was sparkling white. It was so white, in fact, that it was almost blinding. Pedestals were dotted across the hall, and each one held a sculpture grander than the last. Some of the sculptures were so large, they weren't on a pedestal at all. They dominated the marbled floor.

Dozens and dozens of onlookers in their finest summer attire wove in and around the statuary, commenting about and pointing at everything they saw.

Meacham had been right. There was plenty of ancient Greek and Roman statuary to look at as well. I was in awe of it all.

I gravitated to a statue of Romulus and Remus in a fight to the death. There was so much movement in the marble that it looked like they would come alive at any moment and start walking around the room among us.

"Katharine, who was that you were talking to just before we came into the hall?" Margaret asked. She looked over her shoulder as if she hoped to get another look at the mystery man.

"Alberto Santos-Dumont, a Brazilian aviator. He said some very rude things about Wilbur and Orville, and I will not stand for such disrespect."

"Did he make a flying machine too? Is he competition to your brothers?"

I laughed at the very idea. "He can't possibly be competition to Wilbur and Orville because he uses a balloon. Everyone with an ounce of sense knows balloons can float under the right conditions, but they do not fly like my brothers' flyer does."

Meacham joined us. "Ahh, Katharine, I knew that you'd gravitate to the Greek statuary. It is sensational, isn't it?"

"I'm just so grateful to see it," I agreed. "If this is my first night at the fair, I can't imagine what the next day and the days after will hold."

"Do you mind if I take Margaret away from you for just a moment?" Meacham asked in his kindly way. "Several of the men who I work with are here with their wives, and I would like to introduce Margaret to them all."

Meacham's business brought him to participate in the world's fair as he tried to wine and dine inventors and manufacturers to secure their fortunes in his bank. It was stressful work that took nearly all of his energy and left very little time to enjoy the exposition with his wife. He was a kind man and suggested that Margaret should invite me so she would have a friend to see the displays and curiosities with. Even so, I knew there were duties she would have to uphold as a banker's wife, even during my visit.

"Not at all. I am in heaven looking at all of these pieces of art. Margaret, we will have to come back when the hall is less crowded so that we can get a better look at every piece."

My friend smiled. "I expected that you would say something like that. I have a full day of visiting the displays on our itinerary for tomorrow."

I nodded and went back to looking at the sculptures.

I stood in front of a bust of Julius Caesar and wondered what he would have thought of the world's fair. I believed that in his mind the only place to hold such an event was Rome, and he would be disappointed that Rome was no longer the center of the world.

I moved over to the next bust. This one was of Cleopatra, and I noticed a smartly dressed Black man looking at the display. He held his hands behind his back as he bent forward slightly and took in every single detail. It was a lovely piece.

"Paul? I didn't know that you would be here," I said.

Paul Laurence Dunbar smiled widely at me. "Oh, if it isn't Orville Wright's little sister. How is Orv doing? I heard about his flying machine. There are many in Washington who are skeptical about it, but I tell every last one of them that I meet that it's the truth. You won't find a pair of more trustworthy and honest folks than the Wrights."

"We do appreciate your support, Paul. And I am so glad to have seen you here. Did the boys know that you were coming to the fair?"

He shook his head. "I didn't tell them. I didn't tell anyone at all that I was coming. It was very much a last-minute decision. I have been in Washington presenting my poetry, and I needed an escape. My only wish was that my dear mother had been well enough to come with me. She stayed home in Dayton due to family obligations. She so would have loved this." He paused. "She would have loved most of it, that is."

"There are parts that she would not like?" I asked.

A cloud fell over his handsome face. "Yes, I write the poems that others are afraid to write, and am hailed for my bravery, but it is not bravery that spurs me on, it's fear of the past repeating itself."

I wanted to ask him what he meant by that, when a broad-shouldered man with a long white mustache and pale skin came over and stood beside us. He gawked at Paul. "Are you in one of the displays?"

Paul's brow furrowed and he balled his fists at his side.

"What kind of question is that?" I asked. "This is renowned poet Paul Laurence Dunbar. I'm sure any educated man in the country would have heard the name. You should be ashamed of yourself for suggesting that."

His face pinkened. "I beg your pardon. I just came from the Africa Boer display before this, and I thought . . ."

Paul glared at him. "You thought that I broke loose, stole a white man's suit, and passed myself off as a gentleman?"

The man's Adam's apple bobbed up and down. "Please understand that I have nothing against your people. I found the demonstration fascinating. Your traditions are very interesting."

"I was born and raised in Dayton, Ohio. I do not know the traditions of which you speak," Paul said.

The man's face was the same color as the brightest red apple. It seemed to me that he was wishing the marble floor would crack open so that he could fall through and never be heard from again. "I think I see my wife waving at me. I have to go. It was very nice to meet you both." He didn't look either of us in the eye as he scurried away.

"What was that all about?" I asked.

Paul's face was closed off, and I thought he wasn't going to tell me.

He and Orville had gone to high school together, and Paul had been one of the most popular students in their class. He was on the student council, and he won every writing award the school had to offer. He was intent on becoming a writer, and he had done it on his own with the continuous support of his mother and then his wife, who was a poet in her own right. However, I heard rumblings he and his wife had become estranged. I guessed this was one of those times when he wondered if all his successes made any difference as to who he was in the eyes of the world.

"What that man said to you was offensive," I said. "I should have spoken to the steward and had him thrown out. Does he not know what an important person you are? You're likely the most famous person in this room right now."

He gave me a sad smile. "I don't know if I would go that far, Katharine, and I do hope that it is my work that garners fame, not myself." He took a breath. "Don't let the white buildings and smiling faces mislead you. The underbelly of the fair is quite dark. People have been brought here from all over the world to be subjected to scorn. It makes a person wonder if there aren't enough people already in this country who have been on the receiving end of that."

"I do know that there are visitors to the fair from all over the world. Just before seeing you, I met a man from Brazil."

"There is a difference between the fine ladies and gentlemen walking about this room and the people I mean. Those here tonight came to join in the frivolity of the fair. These others were made to come from deserts, small islands, and deep jungles. They were brought here so that people like you can stare at them and watch their primitive and, to some, inferior ways of living. Difference attracts ridicule. It has always been that way in this world." He looked me in the eye. "You will want to be careful, Katharine. This place is not as safe and wholesome as it appears to the eye of a white man."

CHAPTER 4

Paul excused himself to rejoin his party. After he stepped away, I looked around the grand hall and realized that I had lost track of Margaret and Meacham. Margaret was fond of the Impressionists and a sign on an easel to the side of the room said that the paintings, including one by Monet, were on the second floor of the palace. I knew that was where I would find my friend.

I followed the signs to a set of wide marble stairs. I waited as a finely dressed couple came down the stairs, and when I looked up at the landing I saw, to my surprise, the young woman who had bumped into me at the train station.

She was wearing men's coveralls, and a scarf covered her curly hair, but it was most definitely her. I couldn't forget those dark, frightened eyes. She must have recognized me too, because her eyes widened and she turned to run up the flight of stairs.

"Miss!" I called. I lifted my skirts, dodged around the bewildered couple and ran up the steps behind her. As I got to the second floor, I was out of breath, and the young woman was nowhere to be seen. She'd melted into the guests who were floating from painting to painting and admiring the work.

I let my skirts fall to the top of my shoes again. There was something about that young woman that didn't sit well with me. It could be that she reminded me of my students who had been in trouble over the years and whom I have tried to help. She had the same look of pleading desperation in her eyes, and she had asked me for help. Yet now that I was in the position to offer help, she fled. What was she running from?

Margaret stepped through the crowd on her way to the stairs when she found me. "Katharine," Margaret said. "I'm so glad to see you." She lowered her voice. "Meacham's colleagues are a bore. All they speak of is money and investment in new ventures they are seeing at the fair. It makes my head spin. Please tell me the conversations that you have been having were more interesting."

"I spoke with Paul Laurence Dunbar," I said, thinking it was best to leave out the part of chasing the nameless young woman up the stairs.

"Oh, is he here? I would love to speak with him again. I only met him the one time at your home during our college days. I admire his poetry so much. He writes with so much feeling." Her eyes were bright. Nothing made Margaret happier than talking about writing and literature. She had the same gleam in her eyes when she spoke on that subject as my brothers did when they spoke about flying.

"If we see him again, I will introduce you," I said as my eyes continued to scan the room for the young woman in coveralls. One would think that a young woman dressed in such an unexpected manner would stick out in a crowd like this. "Did you see a young woman in coveralls?" I asked.

She blinked at me. "Coveralls? Why would a young woman wear coveralls, and at this gala of all places?"

Before I could answer, an usher in a red jacket with tails came up to us. "Please, we are asking everyone to meet in the grand hall for speeches," the usher said.

I wrinkled my nose. There was nothing I detested more that boring speeches.

Margaret and I made our way back down the marble stairs with a large group of other guests. We all crowded into the room where the speeches were already in progress.

When we arrived in the hall, the once spacious place felt small and close with so many people assembled. I pulled at the cuffs and collar of my dress as I began to perspire beneath my clothing. Margaret looked just as uncomfortable.

A platform had been set up to the right of the hall, and several dignitaries stood there. All the men were in tuxedos or fine suits, and every last one of them appeared to be terribly hot.

A man stood at the podium. He was a tall, mostly bald man with a mustache that would have made my brother Orville envious. "Good evening, ladies and gentlemen. Like the other men who have spoken to you before me this evening, I'd like to say," he began, "on behalf of the Louisiana Purchase Exposition, I welcome you to the Gateway to the West and wonderful city of St. Louis. My name is Carl E. Myers, and I was the director of aeronautics here at the exposition, but due to short-sighted leadership, I have been replaced."

There was gasp from the crowd as he continued to speak. "Nevertheless, they have allowed me the opportunity to introduce you to one of the stars of the fair's aeronautics competition, Alberto Santos-Dumont."

Myers stepped back from the podium and the slight Alberto Santos-Dumont stepped forward. Myers stood with a large, stern-looking woman at the end of the stage.

Alberto began to speak about his plans to fly on July first and that he had every expectation that he would win the one-hundred-thousand-dollar prize. As he went on about the particulars of his airship, Meacham joined Margaret and me. "I cannot believe that they allowed Myers to speak at such an event. He is just going to embarrass the fair committee again. He has many times before."

"Why was he replaced as the director of aeronautics?" I asked.

"Because the man is obnoxious," Meacham said. "Wasn't that obvious from the words that he said?" He nodded at the woman standing next to Myers. The woman glared out at the crowd. "His wife, Carlotta, is no better. Truly, they are a perfect match in spitefulness and vulgarity."

Margaret placed a hand on her chest. "Meacham, you should not speak so."

He shook his head. "You are right, my dear. I do apologize."

I wasn't nearly as offended as Margaret had been, since I loved a little bit of gossip now and again. "Then, why would the fair committee allow him such a public platform?" I asked.

"My only guess is that they are trying to keep him happy enough that he won't cause more problems at the festival," Meacham said. "However, what I can tell them is that men like that are never happy, and problems follow them wherever they go."

Carlotta locked eyes with me for a brief moment, and I felt like she was taking stock of the inner workings of my soul. "That goes for women like that too," I said.

CHAPTER 5

"Meacham, it is good to see you," a large bear of a man said. He was well over six feet tall, had ruddy skin and a beard that was full and dark and surely the envy of every other gentleman in the room.

"Mr. Beard, I did not know that you were coming to the reception tonight," Meacham said. "Had I known, I would have made sure that I made time to speak with you."

My lips twitched to stifle a laugh. The large man in front of me was named Beard and had the most impressive beard I had ever seen. I could not help but wonder if he chose the facial hair to correspond with his surname.

"About my portfolio, no less. You are a persistent man, Meacham. I will give you that, but I must say persistent and courteous. I cannot say the same for the other bankers I meet."

Meacham cleared his throat. "May I introduce my wife, Margaret, and this is her dear friend, Katharine Wright of Dayton. Ladies, this is Mr. Joshua Beard; he has a very successful steel company in Cleveland, Ohio. The innovations that his company is doing in metals cannot be underscored enough."

Beard chuckled. "Meacham, you make me sound like some

kind of hero. In reality, as the president of the steel mill, I sign documents and shift paper around my desk. I can't say that I do much more than that. I don't make anything with my own two hands. I pay others to do that. The men in the refineries are the ones who do the real work. I believe it is always important to give credit where credit is due."

"Don't sell yourself short, Mr. Beard," Meacham said. "You started out inventing things. You have several patents, don't you?"

Beard nodded. "Just for small things. I have never invented anything memorable, as much as I would have liked to."

"But to have a patent is an accomplishment in and of itself," I said. "My brothers are going through that process, and it takes lots of time."

Beard grinned. "That's because it's your American government at work. Everything has be checked and rechecked a thousand times before its pushed through. It's fair in theory, but it's infuriating, nonetheless. I'm happy to be done with patenting, and your brothers have my sympathies." He turned to Meacham. "I didn't realize you know about my patents. I see you have done your research. I like a banker who is thorough." Beard nodded at us both and spoke to Margaret. "Your husband has been on a quest these last many weeks for me to move my fortune to his bank."

Meacham blushed.

"What brings you to the fair, Mr. Beard?" I asked, hoping to distract from Meacham's embarrassment.

"I am here for the same reason that I believe most of us are. This is the one place in the world where culture and ingenuity from the four corners of the earth are combined. As a businessman, it is a gold mine. I am always on the lookout for my next investment. I have a keen interest in innovation. I may not do that kind of work any longer myself, but I am in the position to fund such work."

Meacham cleared his throat. "There are several machines

in the Palace of Transportation that Mr. Beard funded. Without his support those inventors would not have been able to make their inventions."

Beard smiled. "You give me too much credit, Meacham. Those inventors would have found ways to make their inventions with or without my help. I simply eased the financial burden."

"That is quite impressive," Margaret said. "I'm sure that everyone you have helped is most grateful."

Beard pressed his lips together. "Yes, of course, they are. If you all have the time, I would love to walk you through the Palace of Transportation to show you those machines I had a very small hand in."

Margaret glanced at her husband. "Meacham has a very busy schedule while we are in St. Louis, but Katharine and I are really here as tourists. We would love such a tour!"

He nodded. "Very good. I will have my secretary reach out to you when a time can be set. And, Meacham, I am very much looking forward to your dinner party later this week. I must say that I have eaten fine meals all over the world but never on the top of a Ferris wheel. It's a clever idea indeed." He nodded at us all in turn. "Now, if you'll excuse me, I see a friend I must say hello to across the room."

After Beard stepped away, Meacham said that he wanted to look at some of the paintings. Margaret went with him while I excused myself to search for a lavatory. When my friends stepped away, I did not walk in the direction of the lavatory, but back to the marble stairway. I knew it was a futile hope, but I wondered if the girl in coveralls would go back there after she disappeared.

I stepped onto the landing where I had seen her, but of course, she was not there.

"Are you looking for someone?" a man asked from above.

I looked up and saw Mr. Joshua Beard coming down the stairs alone.

"Hello, Mr. Beard. No, I—I was just making my way back to the hall of statues. I am a teacher and my specialties are ancient Greece and Rome. I was not able to observe the statuary in detail before the speech began. And I had hoped to look at them all."

"I too have an interest in those cultures. Care if I join you?"

I did care, because I couldn't continue to look for the girl if Beard was with me. That was assuming that she was still at the reception at all.

But I nevertheless gave him a polite nod before I turned and walked down the stairs and back to the hall of statues. I stopped at a depiction of Julius Caesar. I noted Caesar's clean-shaven face and long, prominent nose. The face was in strong contrast to the man standing beside me. Beard was far from clean-shaven, and I would call his nose petite for his size.

Beard stood beside me and took in the statue in silence. After a few moments, he said, "It was not until I had walked away from you and the Meachams that I realized that you must be from the Wright family in Dayton that Wilbur and Orville Wright belong to."

I turned to him. "I am their younger sister."

"Ahh, that makes sense. I am quite interested in their attempts at flight and was thrilled to learn of their success in Kitty Hawk. I assume the patent they are pursuing is for their flying machine."

I nodded, as I didn't see any point in denying it.

"My business is in steel in Cleveland. I have written them many times asking if they would want an investor in their pursuits, but I have received no response. I believe it would be remarkable if we could keep all the success of flight in the great state of Ohio."

"I'm not surprised you didn't get a reply," I said. "My brothers do not believe in having an investor or patron. They fund everything on their own."

Beard cocked his head as he considered this. "That seems to be a particularly difficult way to fund an invention. Would it not be easier to focus on the work, instead of laboring to make the money to fund it oneself?"

"The Wrights are never ones to take the easy way out, and if my brothers had financial backers, they would have to relinquish some of the control over the project to that person. They will never be willing to do that."

He smiled. "I see. You are a stubborn bunch, down there in Dayton."

"I prefer *self-sufficient*."

"As you should. I am sorry if I spoke out of turn. I find your knowledge and your family's work ethic quite appealing. It is refreshing to speak to someone who is not conversing with me simply to have access to my wallet."

I smiled. "You didn't speak out of turn. We can be quite stubborn too." I looked over my shoulder. "But I should get back to my friends."

"Yes," Beard said. "I do hope that I see you again about the fair, Miss Wright. I was serious when I said that I wanted to give you and Mrs. Meacham a tour of the Palace of Transportation."

I nodded and stepped away.

After a bit of searching, I found Meacham and Margaret waiting for me just outside the main doors.

"Katharine, there you are. Where have you been all this time?" Margaret asked.

"I went back to the hall of statues and ran into Mr. Beard there. He knows of my brothers and wanted to talk to me about them."

Meacham pulled at his collar. "I do hope your conversation went well, Katharine. The president of my bank is keen on Mr. Beard moving his fortune to our bank. He has as much money as Carnegie."

"Is he married?" Margaret asked.

Meacham shook his head. "No."

Margaret turned back to me. "Well, that is most interesting."

I narrowed my eyes at her and changed the subject. "After this long day of travel, I am tired. Shall we return to the flat?"

"Yes, of course," Meacham said and took his wife by the arm as they made their way down the steps.

I followed a few paces behind. I knew Margaret would want my thoughts to be preoccupied with Beard, but they were not. Instead, I couldn't get the young woman's face out of my mind. She had been frightened and, dare I believe, on the run from something.

CHAPTER 6

The next morning, I was up early. I was always an early riser, but this morning I was especially wide-awake because it would be Margaret's and my first full day at the fair on our own. I sat at the small dining table sipping my tea and looking at the Meachams' map of the fair. I formulated a plan. I knew Margaret wouldn't mind in the least if I planned our day just as long as I took into account the things that she wanted to see. I knew my friend so well; I had those places she'd prefer to visit listed in my mind.

I decided that the best course of action was to go to Alberto's hangar first. I had been frustrated at the way that he spoke of my brothers, but I knew if Wilbur and Orville learned that I had an opportunity to see Alberto's airship up close and did not take it, they would be furious. They would have wanted me to take notes on everything that I saw in the hangar. It wasn't because they wanted to copy Alberto's method of flight, but because they would want to know what they were up against.

After that, Margaret and I could enjoy the sights and sounds and food of the festival without a care in the world. I was interested in the aeronautics competition because of my brothers, but there were so many other things that I wanted to see at the fair that had nothing to do with aviation.

Margaret walked into the kitchen fully dressed and ready for the day. "Katharine, I knew you would be up and ready to go. The fair will be just waking up, and I thought heading out early would be the perfect way to get the lay of the land." Her eyes twinkled. "And perhaps we will stop and buy a crepe at the sweets stand on the way to the fair?"

Her mention of a crepe made my stomach rumble. "That sounds like the perfect plan. I would never say no to a crepe."

As we entered the fairgrounds, Margaret and I stopped at a French food station and bought crepes and café au lait.

Margaret inhaled the coffee. "I would love to go to France someday. Do you have any wishes to visit Europe, Katharine?"

"Yes, of course, I would love to see it all." I took a bite of my cheese and ham crepe and it was delicious. "Carrie and I have tried to make crepes at home, but they never taste just right. The only other time I had one was when that French chef came to Oberlin and tried to teach us how to make them in the mess hall. Clearly, I wasn't the best culinary student."

"I wouldn't be too hard on yourself about that. Maybe you have to be French to make this properly," Margaret said. "Where to first? I know that you have plans for our day."

I wrinkled my nose. "I do, but I have a bit of business to tend to first."

"Business?"

I nodded. "Yes, I have a meeting with Mr. Alberto Santos-Dumont."

"Wasn't that the aviator at the Palace of Fine Arts last night?"

I nodded. "The one and the same. Before he gave his speech,

I ran into him at the gala. He knows of my brothers, of course, and invited me to see his airship this morning."

"My goodness, Kate, that is quite an honor. I think that also speaks highly of your brothers that Mr. Santos-Dumont wants to meet with you just because of who your brothers are."

"So, you are willing to go with me?" I raised my brow.

"Yes, of course, we always have great fun together on our adventures."

That was very much the truth.

The aeronautics concourse was on the opposite side of the fair, away from all the different palaces that had been built to highlight transportation, electricity, fine arts, and more. It was a pleasant morning, and neither of us minded the walk. When the temperature and humidity rose in tandem in the afternoon, we would be much more inclined to take a hansom cab or one of the trolleys that were traveling in a loop around the fair.

The concourse lay ahead of us, and the first thing that caught my eye about it was the thirty-foot fence that encircled it. My brothers had much to say about the fence. It was one of the many reasons that they didn't enter the competition. They claimed that there wasn't enough room for their flyer to lift above the fence in time to make the flight. Had they entered their flyer into the fray, not only would it damage the machinery, if not destroy the flyer outright, by not being able to lift above the fence, but their reputations would be damaged or destroyed as well.

Behind the concourse, there were at least six hangars that held what I imagined was a collection of airships and other flying machines that were hoping to clear that fence and earn the prize money. One was dedicated to Alberto alone, while other flyers might have to share their hangars with other aviators. Alberto was surely the star of the competition.

I knew my brothers had made the responsible and right choice not to enter the competition. Entering would have put too much at risk, but at the same time, I wished that they had so they could show the world what they'd accomplished. Wilbur, the older of the two, would have said to me that I was too impatient and any invention takes time. It must be honed to perfection through trial and error. Perhaps this was the reason I was a teacher and not an inventor.

I shook my head. "There is no way that a flyer or airship will have the speed or lift to clear that fence in the short distance that the fair has allowed them."

Margaret looked at the fence. "Didn't Mr. Santos-Dumont circle the Eiffel Tower?"

"It was with a balloon attached to his airship. That is so much different than a flyer like my brothers have invented. How can they compete with each other? They aren't even in the same class of machine."

"To the Louisiana Purchase Exposition, they are," my friend replied.

I pursed my lips together. Margaret was only trying to be rational about the fair's plan for the competition. I was too closely tied to my brothers to be the same way.

"I must admit, Katharine, I was surprised when you said this was the first place that you wanted to go." She spun her parasol over our heads. "I have never known you to be interested in mechanical things."

"A lifetime of living with Wilbur and Orville will do that to you, through osmosis. Whether I know of mechanical things or not, I can't avoid them. I will never comprehend as much as they do, of course. They have been working on the problem of flight for so long, and for my brothers' sake, I can't disregard Alberto's invitation. My disregard would look worse on Wilbur and Orville than it ever would on me."

Margaret and I walked around the fenced concourse. There was no way to get inside of it from what I could tell. The fence was double-bolted closed. I wrinkled my nose at the extra precaution that the fair was taking. Why was the concourse so secure? I could certainly understand that if the air machines and airships that had entered the competition were inside, but they were housed in a number of hangars and sheds behind the concourse.

We stood in front of those rows of hangars at the moment, and I didn't even know where to start when it came to finding Alberto's. Nothing was labeled, and there were no signs from what I saw. I was just about to suggest to Margaret that we come back later in the day when there were more people about, when I heard footsteps on the gravel behind us.

Out of the corner of my eye, I saw someone peek his head out from around the side of the hangars. I was led to believe that it was a man due to his brown felt hat that cast a shadow over his face. Before I could even point him out to Margaret to tell her that he might know how to find Alberto's hangar, he disappeared around the side of the hangar again. It happened so fast I wondered if he had ever really been there at all.

"Miss Wright, I am so glad that you took the time to meet me this morning."

I turned to see Alberto Santos-Dumont walking toward us. There was something spritely about his gait, and he swung a long umbrella from his arm, even though there was no sign of rain.

"Ahh, Miss Wright, I did not expect you to come or be so very early. It is barely a quarter past seven," Alberto said. Despite his accent, he spoke perfect English. I could tell from his formal style that he was careful with his words, as if he didn't want to make a mistake.

Many of my students back in Dayton spoke in the same way when they spoke Latin for the first time. It was the type of speech in which the speaker thought of the pronunciation of every syllable of every word.

"I thought it would be a good idea to come, as my brothers would have advised me to take your kind invitation had they been here," I said.

He chuckled at my blunt reply. "And who is this with you?" he asked.

"This is my friend, Mrs. Margaret Meacham."

"Meacham, you say. I believe I met your husband W.C. just a day or two ago. We had a nice chat about automobiles. He almost convinced me to buy one." He chuckled again. "Not that I can spare the funds. Every penny I earn goes back into my airships. I imagine your brothers are much the same, Miss Wright."

I didn't say anything. My goal was to say as little as possible about my brothers' flying and how they made flight possible. Wilbur and Orville were in constant fear of their discoveries being stolen, and their patent had not yet been approved. They hadn't said it to me, but I thought that was another reason that they decided not to enter the aeronautics competition at the fair. With all the aviators in one place, the risk was too high that their discoveries would be found out before the patent made everything official. Without the patent, their inventions had no legal protection.

"It's very kind of you to show us your airship," I said. "I know if my brothers had been here, they would have had great interest."

He studied my face as if he was trying to decide if I was poking fun at him. "I very much wish that they were here, so that we could talk and share ideas. I met with them once and was impressed with their expansive knowledge. However, they did talk of birds flying much more than their own flyer, which I found to be off-putting."

There had been a reason for that, I knew. Sharing ideas was the very last thing that Wilbur and Orville wanted to do.

"Please follow me," he said, and started down the line of hangars.

When we didn't immediately follow him, he said, "This way. Please hurry, ladies. I am a very busy man, and I must put my airship back together today. It's important that I make sure everything in the hangar is in order." He increased his pace.

He was not a tall man, but he was in a great hurry, and Margaret and I had to quicken our pace to keep up with him.

Ahead of us were four small hangars made of wood, thirty feet long and twenty feet high. They looked very much like the shed that my brothers had built on Huffman Prairie back home to store their flying machine and keep it safe from the elements.

Alberto walked to the very last hangar. The sliding barn door was cracked open just wide enough for a man to slip inside.

Alberto looked over his shoulder. "You are about to see a wonder." He put his hand on the side of the door and pushed it open.

When the door was open and the sunlight illuminated what was inside, we all gasped, but it wasn't because we saw something wondrous. It was because we saw something disturbing.

A large man stood bent at the waist and was hyperventilating.

"What's going on here?" Alberto shouted at the man.

The man wore a blue uniform, as though he might have been a police officer of sorts, but there was no badge. He remained bent at the waist.

"I asked you a question," Alberto said in a furious tone.

I stepped forward. "Give him time to speak. Is it not clear to you that he's having some kind of fit?"

Alberto glared at me. "I don't care if he's having a fit or not. He was hired to watch over my airship, and he can't even stand up straight."

I walked over to the man. "What's your name?"

"Lucian Gilliam, ma'am," he managed to say. For as big as he was, he had a very high-pitched voice.

"And you are here to stand guard over Mr. Santos-Dumont's airship?"

"Yes, ma'am, but I failed." He started to bend over again.

I cocked my head as I looked around the hangar. Nothing seemed out of place from what I could tell. The hangars were full of open wooden crates that held the parts and pieces of the airship. Like Alberto had said, he'd need to assemble it before he could fly it on July first.

"How did you fail?" I asked.

"The airship is torn," Gilliam said, and his large body crashed to the floor.

CHAPTER 7

Margaret and I immediately knelt by Gilliam to make sure that he was still breathing. Alberto climbed onto a ladder that leaned up against the largest of the crates and began swearing in a mixture of French and Portuguese.

"Mr. Gilliam." I touched the guard's shoulder. "Are you all right? Do you need to see a doctor?"

He groaned and after a moment, his eyes fluttered open. "I was having a nightmare."

Alberto continued to yell and swear. "The balloon casing has been slashed!"

Gilliam paled under his sunburned complexion. "It was not a nightmare. It is real!" His head wobbled back and forth as if he might lose consciousness again.

Alberto reached into the crate and pulled out part of the heavy silk that made up the balloon of his airship. "See!" he cried.

There was a large slash in the fabric. The tear was clean, as if it was made by a knife, not simply a snag that had happened in transit from Paris. From where I knelt on the dusty ground by Margaret and Gilliam, it looked intentional.

Whoever had tampered with Alberto's airship meant to do exactly what they did.

Tears came to Alberto's eyes. "My darling!"

Margaret and I looked at each other, and together coaxed Gilliam to his feet.

"Police! Police! I need the police." Alberto pointed at us. "Stay here. I will get the police."

Before Margaret and I could agree, he ran off yelling in Portuguese. I didn't know any swear words in his native tongue, but I suspected he spoke more than a few.

Margaret had Gilliam sit on an unopened crate. "Just rest there," she said. "And if you feel woozy again, put your head between your knees. It will help."

"How can it help me?" he moaned. "I am going to be arrested and thrown into prison!"

"Did you slash the silk balloon?" I asked.

His eyes watered as he was on the brink of tears. "No! I would never do that. I have no reason to do that, but it most likely happened when I was supposed to be here guarding the hangar."

"You left your post?" I asked.

He shook his head in the same way a toddler does when denying that he stole the missing cookie from the tray, not considering all the chocolate on his young face that gave him away as the culprit. "No, no! I never left my post."

"Then when could this have happened without you witnessing it?" I asked.

He rubbed the back of his sunburned neck. "When we changed shifts, the day guard and I shared a smoke. We talked longer than we should have."

"Who is the day guard?" I asked.

"His name is J. H. Peterson. We went to school together and always use the shift change to catch up." He looked at his scuffed work boots.

I wrinkled my brow. He wouldn't look me in the eye. I suspected that there was a bit more to the story than that, but I wasn't going to press him on it at the moment. I didn't know how much time we had before Alberto returned with the police.

Margaret touched my arm and whispered, "What do you think we should do? Should we stay here like he asked? I really don't want to become embroiled with the police . . ."

"I have dealt with police officers before," I said. "Leave all of that to me." As I spoke, I circled the large crate that held the balloon silk. Then I climbed the ladder like Alberto had and looked inside.

I blinked. I saw the slash in the fabric that Alberto showed us, but that was only the beginning. There were many such slashes, so many in fact that I didn't know how it could be repaired.

I didn't touch the silk. I didn't want to get any fingerprints on it.

"Katharine, what are you doing?" Margaret stood at the foot of the ladder and looked up at me.

I glanced over my shoulder at my friend. "What does it look like? I'm looking for any evidence that might give us a clue as to who did this."

"It wasn't me," Gilliam said in a whiny voice.

"How can we possibly know who did this? We don't know anything about anyone that may be involved. The only reason that Mr. Santos-Dumont invited you to see the flying machine is because of your last name."

She had a very valid point, but I still wasn't going to pass up an opportunity to take in the scene, just in case. As soon as the police arrived, I would not have this chance to see the balloon again.

I climbed down from the ladder and began searching around the crate for anything out of the ordinary.

"The police will know what to do." Margaret's voice was almost desperate, as if she was well aware that I wasn't listening to her. She was right, I wasn't.

To my surprise, I did find something that I didn't expect. It was a silver cylinder. I removed a handkerchief from my pocket and picked it up. I opened it to find a pink lipstick inside.

Margaret wrung her hands. "Katharine, I really think that you shouldn't be touching anything."

"Do not worry. I'm being careful." I stood up. "What do you make of this?" I kept my voice low so that Gilliam could not overhear us.

"It's a lipstick," she whispered. "I have never known you to wear lipstick."

"It's not mine. I found it here on the ground."

She wrinkled her brow. "That doesn't make any sense. That would imply that a woman was here."

"Or that a woman was the one who slashed the balloon, and the lipstick fell from her pocket during her rage, because I can tell you whoever did all this damage was very angry." Well, that was my theory anyway. Those slash marks were deep and numerous.

"What are you going to do with it?" Margaret asked.

I looked down at the cylinder in my hand. "I have to put it back. It's important that the police find this bit of evidence. It will push them in the right direction."

I leaned down again and set the lipstick in the exact place where I had found it. There was no way that the police could miss it, or so I thought.

I wasn't so sure about the level of ability in the St. Louis Police Department. I knew from past experience that the police weren't always the best at getting to the truth.

As I stood back up, I heard a shuffling sound just as the door behind Margaret opened. A small face was peering around the side of the door, and I recognized it immediately. It was her again.

She caught my eye and recognition filled her eyes. She turned and ran.

"Hey!"

Margaret jumped. "Why are you yelling at me?"

I ran past her. "I'm not yelling at you. I'm yelling at her. The girl from the train station."

"What?" Margaret asked, because of course I had not told her about the incident on the train platform the day before. I had not wanted her to worry over it.

I ran out of the hangar and saw the young woman darting in the direction of the other hangars. She was in men's coveralls again and was not hindered by a woman's skirts like I was. How I longed to have the freedom to run so fast!

She disappeared around the side of the third hangar. I followed her and pulled up short. She lay on the gravel on her back between the two buildings. There was blood pooling under her body, a light pink smear on her right cheek. How could this be? She was running just a moment ago.

The pinkie finger on her right hand moved. She was still alive. I knelt down on the gravel next to her and I ignored the blood that seeped into my skirt.

"Help," she gasped.

"Where are you hurt? I can help you." I removed my jacket, ready to use it to stop the bleeding.

With that right hand, she grabbed my arm. "Air."

"Air? You need air? Are you having trouble breathing?"

Frustration creased her sweaty face. "Aero . . . nautic."

"Aeronautic," I repeated. All the while I looked around her to see where the wound was. It must have been on her back and she was lying on it. I was afraid to move her. What if I did and made the bleeding worse?

"Competition," she whispered.

"Aeronautic competition," I said. I wanted to confirm with her I'd heard the right thing, that what I heard was what she truly said, but it was too late. Her head lolled to the side, and her grasp on my arm went lax. She was gone.

CHAPTER 8

I don't know how long I knelt in the alley between those two hangars until Margaret came and found me. She screamed. It could have been the dead woman on the ground or the blood on my clothes.

"Katharine, what has happened?" Margaret cried. "Is that the woman that you were chasing?"

I looked up at my friend. "It was. I don't know what happened. I came around the side of the building and there she was. It makes no sense at all. I was just a few seconds behind her."

"What are we going to do? I came to fetch you to tell you that Alberto and the police are back. They are questioning Gilliam, so I slipped out."

"Go get the police officer," I said. "We need his help."

"But what if they think that you had something to do with this?"

"I will deal with that in time," I said. "We can't leave this poor woman in the alley for someone else to find. Besides, it's not like I will be able to walk back through the fair with blood on my skirt and be unnoticed."

She nodded, and then without a word turned on her heel presumably to go back to the police and Alberto.

All the while, I wondered if I had heard the woman's last words right. *Aeronautic competition.* Could that really have been what she said, or was it what I had heard because it was on my mind when I found her?

I shook my head. No, those were the words that she said. I was sure of it, and to me that could only mean that something to do with the flying contest was what led to her death.

I reached down and closed the woman's brown eyes. I felt like it was the least I could do and that I was giving her dignity in some way by doing that. I didn't want a bunch of coarse men looking her in the eye.

I stood up, and when I did, I saw the state of my clothes. They would have to be thrown out. Even if the stains could have been washed, I could never wear them again without thinking of this event. It was not an event that I wanted to visit in my mind time and time again, but I knew that I would.

A few moments later, Margaret, Alberto, and a sturdy young police officer came around the side of the hangar. I noted that Gilliam was not with them.

"Good golly," the officer said with his eyes bugging out of his head. He wasn't much older than my students. His skin was pink and slick with perspiration. A bead of sweat dripped down the side of his face. He licked his lips and turned to me. He looked even more shocked to see the state of my skirt. "Ma'am, are you all right?"

"Not really, as a woman just died in my arms."

He turned a particular shade of green, as if he just might be sick with the small provocation.

"Who is she? Do you know her?" he managed to ask.

We all shook our heads.

"I'm going to have to call the station. I—I can't handle this alone. I only just finished at the academy and we never saw something like this."

"Shouldn't you stay here as the police officer to secure the scene?" I asked.

Alberto and the officer both stared at me as if they never expected a question like that to come from a woman. I gave the officer a leveling look and waited.

"I—I suppose you're right. The sergeant wouldn't like it if anything was out of order. He takes that sort of thing quite seriously. He likes to tell us that science will be the thing to solve the most cases in the future."

"I can go," I offered. I felt like I had been standing over this woman for far too long. And though I didn't know her, seeing the life leach from her body left me deeply saddened and feeling uncertain. Could I have saved her if I had answered her first call for help yesterday? Should I have tried harder to find out who she was and what she was running from? Guilt seeped into my mind. I did not know her, but I had failed her.

"No, I—I think that you should stay since you were the last one with her and all." The officer wiped sweat from his eyes.

"I can go," Margaret offered. "What is your name? I will call the station and tell them what has happened."

The police officer looked at her as if noticing she was there for the very first time. "And you are?"

"Mrs. Margaret Meacham." Margaret gripped her parasol. "I was the one who showed you where the unfortunate young woman was."

He nodded. "Yes, yes, you should be the one to go. I would like Mr. Santos-Dumont to stay here with us. As his airship may be in some way involved."

Alberto's cheeks flushed red. "I don't for the life of me see how my flying machine could be involved in this mess."

"It was broken apart and this dead woman is just a few hundred yards away."

Alberto folded his arms as if to say that he didn't believe it, but he was willing to humor the officer.

The officer turned back to Margaret. "My name is Officer

Jeffries. They already know that I'm here because I had called in when I heard the complaint that Mr. Santos-Dumont had about his hangar."

Margaret nodded and hurried away. I knew that now that she was over her shock of seeing my bloody skirts and the dead woman, she would be able to rise to the occasion and help out any way that she could. In fact, I trusted her to deliver the message to the police station much more than I would have trusted Officer Jeffries to do it. He looked as if he was going to pass out at any second, just like Gilliam had in the hangar.

Officer Jeffries licked his lips and rocked back and forth on his heels.

"Are you going to ask me any questions?" I asked.

He blinked at me. "Oh, right, do you know the woman?"

I shook my head. "I have seen her a few times at the fair. At our first meeting, she had asked me for help, but she had not stayed long enough for me to give her assistance. She had been running from someone."

"Who?" the officer asked.

"I don't know."

"Where were you when you saw her for the first time?"

"The train station. I had just disembarked from the train. I could not see who was chasing her in the crush of people, but I do know she was frightened."

He nodded. "There are a lot of people at the fair." He licked his lips again. "It's a bit overwhelming. I have never seen so many people before. I was a police officer in a small township in the country, and when I heard how much they were paying trained policemen to come to St. Louis to work at the fair, I jumped at the chance." He glanced down at the dead body. "Now, I wish that I'd never come."

Alberto rolled his eyes at the young officer, as if he couldn't believe that this was the man who was supposed to help him.

I felt much the same but didn't show it outwardly. It was perhaps because I worked with high school students and had met just about all types of young people, from the most confident to the most timid. All I knew was young Officer Jeffries was in way over his head. I hoped that after the fair was over he would be able to return to his small rural township where the biggest crimes were children's pranks and tomfoolery. Nothing like what he was dealing with here.

The young officer shook his head as if he was convincing himself to get some sort of handle on his emotions. I thought that was the best thing for him to do before his superiors arrived.

Officer Jeffries cleared his throat. "The woman is wearing trousers."

I blinked at him. Of all the remarkable things revealed about the woman lying dead on the ground, the fact that she was wearing men's clothing was the most noteworthy? I must admit that it was of interest, but it wasn't the first thing that I would have noted. That would have been the blood under her body. It seemed a little more pressing to me.

"That's a mechanic's uniform," Alberto said. "There are dozens of mechanics around the fair who help with the machinery and displays that need maintenance. Most of them work around the Palace of Transportation and the Palace of Electricity."

"A woman mechanic?" Officer Jeffries asked, as if he had just been told that a live unicorn pranced inside the Palace of Transportation. "The fair is just one surprise after another."

"There are a few female mechanics at the fair," Alberto said. "I don't use them because I want my work to be done right, and I don't trust anyone—woman or man—who I have not personally trained, to touch my airship."

"I can see why, since it has been attacked," Officer Jeffries said.

Alberto scowled at the young officer.

If Officer Jeffries caught on that Alberto was frustrated, he didn't show it.

"When you saw her before, was she wearing trousers?" he asked.

I nodded. "She was the second time. She was wearing a plain dress at the train station."

"And when was that?" he asked.

"Last night at the Palace of Fine Arts reception. I saw her on the stairs. She stood out because everyone there was finely dressed and she wore the same coveralls that she has on now."

There was a screech of a police whistle, and Officer Jeffries jumped. He ran out of the alley and a moment later reappeared with three officers and a sergeant. I wasn't surprised. I knew Margaret didn't want to be involved, at all, in this mess that I had become entangled in.

The sergeant puffed out his chest, and when he spoke, I expected him to have a booming voice. That wasn't the case as he was very soft-spoken. He barely spoke over a whisper, but his tone oozed authority. A shiver ran down my spine.

"Jeffries, tell us what has happened," the sergeant said.

Officer Jeffries looked like he was going to melt right into the gravel. His legs shook, and his knees knocked together so hard it was very possible that he was going to have a bruise on the inside of both of his knees. Officer Jeffries repeated the events to the best of his ability, and I thought he did a fine job considering how nervous he was.

"And her name?" the sergeant asked, pointing at me.

Officer Jeffries paled as he came to realize that he hadn't asked my name. Taking pity on him, I answered. "I am Miss Katharine Wright of Dayton, Ohio."

"A tourist," the sergeant said with some disgust.

I frowned. The majority of the people in St. Louis that summer were tourists. I guessed they had to outnumber St. Louis natives at least three to one. However, from past experiences, I had learned that it did not help my case to back-talk to the police, at least not until it became absolutely necessary.

"Yes, sir. I am here for the fair. Mr. Alberto Santos-Dumont invited me to see his airship as we both have an interest in aviation. When we arrived at this hangar, his machine had clearly been tampered with." I made no mention of Margaret because I knew my sensitive friend would want to be left out of the police investigation if at all possible. "When we found out what happened, he went in search of help and I stayed inside the hangar with the guard. While I was there, I heard someone. I went to see who made the noise. As soon as I was outside of the hangar, I saw her, this woman. She ran into the alley between the third and fourth hangars. She seemed to be upset, so I followed her to find out what might be wrong. Unfortunately, I found her like this." I glanced at the body. My stomach lurched at the sight. I looked away.

The sergeant examined me up and down in a clinical manner. It was the same way that my brothers inspected the mechanics of their flyers. There was no emotion, just judgment. "I'm Sergeant Wardon, and I will take the lead on this case." He glanced down at the dead woman in the alley. "People come to the fair at times to end their lives. Maybe they believe its makes them memorable."

How could he not have a case? The young woman was lying in her own blood. There were no visible injuries on the front of her. The injury had to be on her back. If that was true, it was impossible for her to have inflicted it on herself. I balled my fists at my sides as my anger boiled. Just because she was young and clearly not wealthy, that didn't mean that he could just dismiss her death as a suicide because it was easier for him.

Sergeant Wardon turned back to me. "Did you hear anything before you saw her on the ground? A cry? A scream? A gunshot?"

"A gunshot? Was she shot with a gun?" I asked. "I did not hear a gun go off."

"Did you hear anything out of the ordinary at all?"

"Running footsteps of her running away from me."

He eyed me. "You were chasing her?"

I swallowed. "Yes. She was in the hangar where Mr. Santos-Dumont's airship had been destroyed. I thought that she might know something. When I came into the alley, she was already lying on the ground. I don't know how she could have been injured so quickly. It was a matter of seconds. The amount of blood on the ground would normally make me believe that she had been there for a long while. I'm not a doctor, but it seemed like a great deal of blood in a very short period of time."

He cocked his head. "You chased her and then found her lying here."

I nodded, and I bit the inside of my cheek to keep myself from making a smart retort about repeating myself too many times.

He narrowed his eyes as if he didn't quite believe me. I knew it sounded unbelievable, but it was the truth. "She was already dead when you found her."

"She was still alive," I said. "That's why I sat on the ground next to her. I was trying to help her."

"And did she say anything?" the sergeant asked.

"Yes." I looked Alberto in the eye. "She said *aeronautics competition*."

CHAPTER 9

A medical team in crisp white uniforms arrived and rolled the woman into a body bag and onto a stretcher. As they moved her, I saw the large bloody slashes in the back of her coveralls. I was not a doctor, but it was clear to me that she had been stabbed more than once. The marks were reminiscent of those I saw in the balloon's silk.

I was grateful that I had thought to close her eyes before the police arrived. Even though it was of no matter, it made me believe that she could not see the indignity that her body was being put through.

An older man walked over to the sergeant. He was also in white but wore a long lab coat over his uniform. "She has several stab wounds in the back. It's a wonder that she lived so long. I guessed she was lying there for a few hours. With so many people at the fair, I'm surprised that she wasn't discovered until now."

"Oh, I wouldn't be shocked if someone saw her and kept walking," one of the younger officers said. "The fair has made St. Louis a transient town. People are moving through to see the fair, and then most definitely don't want to get involved with any kind of trouble."

The doctor gave the young officer a glance but said nothing.

Sergeant Wardon frowned. "That doesn't match up with what the witness has said. The woman who found her said she had been following her. She came around the corner and found her on the ground."

The old man, who I assumed now was a doctor, shook his head. "Not possible. She had to be down for a good amount of time. I have seen injuries like this before. I used to be a doctor in Five Points in New York City. Unfortunately, knife fights were something I came across fairly often. Some of the blood on the ground is already dry. She had been there for a long while. A few hours at least. There's nothing that you can say that can change my mind on that. Your witness is wrong."

The sergeant nodded.

I swallowed and slipped back behind the hangar's side. If the police thought I was lying about what I saw, would they assume that I knew something about the woman's death?

I frowned. Had I thought I had been following the woman on the ground and been completely wrong? I shook my head. No, that wasn't true. She looked exactly like her.

Doubt creeped into my thoughts again. Could someone who looked like her also be at the fair? But she was in a mechanic's uniform. How many female mechanics could there be at the fair who look exactly alike?

The sergeant called for me. I took a deep breath and walked over to him. I expected to be questioned further, but Sergeant Wardon dismissed me.

Before I left, I had a question of my own. "What is the young woman's name?"

He looked at me for a long moment. "Right now, we are calling her Jane Doe. If she worked for the fair, we will learn her name soon enough."

Not soon enough for me, I thought. It didn't sit right with me that she was nameless.

I was happy to get away from the alley. I didn't know if I would ever be able to wipe the memory of the woman in the last moments of her life. I tormented myself by asking what I could have done for her. Should I have told her not to speak and conserve her energy? Could I have been quicker in getting help? Those unanswered questions were ones that I would have to live with for the rest of my life.

I found Margaret and Alberto in the hangar. Gilliam, who still looked a bit green, and Carl Myers, who had given that awkward speech at the reception the night before, were also there.

Alberto was looking at the many crates around him in disgust. "It is ruined. It will take me months and months to rebuild." He muttered something in Portuguese, but whatever it was didn't sound like a compliment. "That woman destroyed my chances."

Margaret stood off to the side as if she wished that she could be anywhere rather than where she was at that very moment. When she saw me, relief filled her eyes. "Katharine, there you are. The police kept you for a long while."

I nodded. "I feel awful about that poor woman."

"She got what she deserved," Alberto said.

I glanced at him. "You have no proof that she was the one who tampered with your airship."

"You said yourself that it was why you followed her into the alley in the first place," he said hotly.

"I followed her because I thought she might have seen something, not because I thought she was responsible."

He picked up a piece of wood from one of the open crates. "If she saw something and didn't report it, she might as well be guilty. I have worked far too long and hard to be treated like this." He threw the piece of wood onto the ground so hard that it bounced off of the crate holding his precious balloon. "This is the end of it. I can't go on with the competition after this."

"Alberto, don't be silly," Myers said, speaking for the first time. "You have to go on with the competition. All the world is waiting with bated breath for your success in winning the one hundred thousand dollars."

"I wanted to show the world what I could do, but I can't do that anymore." Alberto sounded as if he might cry at the slightest provocation.

"Surely, it can be mended," Myers said.

"I will not allow anyone to touch my balloon except for the skilled French craftsmen I employ in Paris."

"You are being ridiculous," Myers said. "There are plenty of American balloonists who could fix you up in no time."

Alberto glared at him. "This is not your average hot air balloon. I cannot have amateurs touching my silk."

"You can at least talk to them," Myers said. "The fair is counting on your participation."

"What do I care what your American fair wants when I have worked so hard, only to be violated in such a horrible way? You cannot possibly understand how many coats of sealant and hours of sewing that it took to have the silk of airship number seven in the perfect condition for flight." Alberto stomped out of the hangar, and Myers ran after him.

A moment later, Officer Jeffries, still sweating incessantly, came into the hangar. "Mr. Gilliam, can you please come with me? The sergeant would like to talk to you."

With his head down, Gilliam followed the officer out.

Margaret blinked at me. "Good heavens. It has been a morning. We need to get you back to the flat."

"Me?" I asked. "Why?"

"Because your skirt is covered with blood. Those stains will be hard if not impossible to get out. I will have to send them to be cleaned."

"There's no need. I have plenty of other things that I can wear now that my trunk has arrived. These are going straight into the rubbish." I cocked my head.

It had been nice to wear Margaret's gown to the gala the night before. I loved Margaret's clothes, but her taste was much less practical than my simple skirts and blouses from teaching. I felt much more at home in an outfit that was fit to put a person in detention.

On the other hand, Margaret's collection of gowns and dresses were much better suited for dinner parties and galas, so I certainly would be stepping into her closet again before we attended one of those.

She removed her shawl from her shoulders. "Here. Tie this around your waist to cover up the worst of the blood. We need to get you back to the flat so that you can change and rest."

"Change, yes, but I have no intention of resting. We came here to enjoy the fair and we are going to do just that."

"But, Katharine, you have been through a terrible experience this morning."

"I have, and the best way to recover from it is by embracing the day, and I plan to do just that."

She sighed. "There are times that I believe that you have more energy than a five-year-old."

"Not at all," I said. "I have just trained myself to use my energy to its best advantage."

When we arrived back at the flat, Meacham was gone for the day, and I thought that was for the best. We would have to tell Margaret's husband how our morning had gone, but I thought it best if he did not see the blood on my skirt. I knew how protective he was of Margaret.

I did humor Margaret and agree to sit down and rest for a quarter of an hour before leaving the flat again, but that was all I could tolerate. I had been honest with Margaret that I was eager to see the fair. That was very true, but I also had a plan to solve a murder, because I had a feeling Sergeant Wardon had no intention to. The girl who had died had asked me to help her—I had failed her in life, but I refused to fail her in death as well.

CHAPTER 10

The mere fact that I didn't know the name of the young woman who had died was most upsetting. She had been a person, an important person to someone, I dared to guess, and now she was gone. If the police didn't know her name, how would they tell her family? I hoped the sergeant was right and someone at the fair would know her identity.

I shivered at the thought of anything ever happening to one of my brothers or nieces and nephews and not being told. The young woman's family deserved to know the truth about what happened to her.

Margaret and I took a hansom cab back to the fair. My sweet friend wrung her hands in her lap so much that the delicate fabric was spun around her thin fingers. "Where should we go at the fair? I would very much like to see the Palace of Liberal Arts and Jerusalem."

I nodded. "And we shall. We will see all of it, but before that, we need take a bit of a detour." I leaned forward to the cab driver. "Can you take us to the aeronautics concourse?"

He looked over his shoulder at me. "I would be happy to, miss, but there is no flying today. There was an incident at one of the hangars."

How well I knew, and it was interesting to me that a young woman's death would be referred to as an *incident*. That was not how I would have described it.

"We would just like to look around. I have a great interest in flying machines." Even though I could have, I didn't mention that my brothers were the first in engine-powered flight. For the time being, I thought it best to keep my interactions as anonymous as I could.

The young driver shrugged as if it was no skin off his nose. Margaret shook her head, but I was glad that she didn't protest.

It was approaching noon when we stepped out of the cab. As the driver turned his team around and headed back to the center of the fair, Margaret put her hands on her hips. "What *exactly* are we doing here, Kate?"

I smiled. "I just want to find out the name of the young woman we found in the alley. I hate the fact that we don't know who she is. She was wearing blue coveralls like the men working in the machine shops and hangars on this side of the fair. Talking to one of those men is our best chance of finding out her name."

"Shouldn't we be leaving that to the police?"

"The police are stretched to their limit across the fair. I do not have faith that they will pursue the killer."

She blinked at me. "So, you will?"

I took a breath. "She asked me for help, and I failed her. I should have been looking for her and trying to see how I could help her while she was alive. The least I can do is help her in death. Knowing who she is, is a big piece in accomplishing that."

She patted my arm. "You have always had a big heart and want to help others. That's why I always thought being a teacher was the very best choice for you."

I nodded. "I know that she's not one of my students, but she very well could have been. She was just about their age. I like to think that a Good Samaritan would do the same for my students if given a chance."

"Then, let's find out who this young woman was." She tapped the end of her parasol on the ground to emphasize her point.

I wrapped my arm around her shoulders. "You are the very best friend a girl can have."

She smiled.

As we walked toward the concourse, we had to stop as a cluster of men in shorts and sleeveless shirts ran by us. They moved fast. Much faster than I had ever seen a person run.

We stopped to watch.

"They have to be practicing for the Olympics," Margaret said. "I read in the paper that it will be here during the fair. Isn't that the most incredible thing? It's the first time the sporting event has been hosted in America."

I nodded. "It seems to me that the fair has all the entertainment that a person could want."

"And I would like to get back to it," she said begrudgingly.

"And we will. Let me just see if we can find out her name, and then I am happy to go wherever you would like on the grounds."

Margaret nodded as if that were true, but I knew she had her doubts. My friend knew me well.

There was a sign on the fence around the concourse that read AUTHORIZED PERSONNEL ONLY.

Margaret pointed at the sign.

"It's just a suggestion," I said. "Besides, I am Katharine Wright. I can say that I am here scouting for my brothers if anyone asks."

She made a face, but I was happy when she didn't argue

with me and followed me through the gate, which had conveniently been left open. If the powers that be really wanted to keep people out, they should have done a better job securing their grounds.

The concourse was little more than a wide grassy field that was fenced on all four sides. It was as large as a city block, and I imagined that it had to be this large so that flyers or balloons would have the required space to lift off the ground.

There wasn't much to it really, but there was a deflated hot air balloon in the middle of the field. Its basket was overturned onto its side. Men in blue coveralls just like the ones the dead woman wore clustered around it. This was going to be my best chance to learn her name. After I did, I didn't know what the next steps were, but I was willing to find them out.

Wilbur and Orville had visited the concourse earlier in the year when they were considering entering the competition. I had not been able to come at that time because it had been in the middle of the school term. I couldn't leave my students.

Young men lounged on the grass and were eating their lunches from metal pails.

I pointed at the workers. "See there, they will know who the young woman is. I will ask them, and we will go about our day."

Margaret held her parasol high as she attempted to shield us both from the blazing sun, but the narrow dome did little to protect our faces.

I plastered my no-nonsense teacher look on my face, straightened my shirtwaist, and marched with purpose toward the group of men.

Margaret stayed a few steps behind me.

"Good afternoon, gentlemen," I began. "I see you are enjoying a break."

They stared at me open-mouthed.

A large Black man set his canteen down on the grass next

to him and looked up at me. "Are you lost, miss? There are no events at the concourse today."

I smiled at him. "I am quite aware of that. I'm actually here looking for a young woman who is also working on the concourse as a mechanic, or at least that is my understanding. Since you are all wearing the same uniform that she has, I guessed that you might know her. There can't be many women in your line of work."

As if I stuck the men with a hot poker, they all jumped up, scooped up the remains of their lunches, and scattered around the concourse. It happened so fast that I didn't even have time to process what was going on.

The man who spoke to me from the start was the last one that remained. "You sure can clear a place out," he said.

I wrinkled my brow. "Why did that question make all those men run away with their tails between their legs?"

He slowly packed up his lunch and stood. "This is not a place where people want to answer questions about much of anything. On jobs here at the fair, you learn quite quickly you're replaceable."

"And was the young woman replaceable?" I asked.

He made a face. "I can't speak to that. I suggest that you go back to the Pike with all the other tourists, buy an ice cream, and enjoy your day." He turned to leave.

"My brothers will be disappointed that no one on the concourse was willing to help us."

Margaret shot me a look as if she took issue with the *us* part. She would have happily been left out of this.

He turned back to face us with his eyes narrowed.

"I'm not sure you would have heard of them." I paused. "I'm Katharine Wright, and my brothers are Wilbur and Orville Wright."

His eyes widened to the size of saucers. "Wilbur and Orville Wright are your brothers?"

I nodded.

"We have much to discuss," he said.

"Can we talk out of the sun?" I asked, and pointed to the grandstand. A portion of it was in the shade from a large tree that by luck had been left to thrive when almost all the other natural growth had been ripped away to make room for all the new buildings and venues.

He nodded and headed in that direction. Margaret and I were just a few steps behind him.

Margaret and I sat on the lowest bleacher side by side, and the man sat catty-corner to us one bleacher above.

"I have told you my name, and this is my dear friend Mrs. Margaret Meacham. If we are going to talk about my brothers, I should have your name. What do you go by?"

He set his calloused hands on his knees. "Godwin Landry from New Orleans, Louisiana." There was a slight Southern lilt to his voice as he said this. "You must know that I have insurmountable respect for your brothers and for what they have done in the pursuit of flight. They really are remarkable."

I agreed very much that my brothers were remarkable people, but I was far more curious about the dead young woman. However, I knew it was best not to force my agenda on him, because he might clam up and not tell me what I needed to know.

"It's very nice to meet you, Godwin. I hope I can call you that, and you can call me Kate."

He nodded. "Thank you much, Kate." He said my name as if he was testing the sound of it against his ears.

"How do you know of my brothers?" I asked.

"I met them when they were here, and I must tell you it was one of the highlights of my life. Flying is my passion. I was so impressed by their knowledge, and immersed myself in reading all I could about flight. They suggested a number of excellent books, and I have been reading all those I can find at the library on my free days. I don't have many of those now as it's summer and the fair is in full swing, but I go when I can. They encouraged me to make my own forays into flight. In truth my interest was the very reason I left my home and came to work for the fair. The moment that I heard that there would be an aeronautics competition, I packed up all my belongings and came to St. Louis."

"And you met my brothers then?" I asked.

He nodded. "They were out here in spring to review the concourse. Carl Myers and the rest of the competition's officials very much wanted them to enter their flyer."

I nodded as I remembered, of course, when my brothers had left Dayton in March to tour the fair. They had come back home discouraged and frustrated. They were so much so because the concourse wasn't going to be built to their standards. Orville had even gone as far as to say that the concourse was *built for their failure*. There wasn't enough runway for flight, and the balloons and other flying machines that could lift straight from the ground would have the advantage.

Even so, that didn't keep others from mocking them and calling them cowards. Some even questioned that they flew in the first place despite their eyewitnesses, photographs, and hundreds of documents as proof.

"I was so disappointed when they decided not to participate, but I understood their reasons. Had they entered, I am confident that they would have won. They are so ingenious that they would have discovered a way to make the concourse work to their advantage. If anyone could do it, it was going to be them. I can't see anyone else being so successful, and that also goes for Alberto Santos-Dumont."

That was also my thought when it came to my brothers entering the competition. When I told Wilbur this, he told me not to be so short-sighted. *Yes, one hundred thousand dollars is a great deal of money, but it is nothing compared to what could be obtained with the patent in hand*, my brother had said.

"Perhaps they are making the concourse purposely difficult in order to protect the hundred thousand dollars that are promised to the winner," I said.

Godwin twisted his mouth. "I have never thought about it that way, but you might be right. The fair has gotten so much attention, and I don't believe that the general public could be any more excited about it, but the focus for so many has been the aeronautics competition."

"Rightfully so," I said.

"Because you are a Wright and your brothers were kind to me when many other aviators were not, I'll help you any way that I can."

"You can start by telling me the name of the woman mechanic that we met."

He twisted his mouth as if he was unsure how to answer that, and as if this was the one question he did not want to answer.

"Why would you want to know?"

I wrinkled my nose and knew that he was stalling. I also knew that he knew the girl's name.

"There can't be many female mechanics, and I wanted to talk to her about it. I wanted to know how she got into the field."

"Her name is Camilla Ortiz, and she is from California." He said that last part as if it should answer some kind of unspoken question for me. What the question was, I didn't know.

"Do you know Camilla well?"

"I did." His use of past tense hung heavy in the air.

"I know her body was found this morning near one of the hangars," I said.

His mouth fell open. "How did you hear that? Everyone who works at the concourse was sworn not to say anything about it, and if we get caught telling someone else, we would be fired."

That explained why all the other men on the field had scattered when I first asked about the woman.

"Who told you she was dead?" Godwin asked.

I glanced at Margaret. "We were nearby when the body was found." I had no reason to tell him that *I* had been the one who found the body. "We overheard the police." It wasn't entirely a lie.

Tears sprang to his eyes. "It's awful. Camilla was one of the best mechanics that we had. She taught me so many tricks since she arrived here. She talked about building her own flying machine. She was saving up money so she could return to California and begin her work. You could give her anything that was broken and she could fix it, and not just fix it but make it even better than it was before. The fair didn't know what an asset she was. They made her little more than a tour guide around the concourse area. She was never allowed to work on the machines."

"Why?" Margaret asked.

He looked her in the eye. "For the obvious reason: her gender."

I frowned. It was the answer that I expected to hear.

"Mechanics seems to be an unusual pursuit for a woman," Margaret said.

"It's an unusual pursuit for anyone," I countered. "When my brothers began building their flying machines, they were labeled as lunatics. They proved those people wrong."

"Yes, Kate, but that is the way of men. They are always building something and coming up with new ideas. Women aren't like that," Margaret said.

"What you mean to say," I corrected my friend, "is that

women aren't *allowed* to do that. Camilla Ortiz sounds like my type of person, since she was willing to break the mold. I wished I'd had an opportunity to speak with her before she died. I might not know as much about building a flying machine as my brothers do, but I certainly have picked up enough from them over the years to converse about it in a knowledgeable way." I turned back to Godwin. "I imagine raising the money was the greatest challenge. I know my brothers would not have been able to fund their endeavors without the income from their bicycle shop."

Godwin nodded. "She wrote to possible benefactors, and several of them were willing to support her plans until they learned she was a woman. When they knew that, they withdrew any interest."

"They didn't know she was a woman from the start?" Margaret asked.

He shook his head. "She wrote to them under the name C. M. Ortiz."

"That was a wise move on her part," I said. "Sadly, rich men aren't willing to bet on intelligent women."

Godwin's face clouded over again. "I bet on her, but I am far from a rich man."

He sounded so heartbroken, I wondered if perhaps Godwin had been in love with Camilla, and if that was the case, he was someone I needed to pay special attention to. However, I dismissed that idea when I saw the wedding ring on his left hand.

"Did Camilla have any fears?" I asked. "Was there any indication that she was in danger?"

"There was always danger for her. She was a lone woman in a man's world, a world that wasn't welcoming to her. Many of the male mechanics didn't want her here." He paused. "Just like they didn't want me for the color of my skin. Camilla and I bonded over that. I did my best to look out for her." He hung his head. "I failed her, and I will have to live with that for the rest of my life."

"Even if the other men didn't like her," Margaret said, "why kill her?"

Godwin looked us both in the eye in turn. "She was killed because she was a threat."

"A threat? A threat to what?" I asked.

He turned to me. "To everything."

CHAPTER 11

"Godwin, come on. Break is over. Get back in the shop!" a thin man in a bowler hat yelled.

Godwin winced. "I have to go."

I held out my hand to stop him. "Can we talk to you again about this?"

He looked me straight in the eye. "I don't ever want to talk about Camilla again. The only way to heal from this loss is to let it go. Please let me do that." With that, he walked away.

Margaret touched my arm. "Kate, we should leave before we are kicked out of here."

I sighed and nodded. There wasn't much more that I was going to learn from the mechanics about Camilla Ortiz.

I followed Margaret out of the concourse. My friend lifted her skirts well above her ankles to walk more quickly. I knew that she hated being somewhere she wasn't supposed to be. I never had concerns like that.

When we were outside of the concourse, she gave a great sigh of relief and smiled at me. "Are you satisfied now?"

"Not in the least." I tipped my straw hat in order to block more of my face from the hot Missouri sun. "We have the name of the dead woman but are no closer to knowing what happened to her."

"Why is that something we have to know?"

"Because no one else cares to."

"I think Godwin cares. The man had tears in his eyes." She opened her parasol and held it over our heads. Again, it was no match for the summer sunrays. "I would venture to say that he might have even been in love with her."

"I thought the same, but did you not see his left hand? He is married. It is much more likely brotherly love that he had for her. It's clear that he took it upon himself to look after her and he feels like he failed in that regard."

"He's frightened," Margaret said. "And for such a strong man to be frightened by something, I don't believe that you should be involved with it."

"Yes, he is scared," I agreed. "But I am not."

If Camilla really was a threat, like Godwin said that she was, that was certainly a motive for murder, but I couldn't understand how she was a threat. Had she been the one who tampered with Alberto's airship, and if she was, had she been killed over it? I realized the one obvious point was, I had to make Alberto a suspect. It was very possible that he could have killed her in a fit of rage over his damaged balloon if he believed that she was behind the damage, but why would she destroy the balloon when she had dreams of making such a machine herself? She would know how much work that it would take.

Furthermore, the coroner said that Camilla had been dead for hours. This would mean that Alberto would have already known that the airship was tampered with before I arrived at the hanger. But when he stepped into the hanger, he was as shocked as Margaret and I were over what had happened.

I also couldn't rule out Godwin. I had liked him from the moment I met him. He seemed sincere in his genuine care for Camilla, but his emotions about her were raw. Raw emotions could quickly turn to rage, if he felt betrayed by her in some way.

Margaret propped the handle of her parasol against her shoulder and sighed. "Katharine, we have to get your mind off of that poor woman. Let's go to the Pike. You haven't seen it yet. It will boggle your mind. Meacham would never let me go there alone. He's worried about pickpockets and bawdy men. But he's always believed that you had a good head on your shoulders. No one is ever going to trick Katharine Wright."

I twisted my mouth. What I really wanted to do was find Godwin again and ask him for more details about how Camilla was going to ruin everything, but I didn't want to get him in trouble with his supervisor. The short pasty man in the bowler hat didn't appear to put up with much of anything. I wished I had thought to ask Godwin that man's name.

However, I reminded myself that I was on this trip because of the kind invitation from Margaret and her husband, and Meacham especially wanted me to be here to look after Margaret while he was in his many business meetings. Although Meacham was the ideal husband for her and the kindest of men, I knew that they had difficulties in their marriage. Most of those were due to the fact they had been married several years and not had a child. I knew they both wanted to be parents, but for whatever reason they had not been blessed with a baby. The waiting had fallen heavily on my friend, and I knew Meacham hoped that my time with her at the fair would raise her spirits.

I wanted to ask her about her hopes for a family, but at the time, even having that conversation with my closest friend in the world seemed too personal, and I didn't know if I was the best person to have it with. I had never yearned for a child, like Margaret had. Maybe it was because I found myself at a young age to be a mother of sorts to my bachelor brothers. They were older than I was, but in so many ways, I was running the show at least in terms of the household. They relied on me.

I slipped my arm through hers. "Let's go to the Pike."

She smiled. "Thank you, Kate." She raised one eyebrow at me. "But I know that you aren't done with this murder business."

"I'm not, but I could use a lemonade."

She laughed.

The walk between the concourse and the Pike was close to half a mile, but Margaret and I took our time getting there. We stopped every so often to look at the displays and novelties along the way. Truly there was so much to see that my mind could not grasp it all. It seemed that in every direction there was a new amusement or statue to take in.

There was the British Pavilion with its manicured walking paths, fountains, and gardens that all led up to an impressive replica of the Orangery at Kensington Palace with a brick facade. And one of the statues at the very end of the Pike was of four cowboys riding horses and holding up their pistols as if they were being chased. The placard read, COWBOYS OFF THE TRAIL, and the artist was Frederic Remington.

Even with all the displays that we saw between the concourse and the Pike, nothing prepared me for the Pike itself. It was like any county fair I'd ever gone to, but amplified by at least a hundred. There were women from all corners of the world walking down the Pike. Indian women wore saris, and Hawaiian women wore hula skirts. A man with a clown face walked by us on stilts and another man dressed like a grim reaper had a large crow on his shoulder. The crow narrowed his eyes at me as they passed.

On one side of the road there were restaurants reminiscent of what could be found in the Swiss Alps, and opposite them others from the countryside of Japan.

Margaret nudged me. "I told you it was something."

"It's something all right, but I don't know what that something is. My mind can't take all of this in at once." I made a conscious effort to close my mouth so that I wasn't gaping too much.

Clouds passed over the sun, and Margaret folded up her parasol, hooking it over her arm. "Where would you like to go first?"

I blinked. "I don't even know. Maybe we can walk from one end to the other to see what's here?"

"That sounds like a very good plan." She smiled. "It's what Meacham and I did when we came. In the end, we went to the Cairo exhibition. They have real mummies in there. It was not my cup of tea, but Meacham found it fascinating."

I would have found it fascinating too, as I had never seen a mummy before.

We walked arm in arm down the dirt road that divided the Pike in two. On either side of us were countless businesses and amusements. Carnival workers shouted into the crowded street, trying their very best to entice tourists to come to their booths.

"Fresh sweet corn!"

"Play darts! Win a rose for your sweetheart!"

"Dunk the drunk!"

I was half tempted to cover my ears. There was so much noise.

A young man ran up to us holding a tray of hot dogs on sticks. "Ladies, do you wish to have a hot dog?"

I started to shake my head.

"Don't worry. Don't worry," he said. "It is no cost to you. I just saw you lovely ladies walking and knew you must be famished from your day at the fair. There is nothing better to feed you at a time like this than the finest American hot dog. Try it. You will like it."

I shook my head, but Margaret took the stick from his hand and took a small bite. "Oh, it's very good."

"See, what did I tell you?" the man asked. "You can get three just like that for fifty cents. For a dollar you can feed the whole family. Surely ladies like you must be married with children, no?"

Margaret took another bite.

"Thank you for that, but one is more than enough for us," I said, effectively dismissing him.

The man scowled and walked away. He headed straight for another group of young women with his tray.

Margaret took another bite of her hot dog on the stick. "It really is quite good. I can't say that I have ever had anything like it. Would you like to try it?"

I shook my head. "I don't think so. I'm going to save my appetite for something sweet like ice cream."

Margaret laughed. "Katharine, you have the taste buds of a child."

I smiled. "I don't pretend otherwise."

Margaret and I ate our way down the Pike. I had ice cream, popcorn, and a waffle. All of it was delicious, and I knew all of it was terrible for my waistline. However, I didn't believe that I would ever again be in a place where there were so many foods from around the world at one time. I allowed myself to indulge. Margaret was much more selective after her hot dog. She had an ice cream, but that was all.

I knew that she was constantly concerned about her figure. Why, I didn't know. From where I stood, she looked just fine.

A man dressed as the ringleader of a circus, face painted as a clown's, came up to us. He stood outside of the fun house called the Temple of Mirth. The Temple of Mirth towered two stories high and right in the middle of it was a papier-mâché clown head with its mouth open as if it had been caught in the middle of a scream.

"Ladies! Dear ladies! Please come to my fun house. It's a quick trip through a place of dreams for just a nickel. Now both of you fine ladies look like you have a nickel to spare."

I cocked my head. I had to admit that I was curious about the building.

"I don't know . . ." Margaret said.

A large blue parrot flew down from the top of the papier-mâché clown's head and landed on the man's arm. "Just a nickel," the parrot said.

"What a beautiful bird," I said.

The ringleader smiled. "This is Achilles, the hyacinth macaw. A gorgeous bird indeed, and like me, he encourages you to see the Temple of Mirth. You have never imagined any place like it before."

"Just a nickel," Achilles repeated.

The ringleader bowed. "The Temple will change your reality. When a person goes in, she doesn't come out the same."

Margaret shook her head.

"Come on. Let's have a little bit of fun. How bad can it be if we stick together?" I opened my change purse.

The man's face curled into a smirk. "Sticking together is wise." He held out his hand, and I dropped two nickels in his palm. He bowed and slipped the coins into his pocket in one motion. He gestured to the clown face. "All your dreams are about to come true."

"What if some of those dreams are nightmares?" Margaret muttered.

He smiled. "Only you could be the judge of that. And I am Zeb Dandy, ladies. Remember the name! Zeb Dandy is worth knowing."

I took Margaret by the hand, and we stepped into the Temple of Mirth. The black doors closed after us like a lid to a coffin, and for the first time I was wondering if this had been such a good idea after all.

Margaret squeezed my hand. Up ahead of us someone screamed, but then the scream was followed by a peal of laughter. I let out a breath. There was nothing to really be afraid of; it was all in good fun.

"This was a terrible idea," Margaret said, and tried to leave through the door we came in, but there was no doorknob or handle. We were trapped inside. The only way out was to walk toward the screaming and the laughing.

"Katharine, Meacham is going to be so angry at you for bringing me here." Margaret's voice quavered.

"We don't have to tell him that we were in the fun house."

"And how do you expect to keep that a secret when it's so traumatic?"

I squeezed her hand. "Let's just focus on getting out of here, and then you can tell me what an awful idea this was when we are out in the sunshine again."

She sighed.

I let go of her hand.

"Hold on to the back of my vest. I'll lead, but I will need both hands to feel my way through the dark."

Margaret groaned and did as I asked.

There was a dim light in front of us, and I thought following the light was the best way out. A large crate was to our left. It was a relief to be able to identify anything in the dark space. At least it was, until a giant jack-in-the-box popped out of the crate.

We screamed, and the mechanical jester's head bobbed up and down. "Careful. Be careful," the jester said in a tinny voice before disappearing into the crate again.

I looked behind me, and Margaret was as pale as a ghost.

"It's all right," I assured her. "It's just an amusement. Nothing inside of here can hurt us."

Margaret removed her left hand from the back of my vest and patted her chest. "I'm having palpitations."

With no option to go back, all we could do was walk toward that dim light in the distance and pray it was the exit.

In the next room, two men dressed as clowns jumped out at us in peals of hysterical laughter. It took all my willpower not to kick each of them in the shins. I knew they were only doing their jobs, but clearly they could see two terrified woman in front of them. Common sense should have told them to hang back, in my opinion.

I held my hand over Margaret's head and guided her into the next room.

Margaret's chest heaved up and down. "Katharine, you are my dearest most beloved friend in all of the world, but coming inside of here was a terrible idea."

"I agree," I said with a shiver and dropped my arms to my sides. "You know what I have decided?"

"What's that?" she asked, out of breath.

"I really hate clowns."

"Me too. I never want to see a clown again."

Now that we agreed on something, I moved to the next room. Electric lights glowed dimly high overhead, but it was bright enough to see our way. We found ourselves in a room of mirrors. The door shut behind us and that door had a mirror on it as well.

Margaret pulled on the back of my vest. "How are we ever to find our way out of here? We are trapped!"

I spun around, looking at each mirror that ran from the floor to the ceiling. I grew dizzy and I saw so many variations of Margaret and me standing there. Fear gripped at my throat, but I willed myself to relax. This was an amusement at the fair that hundreds of other people had gone through. There was no report that anyone had been hurt inside of the Temple of Mirth, and I certainly believed we would have heard if there had been.

"One of these has to be a door," I said.

Mirror by mirror I began tapping on the glass. I hoped to hear some sort of hollow sound that would indicate a way out.

Margaret let go of the back of my vest, and also began tapping mirrors.

We were on opposite sides of the large room, tapping and listening.

Margaret let out a yelp, and in the reflection of the mirror in front of me, I saw a door open. Margaret fell through and it slammed shut again. It all happened in just an instant.

I ran to the other side of the room and began pounding on the mirror that I thought Margaret had gone through, but I was afraid that it might not be the spot. Every mirror looked exactly the same. I wasn't sure any longer if I was pounding on the same mirror. I moved to the next mirror and pounded on that.

It opened, and I fell through. I landed on my knees, and even my skirts weren't padding enough to protect them from being bruised.

The floor, ceiling, and walls were all painted matte black. There was a single floor-length mirror in front of me, but that was the only thing in the room. I stared at my reflection. My eyes were wide and my face was pale. "Margaret is fine," I whispered to myself. "It's just an amusement." I repeated it a second time, but it did little to calm me. I prayed that my friend was all right. I didn't know what I would tell Meacham. *I'm so sorry I lost your wife in the fun house. I'm sure she will be home just as soon as she finds her way out.*

Even to deliver that message, I would have to find my own way out of the Temple of Mirth, which at the moment appeared to be an insurmountable challenge. I ran my hands along the edges of the mirror, feeling for some sort of lip or latch that might indicate that there was a door on the other side of it.

Sweat dripped down my back. It was impossibly hot in the closed space. My eyes were focused on the edges of the mirror. I didn't find a lip or latch like I hoped I would. When I looked at the mirror again, a woman stood before me, but it wasn't my reflection.

I stifled a scream. Camilla Ortiz stood on the other side of the glass. I knew it was her. I could never forget her face or her dark curls after seeing her take her final breath.

"Camilla?" I asked in a choked voice.

The electric light above me went out, and the room plunged into darkness. Just as quickly as the lights went out, they were back on, and I could see the woman more clearly. She was young with black hair and dark eyes. She wore a blue and white pinstriped dress. Her hair was pulled back with a matching blue ribbon.

It was the first time in my life that I thought I might actually be seeing a ghost.

"Camilla?" I reached out my hand to her.

Her eyes went wide when she heard the name and then she turned and ran deeper into the fun house. The glass became a mirror again as it reflected my image back to me. I told myself that it must have been a transparent mirror, which I had read about in the newspaper. I pushed on the mirror, hoping that a door would open. Finally, I heard a click and found myself in another room, but this one contained distorted mirrors. Just looking at those mirrors and how they changed the shape of my person gave me a headache.

I saw the girl in the blue and white dress in front of me, but I didn't know if it was her or her reflection.

"Camilla!" I called.

The girl stopped and turned to look at me. Her eyes met mine, and I thought that she was looking into my very soul.

"You're alive?"

She turned and ran from me. Down a dark corridor, and the plain glass turned into a mirror again.

There was creaking sound, and the mirror opened like a door in from of me. Shaking, I stood in the corridor that the woman, that Camilla, had disappeared down.

I ran down the corridor. There was a steel door at the end. I threw the door open and was blinded by the hot Missouri sun on the other side.

CHAPTER 12

The sun was so blinding, I took a step forward, not realizing that I was on a platform. I fell to my knees on the gravel below. The sharp stones dug into my flesh. When I took a bath that night, I would discover that my legs were black and blue from the day's adventures.

I struggled to my feet and rubbed my eyes. I worried about Margaret. I didn't know where she had gone, and I knew that she wouldn't want to be inside of the fun house alone.

I blinked away the black spots that had clouded my vision.

"Katharine, are you all right?" I heard Margaret's voice.

I blinked. "Margaret?" I waved my hands around. "Where are you?"

"What's wrong with your eyes? Can't you see?"

I shielded my eyes with my hand. "I'll be all right in a moment when my eyes adjust."

"What happened to you? You were inside the fun house for such a long time! I was close to asking the man selling tickets to go in there and fetch you."

"I had a hard time finding one of those mirrored doors that opened."

Her blurry image nodded. "I found my way out quickly just

by luck. I would have run away from here as fast as I could go if you had not still been inside. Let's make a pact. No more fun houses."

"That's fine with me." Her face finally came into view. I was much relieved. I was frightened that the mirrored fun house might have done some permanent damage to my vision.

"You're awfully pale. We should return to the flat for the rest of the day." She touched my forehead. "You don't feel like you have a fever, but you can never be too careful when you are away from home. Heat stroke can come on fast." She dropped her hand to her side.

"I'm fine," I said. "Now that I can see again, I feel as right as rain."

Margaret pressed her lips together as if she didn't believe me.

"I do have one concern though," I said.

She leaned forward. "What is it?"

"You are going to think that I've taken leave of my senses, but I saw Camilla Ortiz inside of the fun house."

She gasped. "That's not possible."

"I know that it's not possible, but I am telling you it is what I saw. She was there."

"Katharine," Margaret said in a soft voice. "Camilla Ortiz is dead. We both saw her dead body just this morning."

"I know that, but I'm telling you what I saw."

Margaret pressed her lips together once more. I knew she didn't want to argue with me, but she didn't believe me, either. I don't know if I would believe myself, had I not seen Camilla with my own two eyes. And then the doubts crept into the back of my thoughts. What if my mind *had* played tricks on me? I was disoriented inside of the fun house; anyone would have been. I knew that I had seen a woman on the other side of the glass, but had my mind put Camilla's face in the place of who it actually was?

I shook my head. No, I knew what I saw. I had never been one inclined to manipulation or flights of fancy. Camilla had been in that fun house, and I saw her. And she saw me.

"I need to talk to the ticket man again," I said, and marched around to the front of the fun house.

Now that it was close to the lunch hour, the Pike was full of tourists and locals alike looking for a place to eat. The Asia Market and French Village were the most popular.

I walked up to the man selling tickets in front of the fun house.

"You're back!" Zeb Dandy shouted at top voice. "I take it that you had a delightful time in my house of amusements." He looked down at my skirts. "Looks as if you took a bit of a tumble. It happens from time to time when people enter the Temple of Mirth." He folded his arms. "But that is not my fault if you are unable to keep your feet under you."

I looked down at my skirt and it was caked with dust. I shook it out the best that I could, but there was nothing to be done about it until I could get it laundered. "I'm not here about my fall."

Margaret stood beside me and fiddled with the handle of her parasol.

"Ahh, you will like another go at it. I'm not surprised. There are few that don't fall in love with my amusements." He bowed at us. "And how did you like your rousing trip through the hall of mirrors, my ladies? Is it not the very best part?"

"I'm never going into such a place again for the rest of my life," I said with all the conviction in the world.

His red lips curled in distaste. "It seems that not everyone is brave enough to face their greatest fear, and I have to assume that you saw the fear." He paused. "In yourself."

"What can you tell me about the girl who was inside of the fun house?"

"Girl in the fun house?" he asked. "I don't know what you're talking about. I am very careful to only let one group in at a time and space them out, so that you're not tripping over each other. As you must have seen, it can be very tight inside of those halls and rooms."

"That may be true, but there was a young woman inside, and she hadn't gone into the fun house with us. She wore a blue and white pinstriped dress."

He turned away from us. "The mirrors can play tricks on your mind." He looked up into the sky. "And the sun is beating down. I'm sure the heat is impacting your memory. It would be wise if you left, got a cold drink, and had a little rest. Overheating this time of year is quite easy."

I balled my fists at my sides and hated how he was dismissing me so easily.

"I know what I saw," I said. "There was a girl inside of the fun house. We made eye contact."

"I need to get back to my customers." He began to shuffle away, which was no easy feat in his oversized clown shoes.

"What do you know about Camilla Ortiz?" I called after him.

He turned around very slowly, as if he was moving underwater. "I don't know who you're talking about. The only Ortiz I know is Sylvia Ortiz."

"And where would I find her?"

He walked away toward the back of the fun house. My last question was one he had no interest in answering.

After Zeb left, Margaret touched my arm. "Katharine, let's go back to the flat. I'm not feeling well."

I studied her face and was shocked to find it so white. Beads of sweat gathered on her brow and her upper lip. She was visibly ill. This wasn't the time to argue.

"Yes," I agreed. "Of course. Let me call us a cab. You are in no condition to walk back to the flat."

She nodded and shuffled over to an empty bench. She sat and clutched her stomach.

I walked to the entrance of the Pike and hailed a cab from

there. Then, I went back to collect Margaret. In the short time that I had been gone, she'd slumped over on the bench. I rushed over to her.

She held tight to her stomach.

I helped her sit up. "The cab is waiting. Can you walk to the end of the Pike?"

Thankfully, I could see the end of the Pike from where we sat.

She nodded and let me help her to her feet. "I just don't know what is wrong with me. I have never felt this ill in all my life."

"You likely caught a stomach bug. There are so many people here at the fair and some of them are bound to be ill. It was probably from the briefest contact with one of them."

"Maybe," she whispered and let me guide her to the cab.

The cab driver took one look at Margaret and shook his head. "No, miss, I don't take sick people in my car. You will have to find another way home."

He hurried around to the driver side of the carriage as if he was going to jump inside and drive away.

"Not so fast!" I said, and threw the back door open. I guided Margaret inside. I walked around the car to the man who was dumbfounded that I had forced the issue.

He glared at me. "You can't make me drive you anywhere."

"That's true, but I can pay you to drive us to where we want. It is a short ride to our flat, and I will pay you generously." I handed him several bills.

He looked down at the money in his hand and sighed. "Get in."

On the short ride to the flat, Margaret's coloring was disconcerting as she changed from white to red to green. It seemed to be in that cycle over and over again. We reached the flat. Margaret leaped out of the car and threw up in the bushes.

The driver peeled away from the curb as quickly as possible while I rubbed my friend's back and held her hat.

When she straightened up again, her coloring was more normal, back to the peaches and cream look that I was much more familiar with.

"Do you feel better?" I handed her a handkerchief.

She patted it to the corners of her mouth. "I do, but I'm so embarrassed."

I tugged one of her loose curls behind her ear like I would to one of my nieces back home when they were ill or upset. "Don't be. I have seen much worse. Remember, I live in a house full of men and have for a very long time."

She wrinkled her small nose and tried to hand the handkerchief back to me, but I shook my head. "It's yours now."

She chuckled and curled it into her first.

When Margaret was tucked into her bed, I was relieved. I had been worried about her. I was likely right that it was just a tummy bug that would last a day or maybe two. It couldn't be anything more than that.

That was what I thought, but I had been so very wrong.

CHAPTER 13

An hour later, I went into Margaret's room to check on her. I found her sitting up in bed. Her complexion was still very pale and her face was drawn, but she was smiling.

I tiptoed into the room. "What is it? Why are you smiling?"

She held out her right hand to me, and I took it in both of mine as I perched on the side of the bed. "Meacham has called for the doctor. I think I might be with child. I can't think of another reason that I would be so suddenly ill."

I hugged her as gently as I could. "Oh, Margaret. I know that's what you want most in the world." I pulled back. "But are you sure?" I couldn't help the worry that leaked into my voice. Over the years Margaret had had so many false alarms when it came to pregnancy. I didn't want her to fly too high only to crash down in disappointment yet again.

"It has to be the reason," she said.

There was so much hope in her eyes that it broke my heart.

Before I could say more, Meacham stepped into the room followed by a portly man with round spectacles. The buttons on the doctor's white shirt were pulled taunt against his waist as if he bought the shirt two sizes too small. A stethoscope hung around his neck, and he held a black medical bag in his hand.

"I'll wait outside," I said.

Meacham looked from his wife to the doctor and back again.

"Dear." Margaret held out her hand to him. "You can wait outside too. I know that you are squeamish with such things."

He kissed her on the forehead and followed me from the room.

We walked to the sitting room. Its large window overlooked the fair. From where I stood at the window, I could see the U.S. Government building and the Palace of Liberal Arts. Both were places Margaret and I had yet to visit.

Meacham wrung his hands. "The doctor will be able to tell us what is going on . . ." He trailed off, and I knew that Meacham wondered if it was possible for Margaret to finally be pregnant. It was what the couple hoped and prayed for the most.

I knew from her letters how much he longed for a child, but I didn't ask about it. I only received what she was willing to share. Whether she was ever to be a mother or not didn't change what a good friend she had always been to me.

The doctor came out of the room. "It seems to me that Mrs. Meacham is stricken with an upset stomach."

"And she's not . . ." Meacham asked.

The doctor shook his head. "No. She's not pregnant in my estimation. It might be a few days before we know for certain. I told her not to give up hope, she is young still. There is no reason I see that she won't have a child. Even so, a child is not the reason she feels ill. My guess is she will be as right as rain in a day or two. She just needs to rest. I would restrict her diet to clear liquids until she is feeling more like herself."

Meacham shook his hand. "Thank you for coming out, Doctor. You put my mind at ease."

The doctor patted him on the shoulder. "Chin up, young man. You and your wife have a long life ahead of you."

Meacham nodded.

The doctor went on. "It could have very well been something she ate at the fair. You have to be careful when you are out on the fairgrounds. Not all food vendors are the same. Some do a knock-up job and make fine meals. Others use the same pots and pans dish after dish after dish and meal after meal." He shook his head. "Sanitation is a concern at such a large event."

"Thank you, Doctor, we will be more careful going forward," Meacham said.

The doctor nodded, picked up his medical bag, and went out the door.

There was a black cloud over Meacham's face. "Will you stay here with Margaret? I have to get back to the office."

"Yes, of course." I pointed at the books lining the wall. "There is a fine library here that will keep me amused for hours."

He thanked me and hurried out of the flat, but he didn't leave before I saw the sadness in his eyes.

I went to the bookshelf and found a much-loved volume of the *Odyssey*. It was a perfect selection for me when I needed a comfort read. It was the *Odyssey* that first sparked my interest in ancient Greece and why I chose to study Greek and Latin at Oberlin College. I still hoped to teach Greek at Steele High School in Dayton, where I taught first-year Latin, but as of yet the principal had held that teaching spot for male tenured teachers. It didn't matter to him that I could run circles around those male tenured teachers in the Greek, Latin, and English languages.

I tucked the book under my arm and carried it to Margaret's door. I peeked in the room, hoping that she would have fallen asleep. In illness, I always believed that sleep was the best remedy.

But she was awake, sitting on her bed with tears streaming down her face. "Come in," she murmured.

I stepped into the room.

"I imagine the doctor told you I am not pregnant." She closed her eyes for a moment as if she didn't want to see my reaction.

"He said you are likely not, but it won't be known for sure for a few days."

She wiped tears from her eyes with the sleeve of her night-dress. "He might as well have just said no. It would have been easier to take a *no* than a *maybe*."

"I don't think doctors can really tell if a woman is preg-nant without definitive proof, at least until a woman is showing."

"You would have thought that all the doctors would have found a way to do that. Perhaps because it involves a woman's body, there is no urgency on their part to find a way to know sooner."

I raised my brow. It wasn't like Margaret to speak this way. In fact, it was much more like me to say such a thing. Perhaps I was a bad influence on her.

She shook her head as if she just remembered that she shouldn't be so critical. "I'm sorry. That was unkind. I know the doctors do all they can." She licked her dry lips. "And I will know soon if I am with child. If I'm not, there is no rea-son to lose hope." She said this last part as if she were trying to convince herself that that was true.

I squeezed her hand. "There is no reason to lose hope at all."

She placed a hand on her stomach. "The doctor gave me something for the nausea, and I do feel much better." She licked her dry lips once more. "But I'm not well enough to go back to the fair today."

"Then, I will stay home too. I have letters to write home to the boys and my father. They will be wondering why I haven't written as often as I promised I would. I am looking forward to describing the Temple of Mirth to Orville. Can you image if he had gone in there?"

Margaret laughed and then held her stomach as if it pained her. "Oh. He would either be hiding in the corner or taking apart the jack-in-the-box to know how it worked."

I smiled. "That's exactly true."

CHAPTER 14

The next morning, I was the first one up in the flat and made coffee in the percolator on the stovetop. I loved tea throughout the day, but on groggy mornings like this one, coffee was my drink of choice.

Meacham came into the kitchen dressed to go into the office. His face was drawn.

I held a coffee mug out to him.

"Thank you," he said in a monotone voice. "I need this today."

"Is something wrong?"

"I will let Margaret tell you. It's her story to tell." He took one sip from the coffee and set it on the kitchen table. He gathered up his briefcase and bowler hat and went out the door.

I frowned after him. What has happened that he couldn't tell me?

I tiptoed down the short hallway to Margaret's room. The door was left cracked open. She was on her side turned away from the door, and I thought that she might be asleep. If she was, I knew that I could have let her sleep, but at the same time, I was dying to know what was going on.

I took a step back.

"Katharine, you can come in," she said to the window.

I walked to the other side of the bed so I could see her face. "Are you not feeling well?"

She gave me a weak smile. "I'm still a bit upset to my stomach, but I'm feeling better."

"What's wrong then?" I asked.

"I'm not pregnant."

"How do you know?" I asked. "The doctor said it would be a few days before you would know for certain."

She gave me a look.

"I'm so sorry," I said as I understood her monthly must have arrived.

She propped herself up on her left elbow and wiped her eyes. A tear clung to her fingertip until she flung it away. "I was wishing that it was true, but I knew in my heart that it wasn't." She rolled over and lay on her back.

I slid into the bed next to her.

"I know that you've had no wish of children and must believe that I worry about this too much," she whispered.

"Not at all. I would never judge you for mourning what you want most in this world. Just like you would never judge me."

She looped her arm through mine. "You are a good friend, Katharine, and I want you to enjoy the fair. I want you to go out today and see the sights."

"I'm not going out to the fair without you." I propped myself up on my elbow.

"I don't feel well enough to walk about the fair. I think one more day in bed, and I will feel as good as new. I want you to go out and enjoy yourself."

"I will stay here with you," I insisted.

"No, I will not take no for an answer. You are here for just a few short weeks. Meacham and I will be here weeks more. His bank wants him to return to Chicago with a slew of new accounts. The pressure he is under is great. But there is so much to see, and your time is limited. Please go and enjoy for my sake."

I bit my lower lip because I wanted to do right by my friend when she wasn't feeling well, but at the same time, I hated being so close to the fair and not being able to experience it. And most importantly, there was Camilla Ortiz's murder that occupied a large part of my mind.

As if Margaret could read my thoughts, she said, "Don't you want to find out what happened to Camilla?"

I raised my brow. "You condone my meddling in her death?"

"No, but I know it's what you want to do."

She knew me well.

It took a few minutes more for Margaret to convince me to leave and for my guilt to subside for wanting to leave when she was unwell. However, she was looking much better that morning, and I believed my angst to see the fair wouldn't allow her to rest.

In the end, I gathered up my shawl and Margaret's parasol, which she insisted that I take, and left the flat.

Since Margaret wasn't with me, I decided to walk to the fair. It was a mile or so away, and there was no way that I could make a mistake in which direction I should go as I saw the whitewashed buildings and large Ferris wheel in the distance.

It was a pleasant morning without a cloud in the sky. The sky itself was bright blue and the sun shone on the exposition palaces. I didn't think there was a more beautiful place in all the world, not even in Europe, not that I had seen any part of Europe outside of pictures.

With the bright, cloudless sky, it promised to be another hot day at the fair. I waved away flies and other clouds of insects as I walked. From what I could tell, the summer climate in St. Louis wasn't all that much different from back home in Dayton. Knowing that, it promised to be a very humid summer day.

It was half past nine when I reached the fair, and the exposition halls were open. I looked at the map that Margaret gave me before I left the house. I was so glad that she had. The fair was massive and felt even larger now that I was there alone.

There was so much I wanted to see, but Camilla Ortiz was at the forefront of my mind. I knew that I wouldn't be able to rest until I knew what happened to her. It would also be best if I could learn of Camilla's fate while I was alone, because I knew that Margaret wasn't as keen on investigation as I was. There was a good reason for that. She hadn't been there when Camilla was dying and asked for help. Had she been, I knew she would have felt the same way.

After consulting the map, I saw that there were dormitories near the concourse. It made the most sense to me that those would supply housing for the mechanics who worked in that area. It was the best idea I had to learn more about Camilla.

Instead of taking a cab to the other side of the fair, I continued to walk. My legs still felt cramped from hours and hours on the train traveling to Missouri. When I was home, I rarely traveled farther than could be reached by foot or bicycle. Being cooped up in a train car had been a challenge when I was used to being free in the open air.

The sun was hot again, so I opened Margaret's parasol to shield my face. I walked by the halls that housed expositions by so many other countries of the world—France, China, India, Sweden, and Cuba. The list went on and on. Each hall was built in keeping with the style and tradition of the home country. I stopped in front of the Chinese hall and felt the urge to go inside. The ornate carvings and use of red and yellow on the building were eye-catching, and I read on the map in my hand that the Chinese exhibition included a rose garden that was supposed to be the most beautiful on earth. I had heard that the emperor himself had a say in what China displayed at the fair and it was their first display at any world's fair.

I pulled myself away and made my way to the dormitories. When so many other buildings at the fair were elaborate and meant to make a statement, the dormitories were utilitarian and meant to be hidden.

The building was made of the same hemp and mud as the other buildings at the fair, but there was no effort to make it stand out. It hadn't even been painted white like all the other buildings. Instead, it was a dusty beige that was unappealing.

I walked up to the front door and knocked, but there was no answer. It was midmorning, so I guessed that most of the workers had been at their jobs since the early morning. There was no flight that day as far as I knew, but in two days' time there was to be a test flight. Everyone who entered the competition would be invited to try out the course. I knew that Alberto had to be furious that he didn't have an airship to test. I wondered if he would let Carl Myers's men mend his balloon. He had not been keen on the idea when it first came up. Perhaps he had already left St. Louis and returned to Europe.

The dormitory door opened easily, and I stepped inside. To my right, there was a wall of letter-size cubby holes that had been built in the wall to hold mail. Below each hole was a room number and last name. I found Ortiz at box eleven. I could only assume that meant she was in room eleven.

Could this have been Camilla, or another Ortiz? If it was Camilla, what was it like for her, living in a building with a bunch of men?

Beyond the mailboxes was a staircase, and to the right was a sign that read WOMEN'S HALL.

I went in the direction of the sign and found myself in a

stark hallway. The floor was concrete, the walls were white. It was cold and dank, and I could not imagine living there for the whole year that the fair would go on. Someone had tried to cheer up the space by pinning postcards and pages from magazines along the wall, but the efforts just made the space more depressing. I hated to think this was where Camilla had lived the last few weeks before she died.

I guessed that most of the people in the dormitory simply slept there, so maybe the surroundings didn't bother them as much as it did me.

All the doors along the hallway were closed except for door number six. Not wanting to startle anyone, I stepped in front of the doorway and said hello.

The young woman brushing her hair eyed me from head to toe. "Can I help you?" She kept brushing.

"Maybe," I said. "I was looking for room eleven."

She frowned at me. "Why would you have any interest in room eleven?"

"I'm looking for a woman."

"You found one," she said with a chuckle. "This whole floor is women. Men have the rest of the building as they have work on this side of the fair." She shook her head. "If you ask me, there should have been a completely different building built for the women. Even though we are on a different floor, the men are loud and crude. If I could do it again, I would not have agreed to come here."

"What is it you do?" I asked.

She narrowed her eyes at me. "Why do you want to know?"

I held Margaret's parasol loosely at my side. "I am sorry. I didn't mean to pry."

She studied me as if she was wondering if she should answer that question or not, but it seemed that she decided I was harmless, so she said, "I work in the greenhouses. It's a full-time job to keep all the plants thriving around the fair.

They get trampled and overheated and have to constantly be replaced by other plants. Are you looking for work? We could always use another set of hands."

I nodded. "I enjoy gardening back home, but I don't think I would be interested in working on this scale. You must know that I have been so impressed with the gardens. I wrote home to my father about it just yesterday."

Her face softened. Now that I had complimented her work, she wasn't as harsh with me as I first observed.

"Who are you looking for?" the young woman asked. "If she lives on this floor I know her. We all know each other on the floor."

"Camilla Ortiz," I said.

The skin of her face tightened. "I'm sorry to tell you that she is no longer here. She's dead."

It was the answer that I knew and that I expected. However, what she said next surprised me.

"I'm so sorry to hear that," I said as if I didn't already know. "Her family must be heartbroken."

"Her sister is heartbroken. I couldn't speak to her that long because I could tell she did not want to talk about it."

"She has a sister here at the fair?"

"Her sister is packing up her things to take home. She shouldn't take long. Camilla owned very little. If you like, I can introduce you to her." She stood up and smoothed her skirts. "I don't have much time because I have to get back to work."

"That would be very kind of you . . ." I trailed off.

"Suellen," she said. "Remember the name if you change your mind and want to work in the gardens."

I promised her I would, knowing very well I had no intention of working while I was at the world's fair.

I stepped back as she stepped out of her small room. "I'm Katharine," I said. "Is her sister's name Sylvia?"

"It is." She arched her brow. "How did you know that?"

"I heard someone say her name yesterday," I said.

"I can show you to her room on my way out. I'm already late getting to the greenhouses this morning as it is." She tied a scarf around her hair and walked out of the room.

I followed her down the dimly lit hallway that was as white and sterile as a hospital.

She stopped at a door at the very end of the hallway.

The last door was cracked open, and Suellen knocked on the door frame.

A high-pitched voice said, "If it is the police again, tell them that I don't want anything to do with them. They are just going through the motions and pretending it was all an accident."

"It's not the police. It's a . . ." She paused and looked at me. "A teacher."

She blinked. "It's a teacher asking about Camilla."

I stepped in front of the doorway, and Sylvia Ortiz and I stared at each other for a long moment. She looked just like her late sister. I had many twins come through my classroom over the years, and I usually could find something about the twins to easily tell them apart. Maybe one's forehead was a bit higher than the other's or one was left-handed while the other one was right-handed. There always was a telltale sign that allowed me to distinguish between them, but when it came to Camilla and Sylvia, I didn't see any sign like that. Had they been standing next to each other, there might have been something, but I would never know the answer to that.

CHAPTER 15

Suellen stepped aside. "I have to get to the greenhouses. I will let the two of you sort this out." She hurried away.

"Sylvia?" I asked.

She scowled at me. "Who would like to know?"

"I'm Katharine Wright."

Her eyes widened for a moment as if she recognized my name, but just as quickly the recognition was hidden behind a dark mask. She picked up a shoe that was on the floor and laid it on the bed.

The room was a mess, and more of a mess than just being lived in. It appeared to me that someone had gone through every drawer and dumped the contents on the floor. Was this Sylvia's method of packing? Because if it was, I could teach her a much better way.

"I'm so very sorry about your sister."

She eyed me. "If that's true, then you are the only one."

"What do you mean?"

"No one else is coming in here telling me they are sorry for my loss." She blinked away tears. "My sister didn't have many friends at the fair. I have learned that."

"I'm sorry for that."

"This isn't a place to make life-long friendships. Everyone

working at the fair can be discarded at any moment because they have another ten people wanting that spot. I wish my sister never came out here. We had everything that we needed in California, but she always wanted more."

"She wanted to be a mechanic," I said.

She narrowed her eyes at me. "How would you know that?"

"I spoke to Godwin at the concourse. He said he was a friend of hers."

Her face relaxed slightly. "Godwin spoke to you? He is— was a friend of my sister's. She wanted more than to be a mechanic. Camilla was a dreamer and she wanted to invent things. She had so many ideas of how she could make daily life better. But above all she wanted to fly. I knew when she heard of the aeronautics competition, there was no way that I would be able to convince her not to come here. She had her suitcase packed that afternoon and was booked on the evening train. There was nothing I could do to stop her."

I looked at the small suitcase in the bed. I imagined Camilla packing it and jumping on the train bound for St Louis. It was something my brothers would do. I understood Sylvia's perspective as a sibling. My brothers would stop at nothing to ensure that their next project was successful. Right now, they were determined to fly, but it hadn't started there. At first, they wanted to perfect the printing press for their print-making business, and then they went on to the bicycle shop, which was a good business. It did enough business that they never really had to worry about having enough money to take care of themselves. Finally, their interest fell onto flying, and that's where it stopped, but knowing my brothers, even after the flying business was settled, they would continue inventing and creating. It was in their blood. It wasn't something that they could stop.

"And you came with her to St. Louis?" I asked.

She looked at me. "No, I came a few days later. I couldn't

be alone at home without her. When our uncle found she was gone, he was furious. It was not livable there any longer." She pressed her lips together.

"You lived with your uncle? Not your parents?"

"They are in Mexico," she said, leaving it at that. "Our uncle gave us a place to stay when we needed it, but there was a cost."

I was too afraid to ask her what that cost was, but by her expression my imagination ran wild.

"You were in the Temple of Mirth yesterday. You were the girl on the other side of the glass. I thought you were Camilla," I said.

"How could I be Camilla when she is dead?" Her voice wavered.

"I didn't know at the time that Camilla had a twin sister, so you can imagine my shock when I saw you. What were you doing in the fun house?"

"I work at the Temple of Mirth from time to time when Zeb needs an extra hand. I take work where I can find it at the fair."

"Zeb is the man who runs the Temple of Mirth?"

She nodded. "Zeb Dandy, but I really don't believe that is his given name."

Neither did I.

"What is it that you do at the fun house?"

"Cleaning, mostly. People become so startled when they are in the Temple of Mirth that they knock over part of the attraction, spill things, or even become sick to their stomachs." She made a face. "Zeb isn't going to clean up those messes. I also sell tickets if Zeb is away."

"You didn't live here in the dormitory with your sister?" I asked.

"No." She lifted her chin. "I have a room outside of the fair in a boarding house. By the time, I came out to St. Louis, the dormitories were full. We asked if I could stay in Camilla's room but were told no by the dormitory director. As we were twins, I believe we could have managed to live together with no one being the wiser, but my sister didn't want to take the risk of losing her job."

She turned and went back to packing. Clothes and papers were strewn around the room. It didn't look to me like it had been made by mere untidiness.

"Was someone else in here?" I asked.

She looked around the room. "The police, not that long ago. They were not careful with my sister's belongings."

"The police made this mess."

"Yes." She would not look at me.

"What were they looking for?" I asked.

Sylvia shook her head. "How am I to know? They didn't tell me. They barely spoke to me at all, other than to ask who I was and why I was in this room."

"They had to know you are her sister by looking at you."

"I suppose they did." She nodded and tears came to her eyes. "I don't know how I will go on without my sister. We have never been apart more than a few days our whole lives. I keep thinking that I could live more than half of my life without her. What life would that be? It is impossible for anyone without a twin to understand."

My expression softened. "I can understand to some extent. I have brothers, and even though we are not twins, I wouldn't know how to go on in this life without them. A sibling bond is a special one."

She nodded with tears in her eyes and went back to picking up and folding clothes. She tucked everything neatly into the suitcase.

She picked up a small men's work shirt and stared at it. "Camilla came here to fulfill her dreams. The moment she heard the aeronautic competition was looking for mechanics, she was on the next train from Los Angeles to come here." Sylvia sat on the edge of the thin mattress.

"How did she start as a mechanic?" I asked, prompting her to talk. I thought it might help.

She folded the shirt and set it on the bed. "She worked in my uncle's shop. She was gifted with engines in particular. Anytime that someone came into the shop with an engine problem, our uncle gave it to her to work on. She would have done well at the shop if our uncle wasn't so cruel and hard to work for. At least I was able to escape him during the day as I cleaned houses for ladies in the city. Because I was able to get away, I wasn't jealous of Camilla's talent. She had been interested in flying for so long, and I knew that she saw the fair as a means of escape from our uncle, but everyone told her that the fair would never hire a woman to be a mechanic. They were both right and wrong."

"What do you mean?"

She put the shirt in the suitcase. "The fair hired her as a mechanic, but when she began working no one would let her do anything. She was relegated to be a tour guide of sorts to direct people around the concourse."

I had learned as much from Godwin. "That must have upset her."

"It broke her heart." She shuddered as if she knew exactly how her twin had felt, and maybe she did. I had read before that twins could sense each other's emotions and feelings. "She and I were so different," she went on. "I dreamed of marriage and having a family, and she wanted to build things and achieve fame. If we didn't look alike, I would wonder if we were even related, much less twins."

"You came to St. Louis to escape your uncle?" I asked.

"Yes, and I couldn't be in California without her. She's my twin, my other half. The distance was painful, but it is nothing compared to the distance that I feel now between us. It's a distance I can't cross. She may be very different from me, but she was my closest companion." She studied my face as if she realized for the first time how odd it was for me to be standing in her sister's room with her. "Suellen said you were a teacher."

"I am."

"Why does a teacher want to know who killed my sister?"

"Because I was the one who found her." I dropped my eyes to the floor. "And she asked me for help. I couldn't help her in life, but perhaps I could help Camilla in death."

She grabbed my arm. "Did she say anything in those last moments?"

I licked my lips. "She said *aeronautics competition.*"

Sylvia dropped her hand from my arm and paled. "She was killed because of that? I thought it would be . . ."

"You thought it would be what?"

"It doesn't matter."

I thought it mattered quite a lot.

There was a loud bang in the hallway, and Sylvia went to the door and peeked out. "I have to go."

"Go? Go where?"

She ran to the window, threw aside the curtains, and opened the window. Before I could even realize what was happening, she had one leg out.

"What am I to do?" I asked.

"Just don't tell him that you saw me." She looked me in the eye. "Please." With that she was gone.

I closed the window behind her and put the curtains back in place just as the room's door was thrown open.

A young blond man stood in the doorway. I recognized the young man even though he wasn't in his porter uniform. "John Smith?"

His eyes went wide. "Who?"

I put my hands on my hips. "I knew that you lied to me about your name at the train station a few days ago."

He still looked confused.

"You retrieved my hat that had fallen on the track," I said.

"Oh!" His face cleared. "I remember."

"Why did you lie to me about your name?"

He cleared his throat, and his prominent Adam's apple bobbed up and down. "As a porter at the station, so many people ask me my name. I have learned it's safer to lie. Who are you, and what are you doing in Camilla's room?"

I folded my arms and looked down my nose at him, which was quite a feat considering he was a good foot taller than I was. "You're the one who came bursting into a woman's dormitory room. Why should I tell you that when you haven't told me your real name or why *you* are here?"

He took a step into the room, and I held out my hand. "Don't come one step closer. I haven't invited you in. Has your mother not taught you proper manners?"

He wrinkled his nose as if he was offended by this comment. "I have a very good mother."

I nodded. "I'm sure you do, and I'm also sure that she would be embarrassed to see how rude you are being to another woman right now."

He blushed.

"Now, tell me your name," I said in my sternest teacher voice.

The voice did the trick, as it usually did, because he swallowed and said, "I'm Hal Buckman, and that's my real name, before you ask."

"Very nice to meet you, Hal. I'm Katharine Wright. Now, tell me why you're here."

"I'm looking for Camilla. I was told this is her room." The firmness was back in his voice. "It is urgent that I talk to her. She's making a mistake."

"A mistake over what?" I asked.

He clenched his jaw, and I took that to mean he had no plans to answer my question.

"Where is she? Time is running out."

Time had run out for Camilla, that was for sure and certain.

I cocked my head. "How do you know Camilla?"

He brushed his bangs out of his eyes. His hair was a bit too long to be fashionable, but it was full and wavy. He was a handsome young man, and Camilla had been quite lovely even when dressed as a mechanic. They would have made a nice couple, but I wasn't sure that's what they were to each other.

"From the fair," he snapped. "That's how anyone knows anyone else in St. Louis this year. Now, will you tell me where she is?" He folded his arms over his broad chest.

"Camilla passed away yesterday," I said as gently as I could. "That is why I'm packing up her things."

"What?" He blinked at me as if he couldn't understand what I was saying.

"Camilla is dead."

"H-how?"

"The police are looking into it."

"The police? Did someone kill her?"

"It looks that way."

He slammed his hand against the doorframe. "I told her that something like this could happen. I told her not to be so stupid!" His face turned gray. "Does Sylvia know?"

I nodded, but I didn't tell him that Sylvia had been with me in the room just a moment ago. I couldn't wholly trust Hal. He had lied to me once already. Everything he had to say had to be called into question.

"You claimed that you warned her that something like this could happen. Was she in danger? Do you know why she might have been killed?" I asked.

He ignored my questions, and his lower lip began to wobble. "Are you sure she's dead?"

I nodded. "I'm sorry."

He gave a strangled gasp and ran down the hallway.

I hurried out into the hall after him. He barreled through the hallway and out the door. I followed him outside and watched as he sprinted away from the dormitory. I caught my breath. He was a fast runner; and he should've been one of the competitors in the Olympic games happening on the fairgrounds. It was impossible for me to catch him, so I hobbled back into the dormitory. Running was not an activity to which I was accustomed.

Why had Sylvia run away from Hal Buckman? He was scared of his own shadow. Maybe she didn't want to talk to anyone about her sister. If that was true, why had she spoken to me?

Suellen's door was closed as I walked back to Camilla's room. I hoped that Sylvia had returned. However, when I stepped into the room, I found it empty.

I shook my head and decided to finish the packing for Sylvia. It didn't take long. Camilla had two dresses, a small-size men's work shirt, one pair of shoes, an extra set of coveralls, and a few undergarments. I folded everything as neatly as possible and tucked them into the small brown suitcase.

Sylvia had said Camilla wanted to make a name for herself. If that was true, where were her notes with her plans? If she was an inventor, she would have some sort of way to record them. I knew from my brothers that inventors made thousands upon thousands of notes. It was common, when I would go about tidying our house in the morning, to find my brothers' ideas and notes sprawled all over the dining room.

It steamed me to no end that they wouldn't at least clean off the table at the end of the night. Was that too much to ask? However, by my brothers leaving their scraps of paper behind, at least I knew what they were up to and could get the gist of their flying machine mechanics. I might not have the fullest grasp of it, but I knew more than most laymen, to be sure.

I wished I had spoken to Camilla before she died. Maybe I could have put her in contact with my brothers, and they would have encouraged her or given her guidance.

I closed the suitcase and set it by the window. Maybe I thought Sylvia would pop up and take it that way. The room was stark and empty, but I knew something about being a young woman, even though at thirty I no longer considered myself young. My friends were married and most had children or, in Margaret's case, wanted them. I was the spinster schoolteacher. My future was all but set in stone.

But knowing young women, I knew there was a lack of trust with personal things. This would be my one and only time to search the room. I had to make it quick, because I didn't know if Hal would return—or worse, the police.

I lifted the mattress and peeked under it. Nothing. I opened each drawer again, even though I had looked in them when packing her belongings. Nothing. I ran my hand along the top of the window frame and door frame and came back with fingers covered in dust.

There was nothing there. The last place to look was under the dresser. It was solid oak and covered with nicks and scuffs as if it had been moved many times. I wondered if the fair purchased it from a salvage yard. They weren't going to buy top-of-the-line items for the workers living in the dormitories, and this dresser was evidence of that.

I pulled on the side of the dresser and it wouldn't move. I frowned and leveraged my body against the wall and pushed it with my right foot. It jerked forward, causing me to lose my balance. I stumbled back and the floorboard below my foot made a terrible squeak.

I had to move the dresser enough to see that there was nothing behind it, but by that point, I had lost interest in the dresser and was looking at the floor. I knelt by the board. It looked like all the others around it, but there was a small hole drilled into one end.

I put my pinkie in the hole and pulled back. The board lifted easily.

There was a shallow crawl space below, and I could smell

the dirt beneath the building. There was no foundation to speak of, and that was because, like most of the other buildings at the fair, this one wasn't built to last. When the fair was over, the earthmovers would come in and all would be erased.

Below there was a small black book that could easily fit into a man's jacket pocket. It lay on a piece of burlap. I smiled. Beneath the floor was the perfect hiding spot. I should have thought of it from the start.

Back at my home, there was a loose board in my bedroom floor. It held my childhood diary and my musings from high school. They were the memories that I didn't want my brothers or father to find. They were thoughts of grief over my mother's death and musings about falling in love and marrying—or not. My mother's death was a constant companion of mine, but I had given up on the hopes for love and marriage at this stage in my life. It wasn't something that my father or brothers would abide, and I knew I had a good life. But still . . .

I picked up the book and opened it. I expected to see a young woman's journal with her musings about her days or perhaps comments about her friends or a young man whom she admired. It was none of that. Instead, inside the journal there were detailed drawings of machinery and engines and notes of equations and measurements. I had a rudimentary understanding of such things, thanks to my older brothers. The writing was neat and precise, but it was clear to me that the penmanship had a feminine turn.

I couldn't understand everything that I read or saw on the book's pages, but it was clear to me that Camilla had a gift, a gift that had been snuffed out far too early. I sat back on my heels. What could she have accomplished for herself and other women, had she lived? I was more determined than ever to find out what happened to her.

And I could not help but wonder if this was the real reason

that Hal came into the room. Had he been looking for this? I wasn't sure. Hal had a very emotional reaction at hearing about Camilla's death. I would more likely think that he was in love with her than that he wanted to steal her notes; not that it couldn't be both. Men were unpredictable creatures when it came to feelings. And motives.

Rather than pack the notebook into the suitcase, I tucked it in the pocket of my skirt. This was evidence of something . . . of what, I didn't know, but I did know it was evidence that I would need.

I stood, dusted off my skirt, and started to leave the room. At the last moment, I decided to take the small suitcase with me as well. It would give me an excuse to track down Sylvia, because I had even more questions for her than when we met.

CHAPTER 16

I didn't know where Sylvia was staying or how I would find her. The only person I knew that might know something was Zeb Dandy at the Temple of Mirth. He was the one who had said Sylvia's name to me in the first place, and she admitted to working for him.

The walk from the dormitories near the concourse to the Pike was close to a mile, but I thought it would do me well to walk.

On a whim, I turned in the opposite direction from the Pike. I wanted to return to the scene of the crime. Maybe there was something I could glean from it now that I wasn't in a state of shock over finding a dead body. Maybe there would be police there, and I could ask them questions. I had a feeling that they would be reluctant to speak to me at all, but *nothing ventured, nothing gained*, as they say.

To reach the hangars behind the large concourse, I had to walk all the way around it. All the while I kept an eye out for anyone who I thought might be connected to Camilla, like her sister Sylvia, Godwin Landry—the mechanic that Margaret and I met the day before—and Hal Buckman. I didn't spot any one of them.

I heard shouting just as soon I was within fifteen feet of the first hangar.

"I said no! That should be the end of it."

I couldn't hear the person's response, but clearly, it was not welcome to the man who yelled in top volume in a heavily accented voice. "You are a fool. Do you think I would risk the integrity of my airship to allow your sweaty numbskulls to attempt to repair it? That I would risk everything that I had ever worked for and my very life? A bandage is not going to fix what has happened. I will return to France where I will have the well-trained and skilled balloon makers that I need."

I inched my way to the side of the first hangar and peeked around the corner. From there, I could clearly see Alberto, Carl Myers, the guard Gilliam, and two other men. The men I didn't know were in mechanic uniforms like the one Camilla had worn.

Myers pointed at the men. "They are skilled. I have full confidence that your airship will be like new. No, it will be better than new."

Alberto shook his head. "My mind is made up. I'm going back to Paris. I should have known better than attempt to fly in such a crude place as St. Louis."

Myers's face flushed and he stood just inches from Alberto. He was a good five inches taller than the slim Brazilian. "You will go up in that airship. We didn't pay all this money to advertise that you are flying over St. Louis on July first to pull out now. There is still plenty of time to mend the airship before that date, and you will do as I say."

Alberto seemed unmoved by Myers's speech and held his ground. "That is something that you should have thought of before you hired incompetent guards who had only one task, to watch over my airship."

Myers stepped back, but he shook with anger.

Gilliam took two steps back. If I were he, I would have just left the hangar area altogether. Someone would be blamed for the destruction of Alberto's balloon, and at the moment, it was looking like it was going to be that guard.

"I expect justice for what I have endured. Isn't that something that you Americans pride yourself on?" Alberto asked.

Myers glared at him. "The police are in the process of looking for the vagabond who was spotted loitering around the hangar. He is the one that did this, and rest assured, he will be held accountable."

I raised my brow. The mention of this mystery man was news to me. Who was he? And where did Myers learn about him?

Alberto stepped back from Myers and picked a piece of imaginary lint off of his sleeve. "If you can find the culprit in three days' time and hold him accountable, I will *consider* letting your men fix my balloon."

Myers folded his arms. "I have full confidence that will happen."

"I do not," the Brazilian said in return. Then he spun on his heel and marched away.

After Alberto was gone, Myers turned on Gilliam and shook his finger at him. "You had better be right about the stranger, because if you are wrong, I won't just fire you, I will ruin your whole life!" With that he stomped away.

Gilliam's lower lip quivered as if he might cry, but I was happy to see that he had been able to keep it together.

The two mechanics looked at each other and sauntered off. I couldn't say that I blamed them.

Gilliam looked around the hangar area, as if he wasn't quite sure what to do with himself now.

I straightened my back, opened Margaret's parasol with a flourish, and marched out into the open as if I was just out for a stroll at the fair. Not that the hangars were a suitable place for a single woman to stroll, but I had never been the conventional type.

The suitcase I carried—stuffed with Camilla's belongings—would no doubt prompt some questions, but I continued on.

Gilliam's eyes bugged out of his head when he saw me. "What are you doing here?"

"Looking for you. I'm Katharine, if you will recall."

"Yes, I remember," he said. "How could I forget? I can forget nothing of that horrible day, as much as I wish that I could."

"That is a very good point. It's not often that an airship is destroyed and a dead woman is found at the same time."

He looked like he might be sick by the way I put that.

"It was such a terrible day." His voice shook. "And it seems that the nightmare is nowhere close to coming to an end."

"Do you know Camilla Ortiz?" I asked as the sun came out from behind a cloud. I angled Margaret's parasol to shade my head.

He blinked at me as if this was the very last question he expected to hear. "Camilla?"

"Yes, the girl who was found between the hangars just about the same time," I said.

"I knew her as well as anyone at the fair. We are all passing through, you see. No one is setting down roots, and, because of that, we can be whoever we wish to be in the short time we are here."

"Are you pretending to be someone else?" I arched my brow like I did when students whispered to each other in Latin class.

Beads of sweat gathered on his brow. "No, but I wish I had. If I had been more careful, maybe I wouldn't find myself in the place that I am in now. I should have stayed with my job that was close to home, but I thought by coming out here that it would be good and easy money. There has been nothing good or easy about it. My wife is trying to convince me to quit."

"And why don't you?"

He licked his lips. "I suppose it's sheer stubbornness.

When someone tells me that I can't do something I just dig in my heels that much further."

On this point, I could relate to Gilliam. It was a trait that infuriated my brothers to no end.

"And you know Camilla Ortiz?"

"I knew who Camilla was. There aren't that many women wearing men's clothes at the fair. She was always around the hangars. She told me that she was hired as a mechanic, but the only thing that the other mechanics were allowing her to do was to run errands and direct people who wandered into the concourse area."

"Did she ever say how she felt about that?" I asked.

"She wasn't happy, but she was still glad to be here. She was learning a lot. She talked to everyone that she could about flight and engines and all sorts of other things that I don't understand. Every time she asked questions, they went over my head, but the aviators she spoke to seemed to be impressed by her knowledge." He rubbed the back of his neck.

I nodded. "When was the last time that you saw her alive?"

He rocked back on his heels as if he thought that the question was too invasive. Maybe it was, but I asked it anyway. I didn't mind making others or myself uncomfortable to get the answers that I needed.

He cleared his throat. "It was the early evening before she died. Peterson and I were in the middle of a shift change, and Mr. Santos-Dumont and his men were in the hangar and looking over the contents of all the crates that held the parts and pieces of his airship."

I nodded for him to continue.

"She came into the hangar and said that she wanted to speak to Mr. Santos-Dumont about his engine. She claimed to have ideas on how to make it better and lighter. One of the men tried to chase her away, saying they didn't need any help from a woman." He took a breath. "She wouldn't leave until she spoke to Mr. Santos-Dumont. He came over to see what the commotion was about, and as soon as he saw Camilla he cried, *I told you to leave me alone!* He left shortly after that."

"So, he knew who she was," I said.

"It seemed that way. From what I gathered, this wasn't the first time she tried to talk to him."

"Did he say anything else?" I asked.

Gilliam nodded. "He said something like she needed to stop following him. I got the impression that she had made a nuisance of herself with him since he got off of the train."

"When did he arrive by train?"

"The day before Camilla died," he said.

That was the same day I arrived at the fair. I'd not seen Alberto on my train, which didn't mean much. There had been hundreds of people on the train. I certainly didn't see all of them, and Alberto could have been on another train altogether. However, I found it to be telling that the first time that I had seen Camilla on the train platform, she had been running away from someone. It was also the first time that I had seen Hal Buckman when he saved my hat.

My head began to spin as to how this all could be connected, but I did not believe for a moment that it was coincidence.

All in all, it was unexpected news that Alberto knew Camilla. He had shown no signs of recognition when he saw her body. I tried to remember if he'd had any reactions at all. At the time, he was far more concerned about the airship than he was about the dead girl.

Had he intentionally kept the fact that he knew Camilla a secret to avoid getting involved, or was it *because* he was involved? Alberto just jumped up three spaces on my suspect list.

If she was harassing him, that would give him a motive for murder.

If she was the one who destroyed his balloon, he definitely

had a motive. However, if he knew that, why didn't he just come out and put the blame on the dead girl? She made a perfect scapegoat.

"I have to believe that the two crimes are connected to each other. They happened close in time and place," I said. "That is why I'm asking about Camilla."

"I can see how you would think that, but it doesn't make it true." He wiped at his brow with a gray handkerchief.

"I agree." I folded the parasol and dropped it to my side. "But it makes it probable, and probability is all we have to go on at the moment."

"Camilla loved flying. She wouldn't do anything to stop the competition. It was all that she could talk about. She was most excited to see Mr. Santos-Dumont."

"Then she wouldn't tamper with the airship."

"No. I don't think she would." He shook his head. "I know who it was. It wasn't Camilla. The police will find the culprit and put this all to rest."

"Who is the culprit?"

He pursed his lips. "I don't know his name, but he's a vagabond who came to the hangars every day for the last few months. He was always conversing with Camilla too. I could tell at times that she tired of his conversation. Maybe she rebuffed him, and he snapped. That would be my guess."

I wrinkled my nose at his last statement. "And do you know why he was coming to the hangars so much?"

"I had asked him to leave more than once. He said that he wanted to talk to Mr. Santos-Dumont. The vagabond started doing this months before Mr. Santos-Dumont even arrived. There were rumors that he would be flying his airship on the concourse, but no one knew for sure."

"But this man was confident that Alberto Santos-Dumont would be here?"

Gilliam shrugged. "Who knows? He turned out to be right, but how could he have known that? Peterson and I wrote him off as an eccentric. He had to be the one who did this though. He asked about Mr. Santos-Dumont all the time, and the day after Santos-Dumont's airship arrives, it's damaged. I can't think that is a coincidence."

"Why would the man damage the airship if he wanted to see it fly?" As I asked a question, a memory struck me of seeing a man peeking around the corner of one of the hangars just before Alberto arrived to show Margaret the airship that morning. At the time, I hadn't thought much of it. There were so many people wandering around the fair. It was to be expected to see someone just about anywhere, but I wondered if it was the vagabond, as Gilliam called him, watching over the scene. But if he tampered with the airship and/or killed Camilla, why would he still be there? Wouldn't he have wanted to run away and go into hiding?

Gilliam frowned. "I haven't worked out that piece, but it's the only explanation that makes any sense. Besides, I saw him that morning when Peterson and I switched shifts again. He was here early in the morning."

I had to admit that the man's proximity to the hangar, which would also be proximity to the airship and the spot where I found Camilla's body, was suspicious.

"What's his name?"

He shook his head. "I don't know. I never asked. I didn't ask questions of him because it would just encourage him to talk to me more, and I didn't want that."

"What did he look like? How old was he?"

Gilliam shoved his handkerchief back into his trousers pocket. "He was just your average-looking man. He wasn't that tall, but he was thin. His skin was pale but had a leathery quality, as if he spent a lot of time in the sun at one point in his life. He wears spectacles like you do."

"And his age?"

"Middle age, I would say. Definitely old enough to know

better. I don't know much more than that. Like I said, I kept my distance," Gilliam added.

I frowned. If I saw a person loitering in the same spot day in and day out, I would have certainly asked for his name and his reason for being there. Perhaps that was the teacher in me. There are times that I believed I had been jaded by some of my more mischievous students to believe that everyone was up to no good. However, in the case of this man, that just might be true.

CHAPTER 17

I thanked Gilliam for the information. "You have been very helpful."

He wiped sweat from his brow. "Mr. Myers and the police don't believe so. I'm afraid if they don't find that man, they will put the blame for this incident on me."

"Why do you say that?"

"Because someone has to be blamed, in their thinking, and I'm discardable to men like them."

"Will they blame you for the injury to Mr. Santos-Dumont's airship, or for Camilla's death?"

He stared at me. "Camilla's death is not as important as the airship to them. You have to know that by now; they have said next to nothing about her death. In this short time, you have asked me more about it than they have."

I pursed my lips together. It was what I had suspected, but I was disappointed to hear it. I would have thought a young woman's life would have been more important than a punctured balloon, but I supposed that depended on who the young woman was. To Myers and the police, she was just another person passing through St. Louis for the fair. They couldn't care about all of them, or so it seemed.

Although there wasn't much in it, Camilla's small suitcase

grew heavy in my hand. I was eager to find Sylvia and pass it off to her. The only place I knew to look for her was at the Temple of Mirth on the Pike. I wasn't looking forward to going back there. I certainly didn't have any intention of going back inside the fun house.

Before I did that, I told Gilliam to step out of the sun. His skin was growing quite red and the man was in danger of heat stroke, in my estimation. "Drink some water," I added for good measure.

He nodded as if he were taking my suggestions to heart. I didn't know about the drinking water, but at the very least he stepped around to the shady side of the hangar before I walked away.

I walked down the line of hangars until I came to the spot where I found Camilla lying in the gravel. I didn't know what I expected to find there; maybe some kind of marker that noted the spot. I certainly didn't expect to find a grown man kneeling on the gravel in tears.

He looked like he might be praying, so I wasn't sure what I should do. At the same time, I couldn't walk away. He was kneeling in the very spot where Camilla died.

I noisily cleared my throat.

The man, who I guessed was close to my eldest brother Reuchlin's age, in his late forties, jumped to his feet. When he saw who it was, he relaxed slightly, maybe because he thought I was a tourist, or because I was only a woman. In either case, I took offense that I didn't inspire more fear in him.

"Sir, are you quite all right?" I asked as I took in his pale, leathery skin and spectacles, just as Gilliam had described him. I knew this had to be the vagabond that the police were looking for. I had to proceed with caution.

He brushed the last of his tears from his cheeks, but the act did little to hide the fact that he had been crying. "Are you lost? There are no flights on the concourse today."

"I know that. I have been told several times."

He frowned. "Then, there is no reason for you to be here."

"What is your reason for being here? You aren't wearing coveralls like all the other workers on the concourse."

He looked down at his button-down shirt and tweed trousers that were looking a bit threadbare at the knees.

"Are you here because of Camilla?" I asked.

"Who are you?" he snapped.

"Katharine. I know her twin sister, Sylvia." What I said wasn't untrue, but I did imply that Sylvia and I were much closer than we actually were.

"How is Sylvia?" the man asked.

"Heartbroken."

He nodded. "I know the feeling all too well."

"What is your name?" I asked.

"Charles."

I noted that he omitted his last name, just as I had. "How do you know Camilla?"

"She was a friend, my only friend at the fair. She was the only one who would even give me the time of day. She was kind to me when others weren't, and she knew so much about flying and engines. She taught me so much. She had promised to show me her notes for the engine she was working on, but that will never happen now."

Those notes in question were in my skirt pocket at that very moment. I wasn't about to tell him that.

"She was going to show them to me after she met with Joshua Beard and got his input. I was eager to hear what she learned from him."

I wrinkled my brow. "Joshua Beard. Is that the same Mr. Beard with the steel fortune?"

He frowned at me. "The one and the same. How do you know of him?"

"I met him my first night here at the fair. He was quite charming."

"If I had as much money as he does, I would be charming too," he said. His eyes began to water again. "I can't believe that she won't be here to talk to any longer. She was my only friend, the only one who would talk to me about flying. I was meant to fly, and I can't see that happening now without her help."

I wrinkled my brow. "How was she helping you?"

"I knew she would be the one to convince Alberto Santos-Dumont to let me fly with him. I wanted him to take me up in the sky."

Even if Camilla had been able to convince Alberto that this man was worthy of taking up in the air, it would be impossible. The airship was for one person and one person only.

"Alberto's airship was tampered with and it might not fly at all now," I said. "Do you know anything about that?"

"No," he said.

"I think that it has to be tied to Camilla's death."

"If it is, I know who it was. It was that young man who wouldn't leave her alone."

"What young man?"

"Hal is his first name. I don't know any more than that. Camilla told me not to worry about him. She claimed that he was harmless, but now she's dead. I had reason to worry, and he wasn't harmless."

I raised my brow. It seemed that I would have to be a lot more careful when it came to Hal. "Is Hal part of the fair? I thought he was a porter at the train station."

"How do you know that?" the man snapped.

"I saw him working there," I said, leaving it at that.

"I see," he said, mollified.

"When was the last time that you saw Camilla?"

There was fear in his eyes. I had seen the same expression on many of my students when I surprised them with a quiz as soon as they were in their seats in my classroom.

"I saw her every day. She was here every day. That just shows her dedication to the fair, and the aeronautics competition in particular."

"Did you see her the day she died?"

He looked at his hands.

I decided to go with a blunter approach. "Did you kill Camilla?"

Tears came to his eyes. "Camilla? I would not hurt a hair on her head. She was the only one at the concourse that gave me the time of day."

"But you saw her that morning."

He wrung his hands. "I did. I had heard that Mr. Santos-Dumont had arrived, and his airship was in the hangar. I wanted to see it. I didn't realize it wasn't assembled yet, so I was disappointed when I slipped into the hangar and realized that everything was packed in crates. I couldn't see a thing."

"Were the crates open when you saw them?"

He nodded. "They were all open."

"Where was the guard?" I asked.

"There were two guards there. They were out having a smoke together and laughing. Whatever they were talking about had them occupied. It was easy for me to slip by them and go into the hangar."

"Other than the airship pieces still being in crates, did anything else catch your eye?"

He didn't answer.

"Were you alone in the hangar?"

He swallowed. "No. There was someone else in the hangar."

"Who was it?"

He looked me right in the eye. "It was Camilla."

I raised my brow. This information would go along with the theory that Camilla was the one who tampered with the airship. Why would she do that if she was so eager to see it fly? It didn't make any sense to me at all.

"Did she know that you were there?"

"No, she didn't see me. She seemed to be so frightened that I don't know if she would have seen me if I was standing right in front of her."

"She was the only one there?"

"No, there was another person."

"Who?" I asked.

"I don't know. I only heard a voice."

"A man or woman?"

"The voice was too low. I couldn't tell."

"Do you think this second person was the one who killed her?"

"I don't know, but if I had to guess, I would say yes. I blame myself for that."

"Why?" I asked.

"I wish that I had revealed myself and stopped her. I wish that I took the time to talk to her one last time. Maybe that would have changed the course of her fate if I had. I didn't because I was too afraid of being caught where I shouldn't be. I put myself first, and my friend, my only friend, was killed."

There was a shrill whistle. "Stop! Police!"

His face was as white as a sheet. I looked over my shoulder to see four police officers running at us.

He turned to run away, but he wasn't nearly fast enough. Two of the officers tackled him and pressed his face in the gravel.

"Be careful. You're hurting him," I reprimanded.

Officer Jeffries, who was one of the officers who held him down, glared at me. "What are you doing here?"

"I could ask you the same thing. I was having a conversation with this man, and you all jumped on him."

Officer Jeffries pulled the man to his feet. The man spit gravel out of his mouth.

One of the other officers glared at him. "Watch what you're doing."

"Charles F. Morrison, you are under arrest for damage to Alberto Santos-Dumont's airship."

"It wasn't me," Charles said. "There was another person in the hangar when I was there."

"You admit being there that morning." Officer Jeffries yanked Charles's arm behind his back.

Charles's face turned bright red.

"Take him away," Officer Jeffries said.

When he spoke, Charles fainted.

CHAPTER 18

Officer Jeffries stared at Charles lying in the gravel. "What do we do now?"

Another of the officers tapped Charles with the toe of his boot.

Charles's eyes fluttered open.

"Stand up. You're embarrassing yourself," Officer Jeffries snapped.

"I didn't do this." Charles's panicked eyes turned in my direction. "Please tell him that I didn't do this."

I didn't know how he expected me to do that when he hadn't even told me his name. However, it was clear to me that Charles had cared about Camilla, but I also knew that murders of passion were a real thing.

A police wagon came to the stop at the far end of the hanger. The police had known Charles would be here and were determined to arrest him.

"Say something," Charles shouted at me.

I didn't say anything. I was too shocked to speak.

Hurt filled Charles's eyes, and I felt regret, but not enough to speak up for a man whom I knew nothing about.

Officer Jeffries looked at me. "Do you have anything to say?"

I licked my lips and found my voice. "You have to give him a chance to tell his story. He heard someone else in the hangar that morning."

Officer Jeffries scowled at me. "It is to be expected that a criminal would make up lies."

"But what if they aren't lies?" I asked.

He just shook his head as if he couldn't believe that I would be that naïve. He nodded to the other two officers, who half dragged, half carried Charles to the police wagon. They shoved him into the back and closed the door. His pale face stood out starkly from behind the bars.

Officer Jeffries turned to me. "I suggest you stay out of this area. The more you show your face, the more trouble you are likely to find yourself in."

That was usually the case when it came to me.

"I have a question before I go," I said.

He gave me a look as if he couldn't believe my audacity. "What is it?"

"What were the police looking for in Camilla's room?"

He frowned at me. "It's common for officers to search the home of the deceased to look for clues as to what might have happened."

"And did you find any?"

He didn't answer me.

"Do you believe that the crimes are connected?" I asked.

Again, he said nothing.

"You must, because you said that Charles was arrested for tampering with Mr. Santos-Dumont's airship. You said nothing about Camilla Ortiz. Are you giving her case the attention that it deserves?"

"We are following protocol. At this time, the sergeant wants us to focus on the airship tampering, and if it that leads to the person who killed Miss Ortiz, so be it."

I frowned. It seemed to me that the police had it all backward. They should have been focusing on murder and the tampering should be secondary, but Alberto was rich and influential; Camilla was neither of those things.

He leaned forward. "What is your interest in all of this?"

I looked him in the eye. "I saw her die."

He blinked and swallowed. For a moment, the professional demeanor that he put on that morning cracked, and I saw the frightened man who had been with me shortly after finding Camilla's body. "Yes, well, I advise you to stay out of it from here forward. You are only increasing your own chances of being hurt." Officer Jeffries eyed the suitcase in my hand, and I held my breath. I think maybe he wanted to inquire about it, but he climbed into the cabin at the front of the wagon, and the wagon, with Charles in it, rolled away.

My shoulders sank. I owed Charles nothing, but I felt like I let him down all the same, because in my gut I knew that he didn't kill Camilla or tamper with the airship. This was one time where my gut feeling wasn't enough.

Officer Jeffries told me to leave the concourse, but I didn't come this far not to complete my mission. Still carrying Camilla's suitcase, I went to the spot between the hangars where I had found her. If I expected to find some kind of evidence at the spot where Camilla had died, I was sadly disappointed. The only indication that anything had changed in the alley was the fact that the gravel was freshly raked. I was certain that was to cover up any sign of anything amiss.

I sighed. I needed to head to the Pike and look for Sylvia to see if I could hand off the suitcase. I was starting to doubt the wisdom of taking it with me when I'd left the dormitory.

I stepped out of the narrow alley and bumped into a person who crossed my path. I dropped Camilla's suitcase, the latch gave way, and the suitcase popped open. Camilla's things fell on the gravel.

"Katharine, we have to stop bumping into each other like this."

I looked up from the small pile of clothes on the gravel to

find Harry Haskell looking down at me. He had a pleasant smile on his face, and amusement in his eyes. After the morning I'd had, I was instantly annoyed with his expression.

"Are you heading home?" He nodded at my suitcase.

I blushed as I saw Camilla's undergarments on top of the pile of clothes that had fallen out of the suitcase. I knelt down and quickly scooped everything into the case and snapped it shut. In my haste, a stocking stuck out the side of the suitcase, but that couldn't be helped.

I cleared my throat. "This isn't my suitcase. I was taking it to the owner."

He raised his brow. "Is that something that you do now? Deliver suitcases? I would think that you were higher up in society than that. You are a teacher, are you not?" he teased.

I scowled. "I'm not too good for any task and am happy to help any way that I can. If the way to help another person is to deliver a suitcase, then so be it."

He held up his hands. "I'm sorry if I offended you in any way."

I sighed. "You didn't. It's been a long day, and Margaret isn't feeling well. I'm concerned about her, so my thoughts are scattered. Please forgive me."

"Oh, I'm sorry to hear that. Please send her my well wishes. I have always liked Margaret and thought of her as a good influence on you."

I brushed dust from my skirt. "Well, I have to be on my way back to her. Surely, she needs to rub her good ways onto me even more."

He held up his hand to stop me. "I thought you might be here because of the airship. Surely, you know what happened to it."

"Mr. Santos-Dumont's airship." I nodded. "I know all about it. I was with him when he discovered that it was damaged."

"You do get around, don't you, Katharine." He removed his notebook from the breast pocket of his jacket. "That's why I'm here. What good luck that you were at the scene of the crime, as it were. I was assigned to write about it for the *Star*. Everyone loves stories like this." He licked the tip of his pencil. "Do the police have any leads?"

I frowned as I remembered Charles F. Morrison being taken away just a short time ago. It seems that Harry just missed the biggest part of the story.

"The police wouldn't tell me if they did." It was the truth.

He put the notebook away. "I suppose you're right. You were just a tourist that happened to be there."

I put my hands on my hips. "*Just* a tourist?"

"You're not from the fair committee or part of Santos-Dumont's team. How would you know anything about it? The police might give up details to those men because of their position at the fair, but why would they say anything to you?"

My fists were digging so deeply into my sides, I wouldn't be the least bit surprised if I saw bruises there when I put on my nightclothes that evening.

He smiled as if he knew that he had me right where he wanted me. Well, I certainly had a way to wipe that smirk off of his face. "The attack on Santos-Dumont's airship is alarming, but it's nothing compared to murder."

The smirk dissolved from his face. "Murder?"

"I thought you would already have known about that." I made a show of examining my fingernails. "There's not much that I can tell you, since I'm just a tourist."

He took his notebook from his jacket pocket a second time. "You have my attention, Katharine. What is it that you know?"

I cleared my throat. "The same morning that Santos-Dumont discovered that his airship had been tampered with, a woman died just a few yards away outside, between the hangars." My tone became more serious. "I was the one who found her. She was alive, but just barely." I paused. "There was nothing I could do to save her."

His mouth hung open.

"I can tell from your face that you know nothing about it," I said.

"I don't think any of the papers know about it. I would have heard about it by now if someone else got the scoop. My editor would be livid with me if I missed the story, and I was right here. I think you need to start from the beginning."

"I will tell you what I know on one condition."

He tucked his notebook under his arm and folded his arms. "Are you really in a place to put conditions on this?"

I looked up at him. "I am. You know nothing about what I am about to tell you, so I will be requiring something in return for the information."

He scowled.

"Alberto's airship being damaged is a big story, but I think that you should concentrate on the murder. It could be a big scoop for you, as it seems the police and the fair have been able to hide the murder from the press if you know nothing about it."

"What are your conditions?"

"As you're the press, the police may be willing to speak to you more. I want you to share information."

"If this is a murder, Katharine, I don't think you should be involved in it at all."

I folded my arms and matched his stance. "That is my one condition. Take it or leave it."

He sighed. "Fine. I will take it."

I held out my hand. "Shake on it?"

"Are you serious?" He stared down at my hand.

"You are a man of honor. I know this. For you, a handshake is binding, so I suppose that is a second condition as I will require that too."

He groaned, but he also wanted the story, so he shook my hand. The handshake was brief and professional.

With that done, I told him about the last two days. As I spoke, he wrote furiously in his notebook. He wrote so quickly that I wondered if he would be able to read his handwriting after the fact.

When I was done, he closed his notebook and slipped it back into his jacket pocket. "If what you have told me is true, this is a huge story, especially if it can be tied to the attack on Santos-Dumont's airship."

I made a face.

He held up his hands, as if in surrender. "I'm not saying that you aren't telling me the truth. I have never known you to lie, Katharine." His forehead creased. "There are times you have been bluntly honest to a fault."

I grimaced as I knew that he was thinking of the same incident in college that I was, when I told my then fiancé, who happened to be a close friend of Harry's, that I didn't love him and I wasn't going to marry just because it seemed that everyone else at Oberlin was pairing off. I gave him back his ring in the middle of the college green where everyone could see. I could have handled that situation a little more delicately. It wasn't something that I wanted to recall. I shook my head and concentrated on the matter at hand.

"It will be easy enough to confirm with the police about Camilla's death. I have an old source that came to the St. Louis Police Department from Kansas City. He will tell me." He looked me in the eye. "And I will report back to you what I learn."

I nodded. "Thank you. I will be holding you to it."

"I suggest that we discuss this again at the Meachams' dinner party in two days' time. By then, we should both have new information to report."

"Will you write an article about the murder for tomorrow's paper?"

"If I can verify everything, I will." He held up his hand again. "I do not doubt you, but I need some sources connected to the fair or the police to verify the story. My editor will be very careful not to disparage the fair. This fair is not only a boon to St. Louis, but the whole country. We want to impress the world. The United States is still viewed by many nations as a country in its infancy. We have to show the world the global power that we can be."

"I don't believe everything at the fair is good for the country's reputation."

He wrinkled his brow. "What do you mean?"

"I saw Paul Laurence Dunbar at the reception at the Palace of Fine Arts."

He nodded.

"Paul said that there was an ugly underbelly to the fair."

He nodded. "What I have learned in my line of work is that there is an ugly underbelly in all good things, and something as colossal as the world's fair will have the biggest of all."

I had thought the same as well. "I will see you at the party."

He nodded. "I hope that Margaret will be feeling better by then."

"I'm sure that she will be on the mend again before then. Margaret is a charming hostess, and she will know how important this is to Meacham. She won't miss it."

He patted his breast pocket. "Thank you for this information, Katharine. You might just have made my career."

I knew how much Harry wanted to be a well-known journalist. He had great aspirations of being an editor for the paper and even winning national attention as a writer. I didn't doubt for a second that he would be able to accomplish all of those goals. It would be nice to be able to say that I had played a little part in his success.

"Where are you headed now?" Harry asked.

"I thought I would go to the Pike."

"I will escort you there and then make my way to the police station." The corner of his mouth curled. "I don't know if you should be walking around the fair alone. Paul is not wrong that this can be a dangerous place."

I held the suitcase in one hand and opened Margaret's parasol with the other. "Don't worry about me, Harry. I have been getting myself out of scrapes my whole life."

"I know that. I just wish you would avoid the scrapes to begin with," he replied.

CHAPTER 19

Harry walked away from the Pike, and I was grateful to have his support. I felt more hopeful that I would be able to find out what happened to Camilla now that Harry was also on the case, and I trusted that he would share information with me even if he didn't want to. He shook on it, after all, and that meant something to a man like him.

Harry Haskell was a good man. His wife, Isabella, and family were lucky to have him, and I was lucky to call him a friend. The police might not take my questions seriously, but they would have to pay attention to a well-respected reporter like Harry. They would know Harry would write about Camilla Ortiz's murder with or without their blessing, so it was better for them to tell their side of the story as they wanted it to come out.

Camilla's suitcase wasn't in the best shape when I first saw it, but the adventures of the day wore on the piece of luggage. I looked forward to passing it off to Sylvia, and I was kicking myself for taking it from Camilla's room in the first place.

It was midday, and exhibitors and tourists who were all looking for lunch crowded the Pike. There were long lines at all the eateries. My stomach grumbled at not being fed, but after Margaret grew so ill from eating on the Pike, I thought it was best not to eat anything until I was back in the safety of the flat. I wasn't taking any chances. We both couldn't be laid up.

My best chance to find Sylvia was the Temple of Mirth, even though it was the last place that I wanted to go. There was something about the attraction that set me ill at ease, and it wasn't just the garish decorations in and around it.

Just like the day before, Zeb Dandy stood outside of the fun house in his clown costume with his large blue parrot, Achilles, on his shoulder. He waved at passersby and shouted at them. "Come to the Temple of Mirth if you dare! Your dreams or your nightmares may come true."

A group of young men stopped in front the fun house. "It doesn't look that scary."

Zeb nodded at them. "There is only one way to know for sure." He bowed and held out his hand. "It will just cost you a nickel."

The young men hesitated, and Zeb straightened up. His hand was still out awaiting the coins. "Unless you are too cowardly to try."

"We aren't afraid of anything, are we?" the tallest of the young men said. He jostled his friends to make them reaffirm their overall bravery.

"There is one way to prove it," Zeb said.

One by one, the young men dropped a nickel into Zeb's hand. When the very last coin hit his palm, he folded his long fingers around them and smiled. The smile was disturbing due to the clown makeup, and by the shocked look on the young men's faces, I wasn't the only one who thought so.

As the group went into the fun house, Zeb removed a change purse from the pocket of his trousers and dropped the coins inside. That unnerving smile was on his face the whole time.

Achilles bobbed his beak up and down as if he was excited about the coins being added to the coffers too.

I took a deep breath and walked toward them.

Zeb tucked the change purse into his pocket again and threw up his hands. "I always know when a lady wants to give my Temple of Mirth a second round. Do you believe that you can beat the hall of mirrors this time? Few people can. How can one fight against themselves? And if I recall, you struggled the first time." He held out his hand. "Even so, I will gladly take your nickel, so that you can test your mettle. I understand that women are more independent these days and want to prove they have a resolve as firm as a man's. Is that what you wish to do, miss?"

"I do not want to go back inside the fun house. I wish I had never gone inside in the first place."

He dropped his hand to his side. "It is not my fault that you could not withstand the experience. I would have thought from your sturdy build you would have done better, but outward appearance is not everything."

I scowled. "I'm looking for Sylvia Ortiz. I was told that she cleans for you, and yesterday you did mention that you knew her."

He frowned. "You are still asking about the Ortiz sisters. Do you have some sort of odd fixation on them? For goodness sakes, leave them alone."

"Sylvia's sister is dead, and I'm trying to return Camilla's belongings to her." I held up the small suitcase as if it were proof.

Zeb's eyes went wide as he looked at that suitcase. There was a keen interest in his gaze, as if he would love to see the contents for himself. Was he naturally curious, or was there another reason? In any case, I could have told him that there was nothing to be amused by in the suitcase. It was simply women's clothes.

"How did she die?" He arched his black drawn-on eyebrow.

I didn't want to go too much into it because I had a very clear feeling that Zeb Dandy was not a person to be trusted, and I didn't feel that way just because he ran the Temple of Mirth. He made me uneasy, and if I was feeling uneasy, that was something worth noting. In cases like this, I tended to trust my women's intuition. Most of the time, it was right.

"She died near the aeronautics concourse yesterday morning," I said.

"Ahh, that was her who died at the concourse. Now, it makes more sense to me why you were asking about her yesterday. I have heard that she was stabbed. Is that true?"

It seemed that the fair hadn't been completely successful in keeping Camilla's murder a secret, and I wasn't surprised to learn it. It was a big place. There were many people about all the time. Gossip would spread quickly through the staff, and then on to the public at large.

Maybe it was a good thing that Harry was going to talk to the police. It would show them that they needed to get ahead of the news and make some sort of statement before the news broke and rumors were out of control. Honestly, I didn't know if they could even fight the rumors at this stage, but the sooner they said something, the better. The news of a murder could scare off tourists, or some of the countries could even pull out of the displays in fear for their people. It could destroy the fair.

"How do you know about it?" I asked.

He twirled his hands and wrists in the air as if he were casting some sort of spell, and I wouldn't have put it past him that he was doing exactly that. "I know and see everything at the fair. People tell me things."

"What people?"

He smiled. "People like you. Did you not just confirm that Camilla was the young woman killed yesterday morning?"

I hated it when he caught me, and he was right.

I switched the suitcase into my other hand. "Is Sylvia here?"

He frowned as if he didn't like my tone, and again with the makeup, his expression was magnified tenfold.

He balanced his elbow on his right hand and tucked his left hand under his chin. "And why should I tell you?"

"Because I have her sister's things and because I'm worried about her. She just lost her sister. As her employer, I would imagine that you would be concerned too."

He laughed. "Do you know how many people have come to my gilded doors of Temple of Mirth for work? I could not possibly care about all of them. In fact, with all that I have to do, I have no time to be concerned with any of them. Every one of them can be replaced in an instant. That is the charm of the world's fair: one person leaves, another three come in. Take yourself, for example. I would think that you think highly of yourself, but here, you are just another score to make a nickel or two." He dropped his hands to his sides, and his fingers reminded me of spider legs. They were so thin and long.

I tried to shake the image from my mind, but it had taken root there.

"Sylvia is inside. She's working. Someone has to be in there to make sure that no one damages the property and to keep things tidy. I hate a dirty fun house, don't you?" he asked.

I stared at the Temple of Mirth, and again, I was repulsed by the giant clown head with its mouth wide-open as if it was in the process of swallowing you up. "Go inside and see if you can find her. Any way I can get customers to cough up a nickel and get through the door is fine with me." He held out his palm just as he had done to the young men just a few moments ago.

I narrowed my eyes at him. "How do I know that she is even in there?"

"She should be if she wants to get paid. This is her time to work."

"She doesn't get time off for her sister's death?" I asked.

He laughed. "What kind of place do you think you are in? The show must go on, as they say in the circus, and so the temple must be open. If she does not do her job, I can pick another ten girls off the street right now that can."

I sighed and removed a nickel from my satchel. I dropped it into Zeb's hand, and those spider-leg fingers curled around it just like they had around the young men's money.

He stepped back and bowed, pointing at the entrance. "Discovery awaits."

I glared at him, but with a straight back I walked into the Temple of Mirth again. Just like the day before, the door slammed closed behind me, and there was no way to open it from the inside since there was no door handle.

I let my eyes adjust, and I could hear the cries and yelps of the young men who were a few minutes ahead of me. Their screams and peals of laughter made me uncertain if they were having the best time or were completely terrified. From what I knew about the Temple of Mirth, it was likely both.

There was an appeal to being frightened, but it was only when it was in a controlled situation, when you knew in your heart of hearts that you were really safe. I didn't know that I was safe in the Temple of Mirth, but at the same time, I imagined that Zeb Dandy didn't want anyone to be hurt in his fun house, because he might be shut down.

I stepped into the next room. This time I was ready for the jack-in-the-box. I smacked it on the snout with the parasol. I will admit even though I knew what was coming, I still had the urge to jump.

The jack-in-the-box bounced back from me as if it was offended that I dare hit it. I suspected that this was not the first time it had been walloped in the nose nor would it be the last.

I walked through the corridor, and to my surprise, I didn't find myself in the hall of mirrors where I had seen Sylvia—

who I had thought was Camilla—for the first time. Instead, in front of me, the flickering electric lights illuminated a spinning cylinder that lay on its side. The cylinder was wide enough for a man to stand up in. The inside had been painted with red and white stripes, and the spinning design caused a dizzying effect.

There was no other way to escape the room but to go through the giant, spinning barrel. I tried to turn back, but again, the door had close solidly behind me with no doorknob to speak of.

I took one step into the cylinder and promptly fell. I was spun around and dropped on the floor of the cylinder only to have it done twice more; each time I tried to stand.

The suitcase flew out of my hand and was spun away from me back to the entrance. There was a roar in my ears. I was doomed to be in this spot forever. Then, as suddenly as it began, the spinning stopped. I lay sprawled on the bottom of the cylinder in a very unladylike manner.

If I had my wits about me, modesty would have me pull myself together and make sure my skirt was in place. Unfortunately, I didn't even know which way was up.

CHAPTER 20

"Katharine, are you all right?" a woman asked.

I blinked several times, and Sylvia Ortiz finally came into focus. I was relieved to know that my spectacles hadn't fallen off during my ordeal.

She stood at the end of the barrel next to a giant lever. I imagined that was what she had used to stop the spinning.

She stepped into the barrel and held a hand out to me. "Here, let me help you up."

I did my very best to pull down my skirts and was forever grateful that it was a woman who found me in such a predicament.

With all the grace that I could muster, I stumbled to my feet with Sylvia's help. When I was upright, I placed my hand on the side of the barrel for a moment as the whole room spun around me.

Sylvia stood nearby with her hands out, as if she thought I might topple over any second. It was a good bet on her part, because I was unsure on my feet. Another wave of dizziness washed over me until I felt steady enough to leave the barrel. When I was on the concrete floor of the fun house, I caught my breath. "What is that contraption?"

"It's called the barrel of love," she explained. "It's my least favorite part of the fun house. I'm grateful Zeb only routes patrons into it a few times a week." She eyed the apparatus. "Any time I go into it I feel queasy, even when it's not even spinning. I think I have been caught in there too many times when the lever was turned on. I suspect that Zeb does it out of spite and to see me squirm."

I still didn't feel the best and was gratified to see an over-turned bucket in the corner. I sat on it. "Do you and Zeb not get along?"

"That's just Zeb. He likes to see people be put in uncomfortable positions. That's why running the Temple of Mirth is perfect for him. He can spend all day scaring folks."

"And he wanted to scare you? But you work for him," I said.

"Zeb doesn't care who he bothers as long as it amuses him."

He sounded like a such a nice man. Surely, there were other places that Sylvia could find work throughout the fair.

I removed my hat that was no longer sitting square on my head. It was crushed and some of the flowers were missing. Since I had been in St. Louis, the hat had really been through more than its fair share. If I were ever to come back to this city, I would not purchase a new hat for the occasion; it was just too hard on headwear, from my experience.

"It should be called the barrel of tumbles." I placed a hand on my forehead. "I don't know the last time that I have fallen down so much, and I think of myself as having some physical prowess."

"What are you doing back here? I got the sense yesterday that you didn't like the Temple of Mirth." Sylvia leaned against the wall.

"You would be right on that. I hated it, and after today, I hope never to darken the door here again." I stood up and walked back to the barrel; looking down it I could just make out Camilla's suitcase near the entrance to the barrel. Not surprisingly, I dropped it early during my twisty ride. "I brought Camilla's suitcase to give you. That way, you don't have to go back to her dormitory. I would think that it would be very hard to go back there."

"Thank you," she said. "I see it now at the entrance at the other end of the barrel. I will go fetch it. You still look a bit unsteady on your feet."

She was right. I was relieved not to have to venture back into that death trap.

Sylvia stepped into the barrel, and a moment later, she came out with the suitcase in hand. She knelt on the floor and opened it. She rifled through the clothes and seemed to be disappointed with what was inside.

"Is something missing?"

She snapped the suitcase closed. "No, of course not." She wouldn't look me in the eye.

I would bet all of the chocolate that I secretly kept hidden in my desk at school for those tough days when the students were just being horrid, that she was looking for the black notebook that I found under the floorboards in Camilla's room.

I patted the pocket of my skirt to reassure myself that the notebook was still there, but I felt nothing. The notebook was gone. It must have fallen from my pocket while I was jostled in the barrel.

I bit the inside of my lip. Should I tell Sylvia that it was missing? That would be admitting that I took it and wasn't planning to give it to her. I would give it to her eventually, but I wanted to mine it for clues first. It might be just what I needed to lead me to Camilla's killer.

"Thank you for returning this to me," Sylvia said.

I nodded. "Why did you run away from the dormitory so fast when there was a knock on the door?"

She stood and picked up the suitcase as if she was about to leave. "I didn't run away."

"You jumped out of the window. That looks a lot like running away to me."

She cleared her throat. "I had to leave to get back to work, and I didn't want to bump into anyone in the hallway and hear their half-hearted condolences about my sister."

She was lying, and we both knew it.

"Who is Hal? And what is his relationship with your sister?"

"Hal was the one at the door?" she asked like she didn't already know this.

We both knew that she did.

"He was."

She wrinkled her nose at this.

"So how does Camilla know Hal?"

She set the suitcase on the floor next to her feet and folded her arms. "Just like anyone knows anybody else around here from the fair. No one really knows anyone all that well. It is a transient community. Just like all the buildings are illusions of grandeur, the people are illusions of who they really are. You can't really know them at all."

"Hal seemed to know Camilla well. I got the impression that he might care about her."

Sylvia snorted. "That's ridiculous. All Hal cares about is money and how he can make more of it any way that he can."

I arched my brow. "So, you're saying that he came to your sister's room for money?"

"Not Camilla's money. She didn't have any, and neither do I, for that matter. Do you think I would be inside this black hole cleaning up after people if I had any money at all?"

She had a point, and truth be told there was no amount of money that Zeb Dandy could have paid me to take that job inside the Temple of Mirth. It was just too miserable in there. I didn't know how Sylvia withstood the close spaces and the echoing of screams throughout the cavernous building.

Sylvia surprised me by saying, "The only reason that he was there was because he was paid to be there."

I raised my brow. "Why would someone pay him to go into your sister's room?"

She didn't answer the question. Instead, she jumped back into the barrel. A moment later she came out again with Camilla's black notebook in hand. "How did you get this? This is mine!"

"Yours?"

"It was my s-sister's," she stuttered. "So, it is mine now. Everything that she had should go to me. I am her only family in St. Louis."

"I agree with that. I am ashamed to say that I wanted to read through it before returning it to you. I was hoping that it would give me clues as to what happened to your sister."

She opened the book and flipped through the pages. "There are pages missing." Her voice was choked. "You took them."

I shook my head. "I promise you I didn't. I haven't even read the book through yet. If it is your sister's book, how can you know that pages are missing?"

She glared at me and held out the notebook for me to see the ripped edges of paper.

"What were on those pages?" I asked.

"How am I to know?" she said. "As you said, this is my sister's book. However, I do know she wouldn't rip out pages like this."

"Maybe she did because she didn't like the ideas she recorded there," I said, trying to be helpful.

"No, she would not do that." Her tone left no room for argument. "Where did you find this?"

"In her dormitory."

"I know that," she said. "I was there, but where in the dormitory?"

I frowned, but I could think of no reason not to tell her where I found the notebook. Camilla wouldn't be going back to the dormitory room now. "There was a loose floorboard. It was under that."

She nodded and murmured. "I should have known."

"Why should you have known?" I asked.

She ignored my question and snapped the book shut. "What were you going to do? Take my—her—ideas back to your brothers to steal and use for their own flying machines?"

My mouth fell open. "I would never do that, and even if I wanted to, my brothers would never open the notebook in those circumstances. They are honorable men."

"At least some people in your family are honorable," she muttered.

Her words stung, but I knew they weren't untrue in this scenario. I should have never tried to keep the notebook without telling her about it first. I had gotten so caught up in the thought that I could solve her sister's murder that I disrespected her and, worse, I disrespected her sister's memory. Of course, Camilla would want her sister to have the notebook. It's the only person I could think of that she would want to have it.

I swallowed. "I am sorry. It was an error in judgment on my part."

Her eyes narrowed. "You are no better than Hal or anyone else at this fair. I can't believe for a moment that I thought you might be different."

I winced. I'd had every intention of giving Sylvia the notebook, just not so soon. I had wanted to read it over page by page before I did that. There was no way that I was going to be able to get it back from her now. Whatever secrets that it held that might help the investigation were lost to me.

Even so, I persisted in my questions. "Is that notebook the reason Hal came to your room? What is so important that he wanted it that badly?"

"Maybe you can ask yourself that, since you were planning to keep it for yourself."

Her statement was fair.

"I was hoping that it would give me a clue as to what happened to your sister."

She looked me straight in the eye. "Why do you care? You don't know her. You don't know me. What kind of game are you playing?"

"It's not a game, not even close. Your sister asked for my help and died in my arms. I saw the light go out in her eyes. That struck me. I can't just let it go."

"The police say that they already have a killer," she said.

"Charles?" I asked. "And you really think he did it? He was arrested for tampering with Mr. Santos-Dumont's airship. The police would not tell me if they thought he also was responsible for Camilla's death."

"No, I don't for a second think it was him on either count, but that doesn't change the fact that you don't know what you are dabbling in. If you did, you would be as far away from St. Louis as you can get."

"Then, tell me. I really do want to know. I really do want to help."

She shook the notebook at me. "You can help by not stealing."

"I wasn't—" I was about to say that I wasn't stealing, but if I went with the strict definition of the word, to take something that does not belong to you, I was.

What would my bishop father say if he heard of all this? Thankfully, he never would, because I had no intention of writing to him or to any of my brothers about any of this. If they knew the mess that I was in the middle of at the exposition, Orville would be on the next train from Dayton to collect me.

She tucked the notebook into the pocket of her apron. "Did you read it?"

"I leafed through it. I can't say that I understood everything that I saw, but it is clear to me that Camilla had a number of good ideas when it came to her inventions. She had talent. It is a shame that her ingenuity had been snuffed out so early."

Sylvia rapidly blinked tears from her eyes, and the tear-drops clung to her long black lashes. "She was a genius, and now she's dead. Everything that she's worked for all these years will never come to be. That's something that I have to live with. All I can do now is run back home to California and live with what I have done."

"Why is that your burden?" I asked.

"Because my sister is dead, and it's my fault."

Before I could ask her what she meant by that, she pressed on the wall behind her. There was a clicking sound as a latch gave way. The wall moved, creating a small gap that was just big enough for her to slip through as she held her suitcase out in front of her. And then she was gone.

CHAPTER 21

A fter Sylvia disappeared, I was alone in the dark room behind the barrel of love, which if you asked me was a
ridiculous name for such a death trap contraption. I ran over
to the wall where Sylvia disappeared, but I couldn't find any
sort of door handle or any indication of hinges. I pressed on
the wall like I had seen her do, but I must have missed the
exact spot because nothing happened.

I looked behind me at the barrel of love and shivered. I did
not want to go back that way to exit of the Temple of Mirth,
but it was possible that I might not have a choice. In the
room with the jack-in-the-box there must have been another
choice of door to go through.

The barrel was off, and I thought I could make it across if
I was quick on my feet.

What a pickle I had gotten myself into. I leaned against the
wall and heard that familiar click of a latch giving way.

I fell back and found myself in a new room. Yet again, it
wasn't a room that I had been in before. It wasn't the hall of
mirrors. Ropes were strung across every which way in the
room, creating a massive web, but I could clearly see a door
on the other side of the room. I just had to climb through the
web to reach it.

This was most inconvenient. Who thought of these places to drive people batty? There didn't seem to be any way around it if I wanted to get out of there. I ducked under one rope and stepped over another.

I tripped over the next, and another rope caught me from falling on my face.

I struggled to stand up. "This is a monstrous place."

Just as I said that a giant papier-mâché spider dropped from the ceiling and dangled just a few feet from me.

Like any good Midwestern girl, I whacked it with Margaret's parasol and sent it flying across the room. The beastly thing got what it deserved.

After a few more backbreaking contortions, I reached the door.

Before I put my hand on the handle, I prayed that it would open. I turned the handle, and the door swung easily inward. I went through and found myself in a narrow hallway, but at the end of it, there was light coming in from under a door. I looked all around me to reassure myself that another manmade creature wouldn't fall from the sky, but I saw nothing.

I walked to the door, opened it, and stepped out into the blazing Missouri sun. I opened the parasol and shielded my face, as if I had just been out on a quiet stroll and not thrown about head over feet.

Sylvia was nowhere to be seen, but I didn't expect to see her again. She had made it very clear that she was done with me, and I could not blame her. I handled the whole issue with the notebook poorly. My father and my brothers were always chastising me that I was too impulsive when making decisions. They felt like I needed to spend more time thinking things through.

I did think most things through, but there were times like this when decisions had to be made, and I went with the one I most wanted to make without giving much thought as to how it impacted another person.

I blamed this on growing up in a house of all boys. As a girl, if I had wanted my fair share of anything, I had to take it.

The area behind the Temple of Mirth was parking for the hansom cab drivers when they weren't working. There were four cabs parked. Two were horse-drawn and two were automobiles. It was the perfect example of the times we were all living in. We lived in the place of in-between, a breadth of time connecting what was and what was yet to be. My brothers' flyer was a great part of that. The aeronautic competition was a large part of that too. It was the first competition like it in the United States—and most of the world. Perhaps France, in this case, was a few steps ahead of my country.

I wished Wilbur and Orville were here participating in the competition. I knew if they gave it a go, they would have won. Wilbur worried about the distance of the runway in order to take off, but he would have figured it out if he had to.

But I was not surprised when they told me that they had decided not to enter the competition. There was nothing more important than protecting the flyer and their patent, which was still pending.

I stepped around the Temple of Mirth and almost collided with Zeb Dandy, who stood at the corner of the building smoking a cigarette. He took a long drag from the cigarette and blew smoke in my face.

Achilles made a gagging face at the smell of the tobacco. "Foul! Foul!" the bird shouted.

"Hush your mouth unless you would like to be turned into pillow stuffing," Zeb snapped.

Achilles snapped his yellow beak shut.

I waved the smoke away. I agreed with the parrot; it was foul. I hated cigarettes—or any form of tobacco for that matter. It was the biggest beef that I had with my brothers' engine man, Charlie Taylor. The man smoked incessantly. Even when he wasn't smoking, I could smell the smoke clinging to his clothing. It didn't help that he also had a terribly foul mouth.

My brothers didn't care about any of that as long as Charlie could build them a lightweight engine for their flyer.

Zeb dropped the stub of his cigarette on the gravel and crushed it with the toe of his red boot. "My dear, I could hear you screaming all the way outside. I take it that you didn't care for the barrel of love." His lips curled into a smile. "It is not as much fun if you don't go in there with your sweetheart and fall all over each other."

I grimaced.

"You no longer have that suitcase that you were holding so tightly in your hand when you arrived. That can only make me believe that you had luck in finding Sylvia."

"I did," I said.

He nodded. "Very good. Because if I heard that she wasn't inside the fun house, I would have had to sack her."

"Why?"

"The girl is unreliable with her work. When she's here, the Temple of Mirth is shipshape. When she's not, it seems to be the time when the tourists with the weakest stomachs come to the fun house, if you know what I mean."

I did know what he meant, and I didn't want to think about it.

"I've kept her on this long because it's just too much trouble to hire someone new, not that there aren't plenty of people passing through St. Louis right now looking for work. Few of them want to do what Sylvia does for me."

I could understand why. She was inside the dark fun house day in and day out, cleaning up other people's messes. It sounded like the most unpleasant of jobs.

His clown makeup had begun to run on his face in the afternoon heat. It gave the illusion that he was crying. "Enjoy the rest of your time at the fair. You never know what will happen next around here." With that he walked away.

I did my best not to worry over Zeb Dandy's final words

to me. I knew I couldn't continue on at the fair in my current state. My dress was covered in dust, and the hem was torn.

The price that my wardrobe was paying for this fair began to add up. I only had one day dress left that hadn't fallen to a terrible fate. I knew that I could use Margaret's clothes, but I was afraid that I would ruin hers too, and hers were much nicer than anything I owned.

When I was certain that Zeb Dandy was gone, I walked around the Temple of Mirth. As I came around the side of the building, the grotesque giant clown head loomed over me. It reminded me of Zeb in many ways. I hoped that I would not run into Zeb again anytime soon, and, if Sylvia was really returning to California as she said, there was no reason to.

I was so distracted by the clown I almost bumped into a young man who was running toward the Temple of Mirth's entrance.

"Watch where you're going," he cried and then he fell silent when he recognized me.

"Hal?" I asked. "Are you here looking for Sylvia?"

He scowled. "What's it to you?"

"You were looking for her twin earlier. It would make sense if you were looking for her too."

"I don't have to answer you," he said. He then took off at a run down the Pike, running past the Temple of Mirth. Maybe I had been wrong in thinking that was where he was headed in the first place.

The walk back to the flat gave me time to think. I had learned a lot about Camilla's life, but I was still no closer to knowing what happened to her on that fateful morning. I had to believe that it was tied to the attack on Alberto's airship.

Could it have been Charles F. Morrison, as everyone from the police to Alberto Santos-Dumont himself seemed to believe? Should I just accept that resolution and enjoy the fair?

Sylvia made it clear to me today that she didn't want me asking questions about her sister's murder. Who else would I be doing it for, other than her?

For myself, I thought, because Camilla died in my arms. She had said *aeronautics competition*. She was giving me a message to solve her murder. I knew it was her last dying wish. How was I to turn my back on that?

Having made up my mind, I walked to the Meachams' building. A young man was at the foot of the stairs holding a package and looking very concerned. It was the same look that I saw on my students' faces when I announced there would be a surprise oral exam on Latin conjugation that morning. Little else can strike the same level of fear into a high school student.

"Can I help you?"

"I'm looking for Mr. W. C. Meacham's flat, but I don't know the number. I thought the name would be on the mailboxes." Perspiration gathered on his brow.

"Well, I must say that you are in very good luck, because I am Katharine Wright, and I'm staying with the Meachams."

He stared at me in awe. "You're Katharine Wright?"

I cocked my head. "Do I know you?"

He emphatically shook his head. "No, ma'am, but I was asked to deliver this package to W. C. Meacham's flat because it is for you."

"Oh. Who is it from?" I hooked the handle of Margaret's parasol over my forearm in preparation for taking the package.

"I don't know, ma'am. I just run deliveries for the fair." He held the package out to me. It was close to the size of a shoebox, wrapped in brown paper, and tied with twine.

I didn't take it from his hands. "It's from the fair?"

"Yes, ma'am."

"I don't know who would send me a package from the fair."

He shook the box at me. "Neither do I, but you got to take it. I have to get back, miss. You wouldn't believe the number of deliveries there are to and from the fair. I have a huge stack to deliver before my shift comes to an end."

I took the box from his hand and watched as he ran out the door. I watched him jump onto a bicycle and pedal down the street like the back tire was on fire.

Frowning, I tucked the package under my arm and climbed the three flights of stairs to reach the Meachams' rented flat.

I was happy to find Margaret in the sitting room when I walked in. She was up and enjoying afternoon tea. At least she was drinking tea. From what I could gather, she hadn't taken a bite of a single sandwich, and I didn't know how she could pass them up. The little sandwiches were cucumber, strawberry and cream, ham, and tomato, and the desserts were tiny chocolate torts and berry tarts. Had I been alone, I could have eaten the entire tray in one sitting.

There was a sheath of paper on the table next to her teacup with a checklist written on it.

"Meacham had this sent up for me. Isn't it lovely? I'm just not feeling hungry yet. Please join me," Margaret said.

She didn't have to ask me twice. There were few things I adored more than delicate finger sandwiches and bite-size desserts. I filled up one dainty plate with all it could hold.

She stared at me. "Katharine, did you eat at the fair?"

"No, I was in such a rush from place to place, I didn't want to take the time." That was partially true. The other part of it was I was a little leery of eating any of the fair food after Margaret became so ill. I thought it was best to change the subject. "Have you been resting all day?"

"Off and on. On the whole, I believe that it was a good day for me to stay home as it gave me time to prepare for the dinner party on the Ferris wheel. You would not believe all the little details that I have to consider to have this party go off without a hitch. Everything has to be loaded into the Ferris wheel carriage before the party begins." She shook her head. "There is no water in there, of course. That will have to be taken in as well."

I raised my brow. "And you have to do all of that?"

She shook her head. "The fair has a caterer that is handling most of it, but it doesn't mean that I'm not making a list and double-checking everything. I want this to be an event that Meacham can be proud of and his bank be impressed by. He has been under tremendous pressure ever since we arrived in St. Louis."

I poured myself a cup of tea. This was news to me. Meacham always seemed to be calm and pleasant to me. There was no indication that he was stressed.

She turned over the sheath of paper as if she didn't want to see the list any longer—or like she didn't want *me* to see the list. "Enough about that. You must have had an exciting day then." She smiled. "I'm so very glad that you had a nice time. I worried by staying back at the flat that I might have put a damper on your day."

I popped one of the berry tarts in my mouth and savored it. After I washed it down with a sip of tea, I felt more like myself. It was perplexing how an empty stomach can make a person feel so vexed.

She pointed to the package that I had set on the floor beside my chair. "What is that?"

I had been so hungry that I had forgotten about the package.

I patted the corners of my mouth with my napkin. "I don't know. When I came into the building there was a young delivery boy at the foot of the stairs. He said he was looking for your flat because he had a package for me."

"It must be from your father or brothers back home. Or maybe it is from a friend? You have so many close friends, Katharine, I would wager that is it."

I shook my head. "It's not from anyone of the kind. The boy said that the delivery came from the fair."

"The fair?" she asked in shock. "Who do you know at the fair?"

"No one, really. I have met people, of course, but I can't think of a single person who would send me a package."

Margaret clasped her hands together. "Open it, then. This is the most excitement I have had in the last few days, and I will do anything to get my mind off my upset stomach."

I popped another cream puff in my mouth. They were very good. Then I picked up the package and untied the twine. The brown paper fell into my lap with the twine no longer holding it in place.

I lifted the lid off of the box, and inside was a small replica of Alberto Santos-Dumont's airship number six, the airship that flew around the Eiffel Tower.

Margaret leaned forward in her seat. "What is it?"

I removed the note from the box, and then handed her the box. She looked inside. "What is it?" she repeated.

I wasn't surprised that she didn't know. She wasn't surrounded by the talk of aviation all the time like I was back home.

"It's Alberto Santos-Dumont's airship. You didn't see it put together in the hangar, of course. This isn't a model of that particular airship that he brought to the exposition. It is of the one just before." I pulled it out of the box and held it up. It was very lightweight, and I realized that the replica was made of tin. All of it, even the balloon that was molded to look fully inflated.

Margaret tilted her head thoughtfully to the side. "I don't see how something this lopsided can fly."

"It's the balloon," I said. "My brothers' flying machine is different because there is no balloon."

She nodded. "Was there a note with it?"

I set the airship on the table next to the tea tray. I moved around the brown paper in the box until I came up with a card. I opened it and read aloud. *"Dearest Miss Wright, I am so sorry about the troubles that occurred the last time I saw you. The circumstances of that morning were upsetting and unfortunate. I would very much like to make it up to you. Although I will no longer be flying my airship at the fair, I have several speaking engagements that I have committed to at the exposition and will see them through. I would like to invite you and a guest to my lecture at the U.S. Government building tomorrow. You will see in the package that I have included two tickets for you and a guest. It would be my honor if you would attend. Because of your closeness with your brothers and their work, I would very much like to hear your thoughts on the lecture. Sincerely, Alberto Santos-Dumont."* I set the note on my lap.

Margaret reached into the package and came out with two bright yellow paper tickets. "Can I be your guest?" she asked.

"I can't think of another guest that I would want to take as much," I said.

CHAPTER 22

The next morning was a flurry of activity as I helped Margaret prepare party favors for the forty-some guests of her husband's dinner party the next day. It promised to be a huge event for Meacham's bank, and the who's who of manufacturing would be there as well as some personally invited guests of the Meachams, like Harry Haskell and myself.

I was eager to find out what Harry might have learned from the police about Camilla's murder. I hoped that he wouldn't tell me that they had dropped the investigation altogether. There had been very little mention of her murder in the papers. Instead, it seemed that journalists were more interested in reporting about the attack on Alberto Santos-Dumont's airship. I supposed that made sense since Alberto's arrival at the fair had been shouted to the far corners of the grounds.

"Are you sure that you want to go to Alberto's lecture this afternoon?" I asked my friend. "Shouldn't you stay home and rest up for the dinner party tomorrow? I know this is a very important event for your husband. I don't want you to be too worn out to enjoy all your hard work."

Margaret tied another bow around a bag that included a

gift. Everyone who came to the dinner party would receive a thank-you gift.

"I'm going to the lecture," she said with a bit more force than was necessary. "If I stay here in the flat for another day, I will go mad, and I feel well enough to venture out today. The staff from Meacham's office is arranging everything for the dinner party. For today, there is nothing more for me to do other than prepare these gifts. What am I to do the rest of the day if I don't go with you?"

I nodded. It wasn't often that Margaret made up her mind with so much conviction, so I wasn't going to argue with her further about it. Also, I was a strong believer that fresh air was good for a person's health. Being cooped up in the hot flat day in and day out wasn't going to make her feel any better.

When it was time to leave for the lecture, Margaret appeared to be in a much better mood. She smiled at me. "It will be so nice to get out of the flat for a while."

"If you start to feel poorly," I said, "we can even leave the lecture early if it runs too long."

Since I had ruined so many of my clothes during my adventures around the fair, I was wearing some of Margaret's garments. I felt quite sharp in the green floral shirtwaist and brown skirt. I looked like a woman who knew her mind and was ready to face the day. The clothes were similar to what I wore in the classroom, but the fabric was much finer. I would never spend what Margaret did on clothing. I had better uses for my teacher's salary, such as buying the train ticket to come to St. Louis. My father and brothers, though they didn't hold me back, wouldn't fund such an adventure. I was glad to dedicate myself to the family and household and helping Wilbur and Orville achieve their dreams, but Margaret needed me too, and seeing how desolate she became over this latest sickness, when her pregnancy hopes were dashed again, I was glad to be here to support her.

Margaret and I took a hansom cab to the fair, and the driver dropped us off right in front of the massive U.S. Government building. It seemed that everything at the fair was built on a giant scale, but the U.S. Government building appeared to be the largest of them all. The structure was as wide as my neighborhood block back in Dayton. And rows of formidable white pillars ran its length on three sides.

The building was meant to instill pride in American visitors and awe in those from other parts of the world. It was closed to the general public that afternoon, and a line queued to the front door, where a steward checked tickets. I held ours in my hand with a viselike grip. If I lost the tickets, it was unlikely we would get another, as young men walked down the line offering to buy tickets for a pretty penny.

One of those young men came up to me. "I will give you fifty dollars for your two tickets," he said.

"No, thank you," I said, turning away from him.

"Fine. Fine. One hundred dollars. I will give you fifty apiece."

"No, I'm not selling for any amount."

He narrowed his eyes at me. "Money means nothing to you?"

"Why would you say that? Of course, money is valuable. I simply want to attend the lecture."

"That's what all rich women say." He stomped away.

I snorted. I was far from a rich woman.

"What a terribly rude young man," Margaret said. "Why would he want to buy our tickets so desperately?"

"To sell them for double the price that he bought them from us."

She shook her head. "The behavior of some people at this fair is beyond me."

I couldn't agree with her more, especially when it came to those who would take a young woman's life with very little thought.

The line inched forward to the front door of the building. Other young scalpers made their way down the line, but they always skipped over Margaret and me after that first attempt. I made sure to have my most irritated teacher face in place to scare them off. It was an excellent deterrent for a myriad of requests.

Finally, we made it to the front of the line, and I handed over the tickets for Margaret and me. The steward consulted the tickets. "Oh dear. You didn't need to wait in this long line. You are both in the VIP section." He snapped his fingers, and a boy no more than twelve appeared at his side. "Please show Miss Wright and her guest to the VIP area near the stage."

The towheaded boy nodded. "This way please, ladies."

We followed him into the massive building. Outside it had seemed like the building had been meant to last a thousand years, with its grand entrances and white pillars, but the inside told the true story. The metal beams above were all exposed and the interior looked more like a military hangar than an elegant museum.

Maybe the contractor did not expect people to look at the ceiling or the walls or question the construction. The displays were so large and dazzling, it was hard to look anywhere else. Directly in front of us was the skeleton of a triceratops and behind that was an even larger skeleton of a whale, with a lifelike replica of a whale hanging from the rafters. There was a stuffed giraffe and lion. Every display had been loaded onto a train car and shipped across the country from the Smithsonian in Washington.

"This is incredible." Margaret looped her arm through mine. "I've been to the Smithsonian and seen many of these things, but to have them all together in one giant room is mindboggling."

I guessed that mindboggling had been the government's

goal. The U.S. Government building was meant to show the power of the United States. Visitors were meant to take note.

"Miss, this way please," our young guide said.

I hadn't realized that Margaret and I had stopped in front of the giraffe. We quickly increased our pace to catch up to the boy.

We followed him through the crowd. He lifted a red velvet rope and gestured for us to pass through. We were about ten feet from the stage. While the others in the audience had to stand in and around the displays to wait for the lectures to begin, we were led directly to our seats. "This is you, ma'am," the boy said.

I reached into my satchel and removed a nickel. "Thank you for your help, young man."

His eyes glowed at the sight of the nickel. He stuck it in his pocket.

"Before you go, I would love to know your name, so I can put in a good word for you when we leave."

"That's mighty kind of you, ma'am. I'm Ned Kingley."

"And where are you from, Ned?" I asked.

He puffed out his chest. "Right here in St. Louis, miss. Lived here my whole life. You will find no finer city. It was no surprise to me that my city was chosen for the biggest event the world has ever seen!"

"Mrs. Meacham is from Chicago. There has been a world's fair there before. You still believe that St. Louis is better?"

"I don't just believe it, I know it. Chicago is not a safe place to be. I heard stories of people being shot on the street."

"That is an exaggeration," Margaret said, defending her adopted hometown.

Ned shrugged as if they had agreed to disagree. "All I know is you won't run into any of that in St. Louis. This is a standup place." He paused. "Mostly."

I cocked my head. "Why do you say *mostly*?"

He leaned forward as if he were about to tell us a secret. "I hate to tell you this, but you seem like nice ladies, and it's always good to be on guard. That's what my grandmother says."

"On guard for what?"

"You didn't hear?"

Margaret and I leaned in.

Ned lowered his voice. "A woman was killed two days ago on the aviation concourse. She was stabbed in the back. It was a terrible scene. Blood everywhere."

As I had viewed the scene firsthand, I wouldn't say there was blood everywhere as Ned described, but the particulars were right. Over time those details would change as word of mouth spread. The story would grow more outlandish and grotesque with each passing day. What really happened—that a young woman lost her life—would be swallowed into the details created for garish amusement.

The conversation with Ned told me that rumors about Camilla's death were swirling among the staff around the fair. The fair committee would be doing its best to make sure that those rumors didn't reach the visitors, but with gossips like Ned among the employees it was just a matter of time before the stories spread. If I knew anything from being a high school teacher it was that rumors had a way of getting out of control. Something minor could be blown way out of proportion, and Camilla's death was anything but minor.

"How did you hear about this?" Margaret asked.

I nodded at her as I was thinking the same question. Perhaps Margaret had a bit of investigator in her after all.

"I heard it around," he said vaguely. "I can't help but hear things while I'm working. People talk, and they don't tend to notice me."

"What's your job here at the fair?" I asked.

"Anything they give me to do. I usually run errands for the

fair committee. Take a message here, deliver this there. I like it. It sends me to every corner of the fair. I think you would be hard-pressed to find anyone who knows the fair as well as I do. I know every building, every alley, every inch."

"Did you know the woman who died?" I asked.

His young face clouded over. "I did. She was a nice girl. Really smart. She was always tinkering with things. I was using a scooter to get around the fair faster to make my deliveries and things. A motorcar ran me off the road one morning. I crashed into the Floral Clock and my handlebars were all twisted up. I couldn't buy another one. It would take me the whole summer to earn that kind of money and that's with no eating for three months. Camilla, that's the woman who died, saw what happened and said that she could fix the scooter for me. She did, and it was better than new. I never knew a woman could be so handy with tools."

I felt myself bristle at his last comment. Clearly, he had never met a Wright before. My brothers were great inventors and builders because our mother was. Just like Wilbur and Orville, she was always making things and always tinkering. She made most of our toys when we were growing up. Many of them were more intricate than anything that could be purchased at the store.

Our father the bishop, on the other hand, hardly knew which way to turn to drive a screw home.

"I loved going to the aviation concourse, and I would see Camilla there often. Anytime there was an errand going in that direction, even though it was in the farthest corner of the fair, I agreed to go."

"Why's that?" Margaret asked.

"Because I'm going to be an aviator too. Everyone is all excited about the motorcars around the fair. There were so many models of them in the Palace of Transportation, but how can that compare to being up in the air and flying? It can't. It just can't. I begged and begged to be able to work here today. Mr. Santos-Dumont is a hero of mine. I was so eager to see him fly." His face fell. "That's not going to happen now."

"You don't know that," Margaret said. "He may change his mind about flying. I know the fair is working to find someone who can mend the balloon on his airship."

I wasn't as optimistic. I believed that Alberto's mind was made up. He wasn't going to fly. He was very much like my brothers in that way. The proper preparation for their flyer always came first, and they would not risk the integrity of their design for any amount of money. I wasn't surprised that Alberto was much the same.

"I hope you're right," Ned said. "I have to get back to my post." With that, the boy disappeared into the sea of visitors.

CHAPTER 23

The stage was in the middle of the grand hall just behind the whale's tail. A platform with a podium had been set up, and a group of men stood on the platform. Among them, I spotted Alberto and Mr. Myers. I didn't recognize any other men.

A tall, gray-haired man with a neatly trimmed beard walked to the podium. "Good afternoon, esteemed ladies and gentlemen. I am Samuel Langley, secretary of the Smithsonian. I am thrilled to be introducing our speaker this afternoon, the celebrated Alberto Santos-Dumont. As an aviator myself, I have been in awe of Mr. Santos-Dumont's accomplishments. They are some of the finest that we have seen in the air. Today, he will be speaking about his historic flight around the Eiffel Tower just last year. And . . ." Langley paused as he looked over his shoulder at Alberto as if to make sure that he was still there. "We hope that he makes history again here in the Louisiana Purchase Exposition by flying our concourse and winning the hundred-thousand-dollar prize."

Alberto scowled. It seemed to me that he had not known that Langley would make such a public announcement of the fair's wishes for Alberto to fly.

Langley gestured back to Alberto.

"And now, aviator Alberto Santos-Dumont."

Alberto walked to the podium. "Thank you, Mr. Langley. It is a great honor to be speaking at the U.S. Government building at the Louisiana Purchase Exposition, which is filled with so many wonders from your museum. The Smithsonian has a long history of supporting those men who are working on the problem of human flight. Without the Smithsonian's support in those early days of aviation, we would be so much farther behind. I commend the Smithsonian's dedication to aviation, and personally, the dedication of you, Mr. Langley."

He paused for applause. Langley basked in it.

"However," Alberto continued after the clapping settled down, "I believe that you misspoke. I will not be flying my airship in the aeronautics competition during the fair. As most of you know, my airship was brutally attacked. It is not fit to fly, and it would be far too dangerous to attempt."

Behind Alberto, the men sitting on the chairs, including Langley and Mr. Myers, grimaced. They turned and whispered to each other like little boys in Sunday school.

"What do you mean you won't fly?" a man shouted from the crowd. "That's why you are here!"

Alberto pulled on his collar. "Yes, that is why I came to St. Louis, but events have transpired that make it impossible for me to fly. I will not risk the safety of my airship or of my own life."

"Boo! Boo! Coward! Get off that stage!" the crowd yelled.

I looked behind me, and there was a sea of disappointed and angry faces. They had come to the fair to see Alberto make history, and now in their minds, he wouldn't even try.

Alberto shook his fist at the crowd. "You would rather I crash to my death in a makeshift balloon than not try at all? Not a single one of you has half the courage that I have to fly. You gawk at something that you will never do. I am not a spectacle. I am an inventor, and if I am dead, what good is my ingenuity then?"

"Boo! Boo!"

"Get him out of here!"

"Show us an American who can fly!"

Langley hurried to the podium and gently pushed Alberto aside. The two men spoke, and Alberto gestured wildly before stomping off the stage.

Hastily, Langley took over the podium again. "Ladies and gentlemen. I want to apologize but Mr. Santos-Dumont had to leave the stage on a personal matter."

No one in the building believed that was true, but Langley went on nevertheless. "I would like to introduce our next speaker. Mr. Carl Myers will talk about the parameters of the aeronautics competition. Do not be concerned. We have nearly a half dozen aviators who have shown interest in flying in our competition. The prize pot will be won, and history will be made."

As discreetly as I could, I stood and started to inch out of the aisle. We were so close to the stage it would have been impossible to leave without being noticed at all.

"Katharine, where are you going?" Margaret whispered.

"I'll be back soon," I whispered out the side of my mouth.

She sighed and fell back in her chair. She knew me. She knew where I was going.

I walked in the direction that Alberto had gone behind the stage.

The U.S. Government building was so large and so filled with grand displays from the Smithsonian, I didn't know how I would ever find him. He was a small man, and he could have hidden behind any one of the stuffed animals where I would never see him.

I stepped around a stuffed lion that was caught in mid-roar. My heart ached for the creature for a moment. He could have been wandering free on a savannah, but instead he was frozen in time on the other side of the world. To me, it seemed such a waste of a beautiful wild creature.

I still couldn't find Alberto, but I heard the murmuring of Mr. Myers shouting his speech to the crowd. Even though I couldn't hear the words, I could tell from his tone that he was quite pleased with himself. I found his self-assuredness confusing. If I had been demoted from my position, the last place I would want to be was speaking on behalf of the organization that demoted me.

Having no luck finding Alberto, I went to the side door that led outside. It was there I found him leaning against one of the pillars, smoking a cigarette. His hands shook as he smoked. I withheld my lecture on smoking. It was such a nasty habit that I had no tolerance for, but if I wanted Alberto to talk to me, I would have to put my feelings aside for the moment.

"Mr. Santos-Dumont?" I asked.

He looked up with a scowl, but when he saw me his face softened. "Miss Wright, I thought I saw you in the crowd at the lecture. I was very happy to see you there, despite how the event went." He frowned.

"The crowd did not take kindly to your announcement that you would not fly."

He laughed. "That is one way to put it. I know how Americans are. You tell them no, and they throw a tantrum. It is the way that your people are built. I already had this plan to leave early because of it. They do not care about the path of discovery, of safety. They simply want to see me in the air so that they can tell people that they were there to witness it, and if I crash to my death, all the better." He took another drag of his cigarette. "I am not one of the animals in the zoo or one of those poor people that they have on display on the other side of the fair."

"People?" I asked.

He dropped the stub of the cigarette onto the ground and stamped it out with the toe of his black polished shoe. "Everything is for entertainment around here. I'd like to think it is just at the fair, and not all of America is like this. But I am not so sure."

"It's not," I insisted. "In your case, my brothers would do the same thing. As you know, they opted not to enter the competition at all because they did not believe it to be possible or fair, what the committee was asking them to do."

"I wish I had been as strong as your brothers and not come at all. If I had made that decision, airship number seven would still be intact. It is going take a great deal of money and time to repair it. Money, I have. Time is of the essence. For as many inventors who are trying to fly today, there are dozens more who will join the fray tomorrow. It is the ultimate race, much more valuable than the Olympic Games happening here at the exposition."

"I met one young aviator while I was here," I said. "Camilla Ortiz."

He studied my face. "The young woman who died the same morning that I found my airship's balloon in tatters?"

I nodded. "Did you meet her while she was alive?" I asked, knowing that he had because he had yelled at her to leave him alone. I was testing him to see if he would tell me the truth. I hoped that he would, because when it came down to it, I liked Alberto. His dedication to his goal reminded me a great deal of Wilbur and Orville.

For the first time, a wave of homesickness overtook me. I mentally shook it away to concentrate on the conversation at hand.

"I did not know Camilla. I had just arrived at the fair the day before. I met with all the mechanics before I checked the crates that night. I remember her being there. She stood out because she was a woman. It was not the typical place to find a member of the weaker sex."

I gritted my teeth when he said *weaker sex*, and just when I was thinking of him kindly too. I knew countless women who would still be on that stage, saying their piece instead of letting the crowd run them off like Alberto had. However, I kept these thoughts to myself, because upsetting Alberto would not get me the information that I needed from him.

"I never knew her in life, but her name was familiar to me, so I went back a few months in my journals—I write a log in my journal every day of what is happening in my life. It is crucial for me to see how far I have come and how far aviation has yet to go. Her name was familiar to me because she sent me a letter in February talking about her plans to build her own flying machine. What was holding her back was the weight of the engine. Weight is a constant concern when it comes to flight."

I nodded. I knew this from my brothers. They were constantly looking for ways to make their flyers lighter so that they could achieve more lift into the air.

"She was quite knowledgeable on flying," he said. "She claimed to have a design that she wanted to show me, but I was tired. I did not have time for that. You would not believe the number of people who come up to me and have the next great idea on how to fly. All of them are rubbish. I couldn't believe that a young girl would be any different. She was creating a fantasy to think that she, a woman, could be an aviator."

Again, I bit my tongue, but it was getting increasingly difficult. I respected Alberto, but his views on women left a lot to be desired.

"But you didn't speak to her at the fair."

"No. I didn't even know that the dead girl was the one who wrote the letter until I heard her name."

I frowned. This contradicted what I had heard about him yelling at Camilla on the day she arrived. The security guard Lucian Gilliam was the one who told me, and I had no reason to doubt him. I decided to press the issue. It was unlikely that I would get a second chance. "I don't believe you," I said.

He blinked at me and spurted, "H-how dare you speak to me in such a way!"

"I know from a very reliable source that you shouted at her to leave you alone the night before she died."

"Who is this source? Because I can assure you that they are lying. Everyone in the country had been against me from the moment I set foot on American soil. I am not surprised more lies about me have spread."

"I can't tell you that." Under no circumstances would I say Gilliam's name. He would surely be sacked by the fair for talking about Alberto. "But as you said, your personal staff and many mechanics were around that evening when you were checking the crates in the hangar. There are many witnesses. I could have asked any one of them to corroborate the story."

He clenched and unclenched his fists at his sides. "This is outrageous! Outrageous!"

I shrugged, even though I wasn't completely certain that he wouldn't lunge at me in his fury. "You can tell me or the police."

"There is no reason to tell the police," he snapped. "They have already arrested the man responsible for attacking my balloon. It seems he was a crazed fan of sorts. I have dealt with those before. It's not uncommon when you accomplish the impossible, as I have, that less stable people want to latch on to you. I have had my fair share of them in France. I wouldn't be the least bit surprised if he was the one who killed Camilla Ortiz as well. From what I heard from the police, the man is unhinged."

"They arrested Charles Morrison, but that doesn't mean the police won't to take a second look at you."

His glared at me. "I would never tamper with my own airship. You can't possibly understand how much time and money

I have spent on number seven. If you knew, you would realize how ridiculous that suggestion is."

"I'm not saying that you were the one who tampered with your airship, but it is possible that you thought that Camilla, rightly or wrongly, was the one who did, and you took your revenge."

"You are mad. What I have learned in my time in this country is all of you Americans are mad." He was so angry he wiped spittle from his lips.

I started to walk away. "I suppose I have no choice but to go to the police with what I know and let them sort it out." I started to walk away, and with my back to him I let out a long breath. I was almost certain that he would call my bluff, that he would let me leave and I would never know why he hated Camilla so much or perhaps even why he killed her.

I was almost to the corner of the building when he called after me, "Wait!"

I turned and looked over my shoulder. To my surprise, all the anger that Alberto had spewed at me just moments ago was gone.

His shoulders sagged and his mustache drooped. "Wait. I will tell you."

I walked back to him, but I kept over two arms' lengths between us. I could never be too careful when speaking to someone about murder.

"I have known Camilla through correspondence for well over a year. Ever since the exposition's aeronautic competition had been announced, she had written to me."

"And you wrote her back?" I asked.

He made a face. "Not at first."

I folded my hands over my wrist satchel, unsure if I wanted to know what the correspondence was about.

"I can tell by the look on your face that you believe that correspondence was inappropriate, and I can assure you that couldn't have been farther from the truth. All we ever wrote to each other about was flying. She was very curious about my airship and wished to ask for advice, as she was building her own flying machine. She proved again and again in her letters that she was very knowledgeable about anything and everything mechanical. After some time, I began to take her seriously and we built a mutual respect through our letters." He removed a handkerchief from his pocket and patted it on his dewy forehead.

I wished that I had a handkerchief with me to do that same. It was sweltering in the hot sun, and where we stood there was no shade. Even so, I wasn't going to walk away from this conversation, no matter how uncomfortable I was.

"Then, what happened? Why did you tell her to leave you alone?" I asked.

He shoved that handkerchief back into his pocket. "Because she betrayed me."

I blinked. "How?"

"I knew that she was working here at the exposition. This was in the winter, and I wrote her to tell her that I planned to enter the aeronautics exposition." He looked down at his hands. "She said that I should, but that the Wright Brothers would win the one-hundred-thousand dollars."

I frowned. "My brothers did not enter."

"We know that now, but at the time she wrote that letter they were here touring the concourse and still contemplating if they should enter." He shook his head. "She said that flying machines like your brothers' were the wave of the future, from everything that she was learning at the fair. Airships like mine would be obsolete. She said I should work with her to build a flying machine." He took a breath. "She insulted my airships and my accomplishments. I was offended beyond measure. Here I was, taking a young person—a woman, no less, with no accolades to her name—on as protégé, and she said that she thought that airships would not stand the test of time. I had just successfully flown around the Eiffel Tower.

Could the Wrights make such a claim? I broke off correspondence after that. I wanted nothing more to do with her."

A man's pride was a dangerous thing.

He shielded his eyes from the blazing sun. "It only became worse when I came to this country. It was because of her that I went to Dayton to meet with your brothers."

How I wished I had known about the meeting so that I could have been there. As close as I was with Wilbur and Orville, they still had their secrets.

"How did that make it worse?" I asked.

"Because when I toured their hangar and saw their flying machine, and when I spoke to them, I realized that Camilla was right. She had been right all along. Flying machines like your brothers' are the wave of the future, and my airship and I would be left behind."

"Then I would have thought when you saw Camilla here at the fair you would have wanted to talk to her about a flying machine. Maybe you could work together to invent something great."

He dropped his hand from his eyes. "No. I was too bruised. I would not take back what I said."

I shook my head. Poor Camilla. She finally thought that she had an ally in her pursuit of flight, but when she spoke to Alberto honestly about her thoughts on the matter, he became offended and rejected her. I could not help but wonder if he would have had the same reaction had Camilla been a man. Would he have taken her prediction more seriously then? It seemed that he took what he had learned from Wilbur and Orville seriously.

"Do you think that she was the one who destroyed the airship?" I asked.

He shook his head. "No, even though we had the falling out and I refused to speak to her, I don't believe she would do that. She loved the idea of flight too much. She was like me in that way."

I had to agree with him on that point, which meant that I was nowhere closer to knowing who tampered with the airship or who killed Camilla Ortiz. I could not completely rule out Alberto as the killer, but he did drop lower on my list, now that he was being honest with me about how he knew Camilla.

"What will you do next?" I asked.

"Pack up my number seven and return to Paris. It's all that I can do. It is the only place and the only people that I trust to salvage my balloon. At this point, I don't even know if it can be salvaged or if I will have to start again from the beginning. It takes months and months to make. There are so many coats of varnish on it. Every last one had to dry before the next layer could be applied."

I nodded. "Had they been in the same situation, I know that my brothers would have done the same thing."

"I am glad that I got to meet your brothers on my travel here to your country." He paused. "I saw an earnestness in your brothers. They were doing this for the same reason that I am. Discovery. The joy of discovering a new way of doing things. It's why all of us, inventors, aviators, or otherwise, get up in the morning."

I knew this was true about Wilbur and Orville. They rarely slept in, even on a Saturday morning, because they were so eager to get to work and solve the problems with their plans and designs they'd discovered the day before. Every day there was a new problem and a new discovery.

A motorcar pulled up behind the building.

"Mr. Santos-Dumont, my friends the Meachams are having a dinner party on the Ferris wheel tomorrow evening. We would all love it if you were able to attend."

His mustache turned downward as he frowned. "I have received an invitation from W. C. Meacham to such an engagement. I have not decided if I will attend."

"You should," I said. "It will be a very nice time, and you

can end your Louisiana Purchase Exposition experience on a high note."

"I will think it over," Alberto said.

A young man with a thin mustache was behind the motorcar's wheel. He smiled brightly at Alberto.

"There is my ride. I will bid you adieu." Alberto climbed into the motorcar and drove away.

I doubted that I would ever see him again.

CHAPTER 24

I walked around the giant building to the front again. There was a guard posted at the door, not letting anyone inside. I walked past him, and he stopped me as I tried to enter the U.S. Government building.

"Wait. Where do you think you're going?" he bellowed.

"Back to my seat." I reached into my wrist satchel and retrieved the tickets that Alberto had given to me. "I am a guest of Mr. Alberto Santos-Dumont."

"That doesn't mean anything at all. I heard he ran away from his duties." He stood with his feet apart and arms crossed.

I shook the ticket at him. "I still have a ticket. I would like to go back inside."

"It doesn't matter if you have a ticket or not. You're not going in. No one goes in until the lectures are over. The place is overcrowded, and the fire marshal has ordered not to let anyone else inside."

I scowled at him, but he did not budge.

If I had been alone, I wouldn't have been so concerned to reenter the building, but I knew that Margaret would be getting increasingly worried about my whereabouts. I didn't want her to be stressed. She was still recovering from her illness.

The doorman glowered at me. Seeing that I was going to have no luck with him, I decided to walk around the building and look for another way in. The structure was so large, it was impossible for me to believe that all the windows and doors were locked. I was hoping I would be able to go in through a door. I had a history of climbing into places through windows and it not going well. I didn't want to repeat that.

A group of people pointed at the very top of the pillar. "Do you see a parrot up there?"

"What a beautiful bird! He must have escaped from the birdcage in the aviary."

"Does anyone have a net to catch him?"

"He's too high for any net."

I stepped under the pillar and clapped my hands. "Achilles! Come down from there."

The parrot ignored all the other shouts from the people in the crowd, but when he heard his name, he peered straight down at me as if he were a hawk that spotted a mouse in a field.

His talons gripped the side of the pillar. As the facade of the pillars was made with hemp, like the rest of the structure, he was able to sink his talons into the soft material and anchor himself.

"How is he going to get down from there?" a bystander asked.

His friend shoved him. "He's a bird, you knucklehead. He can fly."

"Achilles!" I called the bird again and clapped my hands twice more like I had seen Zeb do when he was calling the bird back to his shoulder. It took three attempts with me repeating his name and clapping before the macaw spread his wings and let go of the pillar. The parrot swooped down from the side of the building and landed on my shoulder.

He hit me like a baseball bat to the side. I stumbled to keep my balance. When Achilles was settled, he was remarkably light, but the force of his landing was what caught me off guard.

"Is that your parrot?" one of the young men asked.

I shook my head. "But I know who it belongs to."

"You most certainly do," a crackly voice said.

Just the sound of Zeb Dandy's voice caused the hairs on the back of my neck to stand up. On my shoulder, Achilles's talons pricked my skin.

I turned to see Zeb Dandy behind me. "Thank you for finding my bird."

The group of people who had been standing below the pillar to look up at Achilles vanished. It seems that Zeb Dandy had that kind of effect on people. If Achilles had not been on my shoulder, I might have dashed away too.

Zeb clapped his hands twice and Achilles dug his talons into my shoulder. I winced. The shirtwaist was not thick enough to protect me. I was afraid another article of clothing had been ruined when I heard the sound of tearing fabric. This time it was Margaret's clothing, not mine.

Zeb scowled and clapped twice again.

Slowly, Achilles released his hold on my shoulder, and half hopped, half flew to Zeb's shoulder.

Zeb removed a chain from his pocket. He clamped a tiny shackle around Achilles's right ankle. The shackle was connected to a chain looped through Zeb's belt.

Achilles tried to take off from his master's shoulder, but Zeb yanked him back in place with a tug of the chain. My heart ached for the bird. Birds were meant to be free and fly, not stand like puppets on scoundrels' shoulders to sell tickets.

Looking at Achilles in his obvious misery, I thought of the many hours that my brothers would go out into the countryside to study birds in flight as they were just beginning to venture into the problem of human flight. At times when I didn't have to teach, I would go with them. Listening to my brothers comment about the majesty of the birds in the air gave me a new respect for the creatures. They weren't tethered to the earth like humans were; they were free.

Zeb smiled and showed off his yellow teeth. "Thank you for getting my bird back for me. I thought when he took off that I might never see him again, but I should not be surprised that he was with you. He has had a liking of you from the start."

"Achilles is a very smart bird," I said.

"Maybe too smart for his own good. He would do better just to stay put and stay quiet." He knocked the parrot on the beak, and Achilles ducked his head.

It took all my willpower not to punch Zeb square in the nose for how he was treating the bird.

"What brings you to the U.S. Government building?" he asked.

"I was here for the lecture."

"Ahh," he said. "Me too, of course."

I narrowed my eyes. "What lecture were you here for?"

"I was hoping to hear Alberto Santos-Dumont, but I understand that he was booed off the stage. Rightfully so, in my opinion. If you can't deliver on what you promised, you should leave."

I came to the aviator's defense. "It's not his fault. Someone attacked his airship."

"He's not even trying to get it fixed here in St. Louis. We have capable men too, you know."

There was no point for me to argue on Alberto's behalf. He would be leaving for Paris soon and be done with the world's fair for good.

"I'm disappointed that I didn't have a chance to speak to

him," Zeb said. "He was one of the good many people that I wanted to talk to."

"And why is that?" I asked.

The exaggerated smile on his face from the clown makeup curled into a smirk. "Can I not also be interested in flight?"

"Who else did you want to talk to?" I asked.

He laughed. "I do like the fact that you're unafraid to ask questions, even in matters that are none of your concern. You would do well in my line of work."

I eyed him. "And what line of work is that? Do you ask a lot of questions selling tickets for the Temple of Mirth? I don't see how the problem of flight applies there either."

He grinned. As usual the expression was made more intense from his clown makeup. I didn't know how he could wear so much face paint with how thick the air was. Not to mention his full clown costume. I thought I might melt in the light shirtwaist and skirt that I wore.

"Most certainly for my work at the Temple of Mirth. You have to ask the right questions of folks when you engage them in conversation, so they are more likely to do as you wish. Which, in my case, is to buy a ticket and enjoy a few minutes of harmless amusement in my fun house."

I thought about the barrel of love. The harmless amusement piece was in question.

Achilles bobbed his head up and down on Zeb's shoulder, but I didn't think it was because the large bird agreed with him. If his flight to the top of the pillar was any indication, Achilles wanted to be as far away from Zeb as possible. I wished I could help him, but Achilles belonged to Zeb, and there was nothing that I could do about it.

"Have you had any luck finding who killed Camilla?" he asked in such a way that it was meant to sound disinterested, but it was the complete opposite.

My eyes widened.

He smirked. "Ahh, you are surprised that I know about that, are you?"

I didn't say anything in return.

Zeb appeared to be undeterred by my silence because he went on to say, "It seems the police feel the same way, now that Charles is loose again."

I blinked. "They let Charles out of jail?" I asked.

He placed a hand to his chest in mock surprise. His nails were as long as a woman's and painted white. "Oh, I thought you would have known that by now. I thought the reporter Harry Haskell was your *good* friend."

I scowled at him. "I don't know what this has to do with Mr. Haskell."

In my mind, I wondered how he even knew who Harry was, let alone that we knew each other, and I didn't like what he was insinuating by calling Harry my "good friend." It suggested something unseemly when there was absolutely no truth to it. I glared at him and could feel my blood begin to boil. How dare he speak to me in such a manner?

"Just that he surely knows that Charles was released. He was there when the man walked out of the jail." He cocked his head. "I'm surprised that he didn't tell you that. He's not as good of a friend to you as I thought. After all, he is married, isn't that true?"

"I don't know what Mr. Haskell being married has to do with Charles." My voice was sharp.

"Probably nothing," he said with a shrug. "Come along, Achilles, you bad bird. We have to get back to the Temple of Mirth. Our public awaits."

As Zeb walked away, Achilles looked back over his shoulder at me. He had the saddest look on his face. It was almost as if his beak drooped, if that was even possible. I wished that I could take the bird away from Zeb Dandy, but I didn't know how I could do that and not sink to the fun-house man's level.

I fumed as I saw Zeb and Achilles melt into the crowd. I was still so angry by the way that he spoke to me about Harry. But then, another thought entered my mind. Harry knew that Charles F. Morrison was released from jail. He knew, and he didn't tell me. It seemed that the pact we had made was not as binding as I had thought.

CHAPTER 25

Margaret found me outside near the front of the U.S. Government building. After Zeb Dandy and Achilles left to return to the Pike, I'd walked around the building twice, looking for a way to sneak back inside. However, I was out of luck. Almost every door was locked, and the ones that weren't locked had guards stationed in front of them. All of whom refused to let me back in. The fair was taking the maximum occupancy of the building extremely seriously.

Because I could not get back inside, I waited near the front entrance until the lecture was over. I prayed Margaret would come out that way. The fair was so huge if we were separated it would be almost impossible to find the other person.

Margaret unfurled her parasol as she walked outside and walked over to me. "We need to make a rule that if we are split up, we go to a specific meeting place. We will both know to go to the place and the other will be there as soon as she can."

"What should the meeting place be?"

Margaret took time to consider this. "What about the Floral Clock? It's a large landmark and there are open views where you can stand in front of it, so you can see people coming."

"The Floral Clock it is," I agreed, and looped her arm through mine.

She held the parasol over our heads, and again it did little to shade both of us. We would have sunburns on half of our faces at this rate.

"What did Mr. Santos-Dumont say?" Margaret asked.

"What?" I asked.

"Dear Katharine, don't pretend that you didn't run off to speak with the aviator."

I bumped my shoulder against her. "I did, and I learned some interesting information about Camilla while you were inside too."

Her eyes went wide. "What was it?"

"First of all, Camilla wrote to Alberto telling him about her flying machine and asking advice on engines."

"So, they knew each other?" she asked.

"That's what I thought, but Alberto said no. He said he was able to put together that the young woman who wrote him and Camilla were the same person after she died."

"Can you trust that he was telling the truth? Maybe he just said that because he didn't want to be associated with her murder."

"You might be right about that," I said. "Because Charles Morrison, who is the man that was arrested for tampering with the flying machine, said that he saw Alberto shouting at Camilla to leave his hangar."

Her eyes went wide. "Can you trust a criminal?"

"He's not a criminal. At least that's what the police believe. He's been released from jail; that was what I was told."

"By who?" Margaret asked.

"Zeb Dandy."

She grimaced. "I would take anything that he says with a grain of salt. He's creepy and his clown face is off-putting."

I couldn't agree with her more on that.

I kept to myself that Zeb mentioned Harry. I knew Margaret thought I might still have feelings for my old college friend. Nothing could be further from the truth. All I felt about him at the moment was frustration. We had made a deal that we would share information, and here he was not telling me about Charles's release. Could I really trust him? I reminded myself that Harry and I agreed to share information about the case at Meacham's dinner party. I guess I'd have my answer then.

"You do have a point," I agreed. "I don't believe Zeb Dandy is trustworthy, but I don't know why he would make up a lie about Charles's release."

Margaret pursed her lips. "Some men lie for the sport of it." She said this as if she knew it from some personal experience.

I knew that she must have been thinking of her father when she said this. He had not been a kind man. It made me more relieved that she found such a good husband in Meacham. She deserved all the happiness in the world.

She placed a hand on my arm. "I'm so sorry to break up the plans for the rest of the day, but I think that it would be better if I went back to the flat. I feel a little woozy. The air was very close in the U.S. Government building. I'm glad I came. The lectures were interesting, and it was nice to get out after being cooped up for so many days. However, I don't want to push my health too far."

"Understood. I will hail a cab, and we will return to the flat."

She shook her head. "I can get my own cab, Katharine. I don't want you to miss more amusements. I just feel awful that I have kept you away from it so much due to my stomach bug. It's infuriating that I'm not able to shake this sick feeling that I have."

"You will shake it. It will just take a bit of time and lots of rest. At least, let me hail the cab for you. I want to make sure you're safely off before I visit the rest of the fair."

She nodded. "You are a good friend. I don't know what I would do without you."

I squeezed her hand, and then I took her parasol from her hand, as I could tell that she was having trouble holding the handle straight. I held it over her head. My primary goal for this trip to the world's fair was to spend quality time with my dear friend. So many events since I had arrived had distracted me from that.

There was a long line of hansom cabs and carriages in front of the building waiting to take the public wherever they might need to go. I helped Margaret to one and instructed the driver to be careful as she wasn't feeling well.

I watched them drive away, wondering if I had done the right thing to let her go back to the flat alone.

I had no way to contact Harry to ask him about Charles's release from jail. I didn't know what hotel he was staying in and hadn't thought to ask him. My best chance of learning more about Charles was going back, yet again, to the concourse. I was becoming a bit of a fixture on that side of the fair.

The air was muggy, but I still opted to walk across the fairgrounds. I avoided the Pike as I had no desire to run into Zeb Dandy again. Because of that, my walk took a few minutes longer as I went by the Floral Clock.

There was a group of school children in front of the clock and the teacher with them tried to corral them all in place while a photographer waited behind his wooden tripod and camera to take a picture.

"Closer together," the teacher said. "Pretend that you like each other."

I smiled to myself as the children inched toward each other. Moments like these were what the fair was supposed to be about. My experience was tainted by Camilla's death and by the fact that I was the only one who seemed to care.

I knew that wasn't completely true. Her sister, Sylvia, cared very much, but she was scared. If one of my brothers had been murdered, I would have been scared too, but it seemed deeper than that. Sylvia appeared to be scared because she thought she would be next. But I couldn't understand why she felt that way. Camilla's murder had to be tied to the aeronautics competition. In fact, those were her dying words. Sylvia had no ties to it other than her sister.

I walked to the fence that surrounded the concourse and peered inside. I didn't see a soul. It was a vast, empty space. Alberto had been scheduled to make his historic flight in a few days, but now it was a ghost town.

The gate was padlocked. The competition officials weren't taking any chances with unauthorized people getting into the concourse. After all that had happened, I couldn't blame them for the extra precautions.

I walked around the concourse to the back, where the hangars were. I could not believe I was in the place where I had been a few days ago when I found Camilla.

"I told you to leave! You're not allowed back here!" a man shouted.

I peeked around the side of one of the hangars and saw the guard Gilliam standing in front of Charles Morrison.

"Didn't jail teach you a lesson to stay away from here? You have to be the stupidest man alive to come back here. The police are just going to arrest you again."

"I need to ask Mr. Santos-Dumont to take me up in his airship. It is my destiny to fly," Charles said.

"I don't care if it's your destiny to turn into a frog, you're not doing it here. You have already gotten me into enough trouble as it is."

"I don't mean to make trouble. I don't want to make trouble for anyone, but I have to fly. You don't understand; I have to do it. It was the very reason I was born."

Gilliam's face was bright red at this point, and I would not have been surprised if steam started to come out of his ears at any moment. He looked to be a few seconds away from punching Charles in the nose. I knew it was time that I intervened.

"Gentlemen, what is the problem?" I asked.

Both men gaped at me.

Gilliam threw up his hands. "What are you doing here? Is it not possible for me to get any peace on my workday? All I was supposed to do was guard the hangars, and now I have you two to contend with. This job doesn't pay enough."

"Mr. Gilliam, I am here looking for Mr. Morrison." I turned to Charles. "I very much want to talk to you."

Charles fidgeted back and forth from foot to foot. "Everyone wants to speak to me. Everyone thinks I know something that I do not."

"What do you know?" I asked. "Do you know who attacked Mr. Santos-Dumont's airship?"

"The girl," he said in a matter-of-fact way.

"Camilla?" I asked.

"Yes, I didn't want to say it because she had been kind to me, but it was her."

Gilliam shook his head. "I don't care who it was at this point. I just want you out of here, the both of you."

I ignored Gilliam's complaints. "Why do you think it was Camilla?"

"Camilla ran away from the hangar where number seven was. She had a knife in her hand."

"Why didn't you tell me this when we first met?" I tried to keep my voice even, but I was fuming inside. This would have been good information to have.

"Camilla was kind to me."

"There was no knife with her when I found her," I said.

He shrugged. "Nothing is safe at the fair. Anything worth just a penny, people take."

"Did you see someone else there?"

"No, no, I was too scared to come out of my hiding spot. When someone, even if it is your friend, runs by you with a knife you need to keep your distance."

I supposed those were good words to live by.

Camilla couldn't have stabbed herself in the back, so it only made sense that she met someone in the alley or someone went into the alley after her. But it was still hard for me to believe that *she* was the one who destroyed Alberto's balloon. Camilla wanted to fly. She admired aviators and she had written to Alberto sharing her admiration for his accomplishments. Why, then, would she do something so terrible that would make it impossible for him to fly? Was it because Alberto rejected her and told her to stay out of his hanger? I frowned. That would seem to be a rash decision on her part, and Alberto himself didn't even believe that she was capable of that.

"When was this?" I asked.

"At first light."

"First light? So very early in the morning, long before Mr. Santos-Dumont and I arrived."

"Hours before."

I frowned. That was in keeping with what the doctor said when he examined Camilla's body. He said that she had been stabbed hours before. That could only mean the young woman that I had seen running away from the hangar wasn't Camilla at all but her twin, Sylvia. I shivered. Why hadn't Sylvia stopped to help her own sister? Had she thought that she was already dead? Had I mistaken the direction that she ran? Maybe she didn't see Camilla on the ground? My head was spinning.

Gilliam shook his head. "Don't listen to him, Miss Wright.

The police let him go because he is a harmless kook. You can't take anything that he says as true."

Charles did a little hop. "Who are you calling a kook? Someday when I am flying through the air, and you are back here on the ground looking up and wishing you were me, you will know the truth."

Gilliam wrinkled his brow. "The truth about what?"

"You will all see." Charles shook his bony fist.

I shook my head. It seemed to me that Gilliam was right. I couldn't take anything that Charles said as truth.

"I have had enough of this. I have tried to be nice, but this must come to an end." Gilliam grabbed Charles by the arm. "It's time for you to leave."

Charles jerked back from the much larger man. "Unhand me, you rogue."

Gilliam snorted in disgust.

"Gilliam," I said. "Wait just a minute. Give me a chance to convince Charles to leave."

The guard glared at me.

"Please," I said. "If I'm not successful, you can toss him out."

"No one is tossing me anywhere," Charles said.

"Fine." Gilliam folded his thick arms over his chest.

I turned to the other man. "Charles, there is no point for you to be in Mr. Santos-Dumont's hangar today. He won't fly while he is at the fair."

Charles narrowed his eyes at me. "You're lying."

I shook my head. "I'm telling the truth. I just saw Mr. Santos-Dumont a little while ago, and he made a public statement that he would not be flying at the fair because of the damage to his balloon. He believes that the only place where it can be fixed is in Paris."

Charles's chin began to quiver as if he were about to cry.

Gilliam's lips curled in disgust. I knew the guard was thinking grown men shouldn't cry, and certainly shouldn't cry over a balloon, even a very special balloon like Alberto's.

"This just can't fly. I was meant to fly. Alberto was to take me up. I know it. I saw a vision."

"Have you ever spoken to Mr. Santos-Dumont? Did he tell you that he would take you up in the airship?"

"I knew him in my own way. We are kindred spirits. We both think about flying more than anything else. I thought it was the same with Camilla. She is my friend, but she had not been a friend to me of late."

"What do you mean?" I asked.

"She promised to put in a good word for me with Alberto and convince him to take me up in his airship. She said that weeks ago! But where is she?"

I grimaced. It was difficult for me to grasp that Charles really didn't believe Camilla was dead. There didn't seem to be anything I could say that would convince him otherwise.

"Now, can I kick him out?" Gilliam asked.

Charles bent over and reached into his boot. He held up a short knife. The blade sparkled in the sunshine.

Both Gilliam and I backed up.

"No one is taking me anywhere. I will stay here until Alberto takes me up in his airship. I don't care if it will take my whole life long." He waved the knife in the air.

"Is that the knife that you used to stab Camilla?" I asked.

He spun around and looked at me. "No one is listening to me. No one ever listens to me."

I held up my hands. "Charles, we are listening to you now." I paused. "But I have to know if you stabbed Camilla."

"I didn't stab that dead girl, if that's what you're getting at."

"Did the police look at your knife when you were at the station?"

"Yes, they took it, and I was certain that I would never see it again. It was a gift from my older brother from when he was in the war."

"The Civil War?" I asked.

"It is the only war that matters," Charles snapped.

"But the police gave it back." I inched a few steps back. I didn't want to be in range if Charles had a tantrum and starting swinging the knife around.

"They did. They said it was far too small to be the knife that stabbed the balloon or killed the girl."

"They believed that both actions were committed using the same knife?" This was a detail that I needed to know.

"Yes, the knife that the girl had. Its blade was long and sharp. My knife is too short and blunt to have been the tool."

Gilliam spoke up. "It does look too small to have made the cuts through the balloon silk. Those marks went deep, going through many layers at one time."

Charles swung the knife back and forth in the air. "I told you." And then, much to my relief, he tucked the knife back into his boot.

I still wasn't completely comfortable with his having a knife, but I was much happier that it was no longer in his hand.

"That is enough," Gilliam said. "Get out of here. You should feel lucky that you're not spending the rest of your life in prison."

Charles shook his fist at him. "Don't you dare touch me."

"You aren't even supposed to be on the fairgrounds." Gilliam lunged forward like he was going to jump on Charles. Charles leapt back.

"Try and catch me, then. It is a big fair; you can't be everywhere all at once." He ran to the other side of the hangar.

"Get out of here," Gilliam shouted.

"I will for now," Charles said, hopping from foot to foot. "But, miss, you need to remember. I'm the only one who knows, if you just had eyes to see it, but you are blinded by what you believe." He ran away and disappeared around the edge of the fence surrounding the concourse.

"Good riddance," Gilliam muttered. "If I never see him again it will be too soon."

"He needs some kind of help," I said.

"What he needs is to go to an asylum where he can get the treatments that he needs to keep him calm. That is also the best way to keep him from trying to fly. The man is cracked."

I pressed my lips together. I didn't think that was the answer. I knew too many sad stories about asylums. There had been students in my classes over the years who I knew struggled with illogical thinking. I always did my best to work with them, so that they could stay in the classroom. Not all my efforts were welcomed by parents or administrators. It would be easier to ship those children away rather than accommodate them in the public school. I wondered if, when Charles had been a child such as that, a lifetime ago, all he needed was a teacher to try to reach him where he was.

Because one thing was for certain. Everyone had demons. Just some of those demons were more easily seen by the outside world.

CHAPTER 26

"I cannot believe that the dinner party is tomorrow," Margaret said the next morning at breakfast when going over her to-do lists. "I don't know how I will get everything done."

I set my piece of toast back down on the plate. "Margaret, you have had dinners like this hundreds of times for Meacham's investors and potential clients in Chicago. They have always come off smashingly. I don't see why this one will be any different."

"Those were at home." She fanned herself with her cloth napkin. "I know the caterer, the staff, the china. I don't know anything here, and we will be in the Ferris wheel. What if the staff or I forget something on the ground when we are at the very top? It's not like we can jump out and grab it. It would be an embarrassment if one of the gentlemen wanted gin and we only had vodka in the capsule."

"It would be ridiculous for the guests to expect that you have every possible beverage known to man when you're in a Ferris wheel." I sipped my tea. "And might I add that it is quite an impractical place for a dinner party of any kind, and certainly for a banker, no less."

She fanned herself more vigorously. "My dear Meacham

wanted to set the dinner party in the Ferris wheel to impress all of these important men. He said that we had to go big to impress anyone at the fair because we were competing against the fair itself. He is a dear man, but he didn't consider any of the practicalities of actually pulling it off."

"He didn't think of them because he's a man, and we women are supposed to make it work. Hasn't it always been that way since the beginning of time?"

Margaret paled.

I reached across the breakfast table and squeezed her hand. "And make it work we shall. You have thought of everything you possibly can, despite not feeling your best this week. Meacham cannot expect more than that from you. The dinner party will be flawless, and those men will swoon. They will put their money in your husband's bank in Chicago, and the two of you will live a beautiful life."

She relaxed slightly. I released her hand and went back to eating my toast.

"You do have a way of putting me at ease, Katharine. Just you saying that makes me feel better, even though you have no way to know that it will be true. You speak with such confidence that you make me believe it is possible." She lifted her teacup to her mouth and took a sip. "I wish I had just an ounce of your confidence. My days would go by a lot more smoothly if I did."

"My father always said I had the force of will like a herd of elephants." I grinned. "However, I'm certain that he did not mean it as a compliment."

She almost spat out her tea.

Inwardly, I was relieved. A laughing Margaret was much more pleasurable to be around than a worried Margaret. Since her illness earlier in the week, she hadn't been herself. I knew why. To be throwing such an extravagant party and be sick to your stomach at that same time was no easy feat. I would not want to be in her place, and I vowed to do whatever I could to take a little bit of the pressure off of her.

She set her teacup back on the saucer. "You're right that there isn't much more I can do for the party. Everything is in motion."

"Then, we should go out and enjoy the fair," I said. "Tomorrow, you will be far too busy fretting over the final details. But we will only go out if you are feeling up to it. I don't want you to push yourself too hard with tomorrow being such a big day."

"I'm feeling much better today. When I came home from the fair yesterday, Meacham sent a doctor to come over and look in on me. He gave me some charcoal water to drink. He said that it will protect the lining of my stomach. It seems to do the trick. This is the first day that I was able to eat breakfast without feeling a bit nauseous. I believe the worst is behind me."

I sighed. "I am relieved to hear it. I have been so worried about you, and I have felt so guilty to be out and about at the fair without you."

She cocked her head. "Have you? Or have you been poking around still trying to find out what happened to that young woman?"

I picked my napkin up from my lap, folded it, and placed it on top of my empty plate. "You know me too well."

"And what have you determined about her death?" Margaret asked.

"Nothing definitive yet, but . . ." I trailed off. I was afraid to say what I really thought about Camilla's murder, even to Margaret.

Instead, I changed the subject and told Margaret since she had missed much of the fair because of her illness, she could pick where we went that morning. After spending several minutes consulting the map, she said, "I would like to see the other countries. Most of them are near the Floral Clock and not too far from the aerial concourse. You will like that."

I grinned. "I might want to swing by if we are close."

"I thought so," she said. "So many of the countries represented there are places that we will never see in person. Japan, China, and Russia. This will be our one and only time to see their cultures in action."

"Then that is where we will go."

We left the flat a few minutes later, and Margaret insisted that we walk to the festivities.

"I have had very little exercise in the last few days, and I can feel my joints and muscles growing stiff. Walking would do me well."

I wasn't certain that she should be walking the two miles from the flat to the House of Japan, which was to be our first stop inside the fairgrounds. However, I didn't argue with her because I didn't want to baby her like her husband did at times. Margaret was an intelligent woman. She should not be treated as anything else.

The walk was more of an amble as we made our way across the fair. We stopped at several attractions and statues to take them in, and I bought us both iced teas. Iced tea was introduced at the fair. I personally had never heard of it before. I knew that the British in attendance must have been aghast at the national beverage being Americanized. I found it refreshing and just what was needed on a scorching day when a cup of hot tea could cause a lady to melt into a puddle.

The Japanese rose garden was one of the most beautiful places that I had ever seen. There were roses of every color and variety, all groomed with exquisite care.

In the corner of the garden, a group of women demonstrated Japanese tea services. Margaret and I stood a few feet away from the ceremony.

Margaret leaned close to me and whispered, "I can't imagine us doing anything that reverent outside of a church."

"There is certainly a spiritual aspect to it," I agreed. "Every movement has meaning."

When the tea ceremony ended, the ladies stood and smiled at us and the others in the audience. I wished that I could ask them questions about the ceremony, but they did not speak English and I didn't speak Japanese.

After leaving Japan, we went to the exhibits from Morocco, Jerusalem, and France. Every last one of them was fascinating. After being at the world's fair, I had an itch to travel, but I knew I would never have the funds for a round-the-world trip. This was the closest that I would come and the reason the fair began in the first place.

As we were leaving France, my friend Paul Laurence Dunbar was walking at a very quick pace. He was clearly upset and kept looking over his shoulder. I touched Margaret's arm. "Can you wait here a moment?"

I did not wait for her reply and hurried in Paul's direction. As I was right in front of him, I thought he must have seen me, but there was no recognition on his face.

"Paul, are you all right?" I asked.

He blinked and stopped mid-stride. "Oh, Katharine, it is you."

"Who did you think it might be?"

He pulled at his collar. "One never knows who he will bump into or what he will see at the fair. I wish I could un-know what is known and unsee what is seen."

"What do you mean?" I asked. I knew that Paul was a poet and there were times that he spoke in such a way that it appeared as if he was trying out verse.

"The fair is so obsessed with the sky and for they who soar, but it's not they who soar, but they who plod."

The confusion must have been apparent on my face because he spoke plainly then.

"I am sorry," Paul said. "I was shaken by the anthropology exhibit. They have men from Africa there, and unlike the countries of France and Japan, whose cultures are being lauded as sophisticated and refined, the cultures of the African continent, among others, are mocked for amusement. I saw it to make sure that it was true, and it was. I could not stand it for more than a few seconds before I had to get out. It is too much for me to take in, because I am just a generation separated from where those men are. I am sure that Orville has told you that my parents were slaves before the war."

I nodded.

"There are places where that continues on, and one of those is here at the world's fair."

I shivered.

Margaret walked over to us. "It's so nice to see you again, Mr. Dunbar."

He smiled at her. "And you as well, Mrs. Meacham."

Margaret looked from Paul to me and back again. "Is something wrong?"

"I have just seen something that was upsetting to me," Paul said. "But like so many things that make my blood boil over, I will turn it into words and hope that the ones who can do something about it will act."

"Oh," Margaret said, looking thoroughly confused. I could not blame her. If I had come into the middle of the conversation like that, I would not know what he was talking about either.

Margaret cleared her throat. "I am very happy that you accepted our invitation to the dinner party tomorrow evening. It will be nice for Kate to have another friend there as I will be so busy as the hostess."

He nodded. "I will be there. I do appreciate the invitation."

She smiled. "I am sure everyone will be curious to hear about what poem you are writing."

He frowned. "Curiosity appears to be a theme here at the

fair." He nodded at us. "I wish you both good day." With that he walked away.

If what Paul said was true, and I had no reason to doubt him, it was awful indeed. I had no wish to see it.

"Shall we go into the anthropology exhibit next?" Margaret asked quite innocently.

I shook my head. "There are many exhibits at the fair. We can't possibly see them all. Let's choose another."

Ever agreeable, Margaret nodded and said, "Where do you want to go?"

"To the birds," I said.

CHAPTER 27

It might have been my brothers' interest in birds and flying, or perhaps it was because I was still thinking about poor Achilles the parrot, but I very much wanted to see the flight cage at the fair before leaving. I knew Margaret, who had an affinity for animals of every kind, would enjoy it as well.

The walk to the flight cage was short and gave me time to think over what Paul had said. It seemed there always had to be a dark side, even to a celebration of accomplishments and advancement like the Louisiana Purchase Exposition. It was a sad fact that I would do well to remember.

"Oh, my word," Margaret said as the flight cage came into view. "It looks like the world's largest overturned laundry basket."

I had to admit that she was right, if the laundry basket was made with wire.

Even from where we stood, still a good distance away, we could hear the birds singing and squawking inside of the flight cage. And we could smell them too, as there was a very distinct odor to bird droppings en masse.

Margaret held a handkerchief up to her nose. "Are you sure that you want to go in there?"

"Yes, of course. When will I again get a chance to see so many different birds?" I asked.

She nodded. "I think I will stay here and view them from outside. I don't believe that my stomach is well enough to withstand the smell."

"I can skip it too," I said. "There is plenty more to see."

"No, no, you go inside. I know you want to see them, and you spoke of how your brothers studied birds to fly. You can't pass up on this chance. There is a lovely garden just over there with a bench in the shade. I could use a little rest."

I bit the inside of my lip. "If you are sure."

"Of course, I am sure. Don't be silly. Now, go!"

I hesitated a moment longer, but Margaret shooed me away. I walked up to the line to enter the flight cage. After a short while standing in line, the smell didn't bother me as much because I had become accustomed to it. I believed that was a good thing for the keepers working in and around the flight cage. I don't know how they would stand it otherwise.

As I came up to the gate, I gave the man a nickel at the door so that I could step inside, and I gasped in awe as I stood on the path. All around me colorful birds flew here and there. There were birds of every shape and size, from tiny painted buntings at the bird feeders suspended from posts to pink flamingos that stood on one leg in the man-made pond in the middle of the cage.

The small songbirds clung to the top of the cage or nestled in the young trees that had been planted inside the flight cage especially for the birds.

When I was at Oberlin, I had taken an ornithology class for a science credit. I had chosen it, of course, because of my brothers' interest in birds and flying. For part of the class, we would go into the woods or to the lakeshore to look for birds and identify them. However, I had never seen a collection of the winged creatures such as this.

There were two young girls with their mother in front of me. The smaller of the two girls looked up with awe on her face. "This is my favorite place. I love birds. Someday, I will be a bird doctor."

The second girl snorted. "There is no such thing as a bird doctor."

"There is," the first girl argued. "Who do you think takes care of these birds when they become ill?"

"Oh, my sweet Annabelle," their mother said. "That is something that you can have an interest in, but you won't have time for such study when you're married with babies."

Annabelle stopped in the middle of the path and put her hands on her hips. "Maybe I would rather be a bird doctor than be married and have children."

The mother's face grew grave. "Please don't make a scene."

"I have a right to make my own choice." Annabelle said.

"Dahlia," a man said, who stood a little off to the side. "Let Annabelle be."

"Godwin, I don't want to give our girls the wrong idea about their future."

I raised my brow when I heard the name.

"It is not fair to them if we are not honest about their aspirations," Dahlia said.

Godwin nodded. "I understand, but we have two very powerful young girls. I believe it is not speaking to them falsely to say that they might be right in their aspirations."

Dahlia shook her head and sighed.

I hesitated on the walk. I was directly behind the family now. Did I wait for them to move on or did I gingerly step around them?

Godwin looked over his shoulder and waved his family to the side. "Let's allow this lady to pass." As he said this he frowned as if he was trying to place me. A moment later recognition came into his eyes. "Weren't you at the concourse asking about Camilla Ortiz?"

I had not seen Godwin since that day on the concourse when I asked about Camilla. It seemed like it was ages ago but it was just a few days. I nodded. "It's nice to see you again. You have a beautiful family."

He smiled. "Thank you. It's not often that I have a day off of work to spend at the fair with the family, but with no one flying in the competition soon, I was granted a free day."

"I'm glad that you were," I said and nodded at Dahlia and the girls. "I'm Katharine Wright."

"Oh!" the little girl Annabelle cried. "You are the one Daddy told us was the sister to the Wright brothers."

"I am." I could not help but smile.

"I wish they were here to fly," she said.

"To be honest," I said, "I wish that too. I will tell them they have a fan here in St. Louis."

Annabelle's eyes sparkled at the very idea that I would speak to my brothers about her.

"Dahlia, can you take the girls to see the flamingos? I would like to talk to Miss Wright for a moment."

Dahlia pressed her lips together but did not argue with her husband as she tried to usher the girls down the path. The oldest girl went willingly, but Annabelle held back. "No, I want to talk to Miss Wright too."

"Annabelle." Her mother's voice had an edge to it.

The little girl's shoulders drooped as she realized that she couldn't defy her parents without getting into a whole heap of trouble.

I smiled at her. She reminded me quite a bit of myself when I was a child. I supposed it was something about being the youngest that you were more willing to push the boundaries with your parents. It seemed Annabelle wisely realized she had reached her limit. "It was very nice to meet you, Annabelle."

"Don't forget to tell your brothers about me." She hurried after her mother and sister down the path.

"I have to apologize for Annabelle. She is a very strong-willed child," Godwin said.

"Don't," I said. "I like her spunk."

"That doesn't surprise me." He cleared his throat.

"You wished to speak to me?"

He nodded. "About Camilla."

I raised my brow. I had not been expecting that, as it seemed like everyone at the fair was reluctant to speak about Camilla Ortiz.

"Camilla was my friend," he began.

I nodded encouragement.

"I've done so well at the concourse because of things that she taught me. She knew more about engines than any other mechanic there and maybe even more than the inventors."

I waited.

"There are rumors that Camilla is the one that damaged Mr. Santos-Dumont's airship. I know that she wouldn't do that, and I don't want her to be blamed for that."

"I understand."

He swallowed. "That evening after Camilla died, I went back to Santos-Dumont's hangar. There wasn't anyone around. I looked around, and I found something."

My eyes went wide. "What?"

"A lipstick."

I had found the lipstick too after we discovered that the airship had been damaged. I had left the lipstick at the scene with the hope that the police would find it. I had forgotten about it when I found Camilla's body in the alley between the hangars. It seemed that the police had not found it, and Godwin had.

"The only person who would have a lipstick would be a woman, and the only woman around the concourse was Camilla, so I took it."

"You took it? Why?"

"Because if someone found it, she would be blamed. I couldn't let that happen. Maybe she was in the hangar and maybe she did drop it, but she would not tamper with the airship. I know this. She was friends with Alberto Santos-Dumont. She had shown me the letters he had written her."

The look on my face must have given him the wrong impression as to what I was thinking about the letters, because he waved his hands. "It was nothing inappropriate. All that they wrote about was engines and flight."

I nodded. I already knew this, of course, from my conversation with Alberto earlier. However, it didn't appear that Godwin knew that Camilla and Alberto had had a falling-out.

"Are you sure that it was hers? Did Camilla wear lipstick?" I asked.

"I never knew her to, but I would only see her at work with the other guys. I don't believe that she would wear lipstick then. She wouldn't want any other reason to be singled out."

I understood that, but also wearing lipstick wouldn't have made her stand out any more than she did already. She was a woman working in a man's world.

He removed the silver tube from his pocket and held it out to me. "I want you to have it. I have been carrying it around in my pocket for days. It's weighing me down." He looked over his shoulder at his family.

His wife and two daughters were laughing at the antics of one of the flamingos that was stretching out one of its long, knobby legs.

"Camilla was my friend, but I can't be involved in this. I have a wife and children to protect."

I nodded and accepted the tube of lipstick. I tucked it into my wrist satchel.

"You will know what to do with it, because I surely have no idea."

"Daddy, come look!" Annabelle cried from her spot in front of the flamingos.

"I'm coming, sweetie," he said back. He then turned to me. "You will know what to do with it, won't you?"

I nodded. "I will." And I did.

I waited for Godwin and his family to leave the flight cage before I continued to make my way down the path. Just like little Annabelle had, I stopped in front of the flamingos. They were striking creatures.

"I was covering a story in Florida once many years ago and saw them in the wild. It was a thrill to see hundreds of them in flight. They were like a pink cloud in the sky," someone said behind me.

I turned around to see Harry Haskell on the path behind me. "Harry, what are you doing here?"

"I'm here on assignment. The *Star* has asked me to write features on the most interesting structures at the fair, and the articles will be released throughout the rest of the year. As Kansas City is not too terribly far from here, we are trying to convince as many people as possible to come to the fair. It will be a very long time, and likely will never happen again, that an event of this caliber will come to this part of the country."

I nodded. "There is plenty to see here, both good and bad."

He frowned as if he didn't know how to react to my comment. Before he could find the words, I said, "I see a bench over there." I pointed to an empty bench. "I need to talk to you."

He removed his hat and smoothed his hair. "You sound serious."

"I am very serious." I marched over to the bench and didn't wait for Harry to follow me.

I sat on the corner of the bench as far away from Harry as I possibly could without falling off altogether. Overhead a pair of bright red cardinals looked down at us. Cardinals were birds that I saw every day in Dayton, but even so, they were striking creatures with their prominent crowns and bright red plumage. I could imagine visitors from other parts of the world being enamored with them, and finding them exotic, even. It just went to show what was exotic was in the eyes of the beholder.

"Is something wrong?" Harry asked.

"Very wrong. Why didn't you tell me that Charles Morrison had been released from jail?"

His face fell as it he expected me to say something else. "Charles Morrison? That's what you wanted to ask me about?"

"Yes. I saw him yesterday at the concourse and learned he was released. I was told that you were at the station when the police let him go, so it's been a full day since you knew. We made a deal that we would share information on the case, in particular that you would share whatever you learned from the police with me."

"You and Margaret went to the concourse alone?"

"No, Margaret was back at the flat because she wasn't feeling well. I was at the concourse alone."

He slapped his forehead. "That's even worse. Katharine, do you even remember that a young woman was killed in that very place? It's not safe for you and Margaret to be there, and it's especially not safe for you to go there alone."

"Don't try to distract me from the matter at hand. You didn't answer my question."

A mallard flew over our heads and squawked. I took it to mean that the birds in the flight cage were on my side. I would expect nothing less from my winged friends.

"What question was that?"

"Did you know that Charles was released?"

He was quiet for a moment, and then he said, "I knew."

"And you didn't tell me. I am not happy about this, Harry,

not in the least. We had a deal, and you broke it. Why should I share information with you so you can write about what *I* learned in your paper like you were the one who discovered it all by yourself?"

"I didn't tell you because I was afraid that you would go off looking for him. I knew you would want to ask him about Camilla Ortiz. I thought that was a bad idea, so I didn't tell you." He said this all like it made perfect sense.

"I was going to find out one way or another. You not telling me makes me question if I can trust you." I took a breath. "Furthermore, I did not ask for your protection. I am more than capable of protecting myself. I am a logical person. I know how far I can take things."

"You might be a logical person, but there are times you don't think before you act."

"Perhaps that was the way I behaved when I was in college, but you don't even know the person I am now, all these years later."

"You're right. You're right. I made a mistake."

"A big one."

Harry continued to shake his head. "You need to stay away from Charles. The man is off his rocker. He might not have killed Camilla, but there is no telling what he will do."

"Oh, I have already talked to him. Don't worry about that." I stood up. "I would hope going forward that you will keep up your part of the bargain and make no more excuses for not keeping me informed." I brushed pollen that had fallen from a nearby tree from the sleeves of the dress I had borrowed from Margaret. I hoped that it would not stain the fabric. It was going to take my full academic year's salary to replace all her clothes that I had ruined at the fair. "Now, I must continue on my way. Margaret is waiting outside of the flight cage for me, and I don't want her to be there very long."

Harry jumped out of his seat. "I am sorry."

"I'd rather not have apologies. I would much rather have information. If you are so concerned about my safety, the very best way to keep me safe would be by keeping me informed." I marched away with my head held high.

CHAPTER 28

Margaret looked like a picture as she sat under a shade tree on a bench, with the giant Ferris wheel behind her. The wheel moved at a snail's pace from my perspective on the ground, but I knew it would feel much different from inside the Ferris wheel, where we would be the next evening for the dinner party.

My dear friend waved and smiled when she saw me. Her smile made her bright eyes sparkle even more than usual. I was happy to see her looking so well. It had been a good thing for her to skip the flight cage and rest, not only for her health but it also gave me a chance to speak my mind to Harry Haskell. I was still steamed over the idea that he hadn't told me about Charles Morrison's release.

"You were in the flight cage longer than I expected you to be. Was it worth the visit?"

"More than worth it," I said. "There were so many beautiful birds."

She nodded. "Perhaps when I am feeling more fit, I will be able to see it. Today was not the day, but I am happy to tell you I ran into Mr. Beard while I was waiting for you. He reminded me that he had promised to give us a tour of the

Palace of Transportation. He's available now and waiting for us there, if that is all right with you."

I raised my brow.

Margaret pressed her hands into her lap. "I know that you might have had other plans on what to do next, but Mr. Beard is a very important potential client for my husband's bank. I didn't want to be rude and refuse him."

"I understand, Margaret. I think the Palace of Transportation is the perfect place to go." I picked up her parasol from the bench and gave her my hand to help her up.

She smiled and linked her arm through mine. I unfurled the parasol over our heads, taking care to make sure that most of the shade was over my delicate friend.

"You are always so understanding, Kate," Margaret said.

I didn't believe that Harry Haskell would agree with her assessment, and that was just fine. I didn't much care what his opinion would be at the moment.

We could see the many flags flapping in the light wind over the Palace of Transportation from where we stood. It was a short walk from the flight cage, just north of the Pike. I was quite grateful that it wasn't in the Pike. I had no wish to go back there.

Although all the grand palaces of innovation at the exposition were white, the architects and builders took care to make each palace stand out from the others. In the case of the Palace of Transportation, it had a domed roof and huge arched entryways that rose all the way to the roof's edge. In each of the corners of the roof a column rose high into the sky, reminiscent of a lighthouse. Perhaps that was a nod to the watercraft inside of the building.

We found Beard near the main entrance to the building.

"I'm grateful you were able to make the time to meet with me," Beard said.

"We have been looking forward to the tour," Margaret replied, and I agreed.

Like all the structures at the fair, there was a line to enter, but Beard simply nodded at the man at the door and we were allowed inside. I felt a little guilty over the dozens of people still waiting in line, as I knew they must have been waiting for a long while.

However, my thoughts didn't stay on the other fairgoers for long as I gasped at what I saw in front of us. There were at least five locomotives inside the massive building. They were all on enormous platforms that kept them up and off the wood plank floor. It was beyond me how these giant machines were put inside of the building, much less hoisted onto the platforms.

Overhead were the exposed wood beams that held the roof up. While the outside might appear that the building was here to stay, the exposed beams and unfinished walls inside told the real story: It would all be turned into tinder in the coming year.

"It is impressive, is it not?" Beard asked. "What I can tell you is what all those locomotives have in common. Steel, just like we refine in Cleveland, Ohio. Nothing in this building could even exist without the advent of steel."

I nodded. "Are those the machines that you funded?"

He laughed. "I wish that was the case. Had I worked in the railroad industry, I would have retired by now. It seems that everyone who came to the fair traveled by rail, but I do believe that automobiles will be the wave of the future. It will be how we travel across the country in a very short time."

Margaret frowned. "Wouldn't that depend on the distance? My husband's bank gave him a car to use here in St. Louis for his work, but it was brought here by train. It would have taken days and days to drive from Chicago to St. Louis by auto."

"That might be the case now," Beard said. "But it won't always be like that. The American public, for all their optimism and ingenuity, are reluctant to embrace anything new until it has been proven to be successful. Haven't your brothers found that to be the case when it comes to flight, Miss Wright?"

"They have had some pushback from the press and the public, but I know it will be only a matter of time before everyone sees and recognizes their accomplishments."

"Very good," he said.

Margaret looked around the palace. "There are more autos in here than on all the streets of St. Louis. I'm still not sure I believe your prediction, Mr. Beard."

Beard laughed. "I don't know if that is true, and maybe it just seems that way because they are all packed in so closely together."

As we walked down an aisle of motorcars of all shapes and sizes, I asked, "What are the innovations that you had a hand in, in this building, Mr. Beard?"

He smiled ear to ear as if he was pleased with the question. I wasn't surprised if he was. It had been my experience that men driven by achievements, like Beard, also liked to brag about what they have done. This was in stark contrast with my brothers Wilbur and Orville, who were proud and humble at the same time about their successes. It was difficult for me to imagine the man in the expensive suit in front of me being humble about anything at all.

He stopped in front of one of the racing motorcars with its long chassis. The doors were polished wood and the hood was a metallic blue. "I am quite pleased with this beauty, and proud to say I had a hand in her. She will be entered into the 1904 Vanderbilt Cup Race in October, and I have every expectation that she will win. In a test, she got up to eighty-nine miles per hour and we have not yet pushed her to her limit."

Margaret leaned forward and read the sign in front of the car. "It says here on the placard that the maker is a man by the name of Holden Green."

Beard clenched his jaw for just a moment and then the placid expression that always seemed to be there was safely back in place. "Yes, I gave Holden the money to build the race car." He cleared his throat. "Financiers don't get any of the credit, I'm afraid."

"Is that why you are hoping to create an invention of your own?" I asked. "Because you would like the credit?"

"I don't think that I speak out of turn to say that having money doesn't make a man memorable, but creating something with his own hands does. I have always loved to tinker. I just don't have as much time for it in my current life. It was bound to happen as the head of a large company."

Joshua Beard led us up and down the aisles of the palace. Here and there, he pointed at boat engines, other motorcars, and motorcycles that he had financed. We were standing in front of a motorcycle when Margaret said, "Mr. Beard, this has all been very interesting, but I'm afraid that I'm a bit winded from the long day. As my husband's dinner party is tomorrow, I believe that it is best if I go back to our flat and rest."

"Oh my, yes, please do. I'm so sorry if I kept you for too long as I prattled on about the machines," he said. "Let me walk you ladies out."

I took Margaret by the arm. She was looking paler than usual. We followed Beard to the main entrance.

When we were out in the sunshine again, Margaret unfurled her parasol to shield her eyes. "I am sorry to cut the tour short."

"There is no need to apologize," Beard said. "Your health is of paramount importance, and we will have more time to talk at your husband's dinner party."

"Thank you for understanding," Margaret said.

"It was so nice to meet with you both," Beard added. "You have been most charming. I am looking forward to the dinner party and learning more about what your husband's bank has to offer my company. I do not take my money lightly. As you can see from the tour today, I only invest in the very best."

"There is no better man you can trust than my husband," Margaret said. "I can assure you that your company's accounts will be very safe with him."

He nodded. "Then, I will see you at the party." He turned and went back inside the Palace of Transportation.

And I had to wonder what invention he was so desperate to be remembered for.

CHAPTER 29

I realized the Louisiana Purchase Exposition was a true display of America, and maybe even of the world as a whole. It included all the great things that humanity could accomplish with its commitment and ingenuity, but at the same time, it showed the worst of humanity too, by building a hierarchy among cultures in the westerners' eyes, from primitive to superior.

I could not help but wonder what my bishop father would have thought about all this. He would have material for sermons about the fallen world for a whole year.

The fact that I was no closer to finding out who killed Camilla Ortiz also left a sour taste in my mouth.

I wasn't sure that I believed Harry when he said he had not told me that Charles was released because he didn't want me to talk to Charles. He was running all over the fair writing pieces for the *Kansas City Star* as fast as his could. Some of his stories were being picked up by other papers too. People back home who didn't have the time or means to travel to the world's fair were clamoring to hear all about it. It was very possible that, in the pursuit of his career, he forgot our pact. If that was the case, I was not beholden to it either.

I was staying with the Meachams. It would have been easy

enough for him to send a simple note to the flat so that I wasn't blindsided by Zeb Dandy.

I did not have the line into the police investigation that I thought I did. I was more alone in finding the truth than ever.

After leaving the Palace of Transportation, Margaret and I returned to the flat so Margaret could rest, and when she was up to it, make some final preparations for the dinner party the next day.

We walked into the flat. All the electric lights were off, but there was plenty of light coming in from the windows. Meacham sat at the small table where Margaret and I had tea just days ago. He stared out the window. He held a stout glass of amber-colored liquid in his hand. And there was a whiskey bottle on the table. I raised my brow. In all the time that I had known Meacham, I had never known him to drink alcohol.

Margaret took a sharp intake of breath. She was as surprised as I was at the disheveled appearance of her husband.

"I have some letters to write," I said. "I'll excuse myself to my room."

Meacham looked up. "No, Kate, you can stay. You are our friend. I trust you will keep this all in confidence."

Panic gripped my heart. What was Meacham about to tell us that we would have to keep in confidence?

I glanced at Margaret, and she appeared as concerned and confused as I was.

Margaret walked over to her husband and pulled the other chair at the table close to him and sat. "My dear, what is wrong?"

I stood by the door and was ready to bolt down the hallway and hide in the guest room for the duration of the night, but at the same time, I was naturally curious. I wanted to hear what he had to say. In the end curiosity won, as it always did with me.

He shook his head. "I'm sorry that you had to find me like this. I promise you that I have had only one drink. I simply needed something to settle my nerves. I thought you would be at the fair for a few hours more, and I would have time to collect myself before you returned. I hate for you to see me this way."

"Don't worry about us," Margaret said. "I am worried about you. What has happened?"

He set the glass on the table and pushed it away from him. "I lost a large account today."

"How? What account was that?"

He swallowed. "Alberto Santos-Dumont."

"Alberto was going to open an account with your bank?" I could not help but blurt out. I shuffled over to the club chair by the fireplace. I needed to sit down for this.

"He was considering it. Through letters and phone calls I had him all but convinced. He has great wealth from his family's coffee-farm fortune in Brazil. He thought that he needed to have more of a financial footing in the United States since he was confident that he would win the aeronautics competition here at the fair. He said that he planned to be more involved in North America because of it. That isn't happening now."

"Because his airship was tampered with," I said.

Meacham nodded. "I hoped against hope that he would have the airship mended here and he would fly, but he plans to return to France now. He plans to take all plans to start a financial footing in this country with him."

"You will find another account," Margaret said.

He shook his head. "Not one as large as Santos-Dumont's, and I made the mistake of mentioning it to the bank president. That is the very worst part. He is expecting me to deliver the Santos-Dumont account to him on a silver platter. Instead, I will return to Chicago empty-handed."

"There is still a chance though, isn't there?" Margaret asked. "We invited Mr. Santos-Dumont to the dinner party. When he is there and sees everything the bank has to offer, he may change his mind."

Meacham shook his head. "He told me he's not coming. I believe he's leaving in the morning. If I don't go back to Chicago with at least one big account, I could very well lose my job." Tears gathered in the corners of his eyes.

"Then, we will just have to find another account that is just as profitable for the bank." Margaret had a determined set to her mouth. I had seen that look many times on her face when we were in college. When Margaret made up her mind, there was no stopping her.

"You act like millionaires grow on trees," he said.

"They might not grow on trees, but there are a few around the fair still. We just had a tour of the Palace of Transportation with Mr. Joshua Beard," I said. "He is an affable man and seemed to be quite interested in what your bank had to offer. You should have seen all the machines in which he has invested. The man has money and is willing to take risks."

Meacham looked up at me as if he was just remembering that I was still in the room.

"I have met with Beard several times in the last three weeks, and he has not given me a strong indication that he would like to move his company accounts."

"Maybe he's coming around," I said. "At this point, it can't hurt to ask."

"No, I suppose not."

"And the dinner party will be just the thing to finally convince him to make the decision," Margaret said. "We will make it the very best party the fair has seen." She looked at me. "Won't we, Kate?"

I nodded. "We will. All of your prospective clients will be so impressed with the party, they will clamor to move their accounts to your bank."

He held the edge of the table. "I am sorry to be such a

mess, dear. After the last few days, I have been wound so tight. This should not be your concern, especially when you have been feeling so ill."

Margaret knelt by her husband's chair and wrapped her two small hands around his much larger right hand, which gripped the arm of the chair. "Your concerns are my concerns, and mine are yours. I am your helper as you are mine."

He looked down at his wife with so much love and tenderness that I had to look away. It was one of the few times in my life that I wished someone would look at me like that.

I slipped out of the room.

CHAPTER 30

If Margaret wasn't worried about the dinner party atop the Ferris wheel, she certainly was now that she knew that her husband's very career might be riding on its success. The next morning, we rose early and prepared for the dinner party by writing lists and sending notes to the caterer and party planner that were helping with the event.

By the early afternoon, we stood at the foot of the Ferris wheel. I had never seen a Ferris Wheel so large!

Margaret told me this one was one of the largest ever constructed, 264 feet high, and it had been transported to St. Louis from Chicago in 175 individual freight cars. Back home, at the carnival fairs, our Ferris wheels had carriages that held two or maybe three people. Each of these wooden carriages could hold up to sixty!

We waited for our capsule to descend so that we could start loading it with tables, chairs, and linens for the dinner party. We weren't doing this alone. Meacham's bank had hired a small army of staff to make sure that everything came together perfectly. He insisted that the staff could handle everything and Margaret didn't even need to go to the Ferris wheel until right before the party, but my friend heard none of that.

"If this party is not as grand as promised, it will be on me," she had told me that morning as we put together the floral arrangements for the tables. "Not on my husband and certainly not on the bank. I have to do all I can to help Meacham clinch these accounts."

I raised my brow at her.

"It is not because I fear that he will be fired from his position. If that was to occur, then we would address it as a couple. It is because he would be disappointed in himself. There is nothing worse for the male ego than believing that he failed in some way, be it failing his family, his wife, or his employer. Any of these failures can be debilitating. I don't want that to happen to my husband."

It did not make me want to be a wife if one had to be in constant support of her husband's ego. Heaven knew, I would fall short on a daily basis.

"This is yours, miss," the Ferris wheel attendant said to Margaret as the next carriage came to a stop at the platform. He held open the door for us.

Margaret clapped her hands. "Get everything inside," she said to the staffers.

"You will want to hurry. I can't hold the Ferris wheel in place for long. We still have paying customers who are here to ride," the attendant said.

Margaret nodded.

As the attendant held the brake on the wheel, Meacham's staff made a line to hand off all the supplies and load them in the carriage.

We just about had them all inside when the attendant said, "Ma'am, I have to let the wheel go."

The last thing to grab was the flowers. I scooped them up and was the last one to hop into the car as it started to ascend.

Margaret placed a hand to her forehead as we slowly made our way up into the air. "The next time my husband says that he wants to host a dinner party on a Ferris wheel, tell me not to agree. As if we didn't already have pressure enough riding on this party, this extra wrinkle of a moving carriage in the sky is most unwelcome."

I set the flowers on a table and began to unpack the table service with one of the servers.

The car lurched as we came to a stop at the very top. Even with all the flurry of activity around me, I was drawn to one of the many windows. From where I stood, I could see all of the fair, from the U.S Government building to the Pike to the aeronautic concourse. They looked like miniatures of a town, like I had seen in the store windows of downtown Dayton at Christmas. But in this case, they were real.

I wasn't afraid of heights, but I felt a little bit woozy looking down. The car lurched forward again, and we began our descent.

The five staff members who were in the car with Margaret and me, made short work of setting everything up. The serving table was in place, and the two long dining tables were in the process of being set for a total of forty guests.

I stopped gawking and hurried back to help Margaret, but she waved me off.

On the serving table, she set up six vases and fussed over the arrangements of summer flowers in each one. Every flower was carefully selected and set in the perfect spot.

There wasn't much for me to do, so I looked out the window again. I could not help it. I was so fascinated with the view. Was this what the world looked like to my brothers when they flew? In reality, I was higher up than they had ever soared.

It was a little disconcerting that pieces of steel and intricately fit-together gears were all that was keeping us from plummeting to our deaths. I kept those thoughts to myself. Margaret had enough concerns.

As we inched closer to the ground, I could see the Temple

of Mirth in the Pike. The giant clown head with its open mouth, like it had intentions to swallow the whole world, was even more grotesque from this angle.

I leaned closer to the window. I could be wrong, but I thought I saw Achilles the macaw perched on the clown's nose.

Below the clown and Achilles, I expected to easily spot Zeb Dandy in his ringleader suit, but instead I saw Sylvia at the door to the Temple of Mirth.

She was as small as the other ant-sized people. As the Ferris wheel made its very slow descent, my body was thrumming with adrenaline. She said that she only sold tickets when Zeb was busy with something else. I had no desire to run into him again. This might be my only chance to speak to Sylvia again, and my only chance to speak to her with Zeb not around.

When our car finally reached the ground, I threw open the latch and opened the door. I jumped out.

"Katharine!" Margaret called. "Where are you going? I haven't finished arranging the flowers yet."

"You stay here. I'll be right back," I said, and waved to her as the attendant slammed the car door closed and the Ferris wheel was in motion again.

I skipped down the steps of the loading platform, bumping into people as I went. "Pardon me. Pardon me. Excuse me. Please let me through. Thank you."

When I broke free of the crowd, I walked as fast as I dared toward the Pike. I was a good distance away from it, and Sylvia could have melted into the busy street at any moment.

"Miss, you look like you have a strong arm. Play darts. Five darts for a nickel and you could win a rose. What girl doesn't love a rose?" a vendor shouted at me.

I ignored him and hurried by.

"Kebob? Free kebob!" A young gentleman tried to shove a piece of meat on a stick at me.

I pushed it away. "I'm sorry. I'm not hungry."

He went on to the next person with his offering.

Finally, I was within a few yards of the Temple of Mirth.

Sylvia stood outside the fun house and shouted, "Come have the time of your life at the Temple of Mirth. You will laugh and scream with joy. You have never been in any place like it."

She held flyers out and people rushed past her. When she turned to face me, she had a flyer at the ready and froze when she saw who it was. She dropped the flyers on the ground and took off at a run.

"Sylvia!" I called.

She didn't stop running.

A marching band made its way down the main thoroughfare, and I lost sight of her.

I scooped up the flyers and stacked them the best I could. The Temple of Mirth was running a special that night. Buy one ticket, get one free. What I didn't understand was why it was Sylvia standing in the middle of the Pike trying to sell tickets and not Zeb Dandy. Where was he?

I did not want Sylvia to be in trouble for dropping the flyers, so I placed them as neatly as can be by the door leading into the fun house. There was a whooshing sound behind me, and I turned around to see Achilles hopping toward me.

From my perspective, other than Margaret, the parrot was the only one happy to see me at the fair.

I clapped my hands. The bird took flight and landed on my shoulder. I thought about my brothers and their study of birds. They noted how the birds would bend and tilt their wings to stay aloft, and Wilbur and Orville were able to replicate that with the invention of wing warping on their flyers. It was their cardinal secret, the one that they were impatiently waiting for the U.S. Patent Office to protect.

Suddenly, Achilles squawked and took off from my shoulder. He went back to the top of the clown's head and disappeared behind the clown's giant ear.

A moment later, Zeb Dandy came stomping down the Pike. Now I knew very well why the bird flew away. I merged into the marching band and slipped away before he could see me. All I know was he didn't look happy. I didn't know if that was because Achilles was hiding from him or for another reason.

I knew that I should return to the Ferris wheel and help Margaret with the preparations, but I wanted to at least look for Sylvia one last time. Even if it was a matter of walking down the Pike. Besides, I couldn't go by the Temple of Mirth again without risking being seen by Zeb. That was not a risk I was willing to take.

I walked to the end of the crowded Pike and turned onto Administration Avenue back in the direction of the Ferris wheel. I gave up all hope of finding Sylvia at this point, and I doubled my pace to hurry back and help my friend.

Sometimes it was like that: When you give up on something, that's when it happens.

There was a slight young woman with black hair standing in front of the Palace of Transportation. She looked up at it with an expression of determination.

I took care not to startle her or to let her know that I was near.

She was so focused on the building, with so much concentration, that she didn't see me until I spoke. "It is an impressive structure, isn't it?"

She jumped and made a move to run away from me again.

I held out my hand, but I didn't touch her. "Please, don't run away. I want to help you."

"Help me with what?"

"Help you find out what happened to Camilla," I said. "Don't you want to know what happened to her?"

An expression that I could only describe as tortured fell over her face.

I reached into my wrist satchel and removed the tube of lipstick that Godwin had given me. "Do you wear lipstick?"

She blinked and stared at the tube. "No, never. I have no reason to."

"Did Sylvia?" I asked.

"Sometimes. She enjoyed more girlish things than I did." Her face fell as she realized her mistake.

"Is this Sylvia's lipstick, Camilla?" I asked.

Her face paled. "How did you know?"

CHAPTER 31

How did I know? It was a fair question. It was a feeling that Sylvia had been the twin who had been killed, not Camilla, since I met "Sylvia" in Camilla's dormitory room.

I had pushed the idea down because it seemed to be such an awful thing to believe that Camilla would take her sister's identity after Sylvia was killed. However, when Godwin handed me the lipstick, it all fit together in my mind. Camilla never struck me as a girl who would wear makeup, but that didn't mean her twin was the same. And if it was Sylvia's lipstick and not Camilla's, it would place her in the hangar, not her sister.

"We should go somewhere to talk," I said. "Somewhere we can't be overheard."

She nodded. "I know a good place."

I followed Camilla as she led me on a short walk to the edge of the Grand Basin, the man-made body of water in the middle of the fair. From there the Ferris wheel was just a few yards away. I knew if Margaret took time from preparing for the party to look out the window, she would have seen me. I was going to have to make up my absence to my friend. However, I knew when I explained to Margaret why I had to jump out of the Ferris wheel carriage, she would understand.

Camilla sat on an empty park bench that overlooked the basin. In the water were Venice-style gondolas that took visitors for rides up and down the channel while singing to them in Italian. Most of the riders were young couples who were spending much more time looking at each other than at the scenery.

We stared out at the basin for a few minutes more, and when I could no longer take the silence, I asked, "Why are you still here?"

She blinked at me. "What do you mean?"

"Why didn't you go back to California like you said you were going to do the last time I saw you?"

She folded her hands in her lap, and it was then that I noticed that her hands were calloused and her fingernails chipped. What nails were there were embedded with machine grease. They were not the working hands of a cleaning lady but the working hands of a mechanic. I should have notice that from the start. Wilbur and Orville's hands were often in the same condition.

"I couldn't go home. I'm never going back there. Sylvia and I agreed we would never set foot in our uncle's home again." She clenched her fists on her lap. "I have to decide what I am going to do next. I still have this buried hope that I can find the help I need to make my own flying machine while I'm here. Maybe I am crazy for even thinking it, and there is the problem that everyone believes that I'm dead. I feel like I owe it to Sylvia to complete my dream. It is the reason she is dead. I don't want her death to have been in vain."

"Tell me why Sylvia was in your place at the concourse?"

She looked down at her hands like she was searching for her words. She picked at her broken nails.

"Because I asked her to be there. She was there for me. It

was my fault. I should have never asked her to do it, but I was afraid to lose my job. I needed to be somewhere else and had to be at work at the same time. It just made sense to me to ask Sylvia to play me while I was away."

"If you have something more pressing than going to work, why didn't you tell your employer?"

"You don't understand. Mr. Myers, who runs the concourse, does so with an iron fist. He made a rule that you couldn't miss a shift while working at the aviation concourse. If you did, you would be replaced immediately. Hundreds of men come to the fair every day from all over the country looking for work. Everyone is expendable and replaceable at the fair. That is something you learn the moment you start working here."

I wrinkled my brow. "I thought Myers was replaced by the committee."

She shook her head. "In name only. The new head of the concourse is little more than a figurehead. He shows up for the ribbon cuttings and the unveiling of flying machines, but he doesn't manage the concourse. He happily leaves that to Mr. Myers, who is a cruel man. Everyone working at the concourse hates him. He says the most inappropriate things. Honestly, he makes my skin crawl, and I do everything in my power to stay out of his sight."

This was interesting news. I did not have a good impression of Myers myself, but I thought that was just because he made rude comments about my brothers and I found him to be pompous.

"I didn't want to lose my job," Camilla went on. "It wasn't just because of the money. It wasn't because of the money at all. The fair barely pays us a living wage. If they didn't provide housing, I don't think anyone would have worked here at all."

"Was Sylvia in the risk of losing her job at the House of Mirth by taking your place?"

She shook her head. "Zeb Dandy didn't ask her to keep regular hours. As long as the fun house was clean, he didn't care when she cleaned it. She also cleaned for other amusements around the fair but usually at night."

I nodded. "If you weren't working here for the money, then what kept you here?"

"The aeronautics competition."

A shiver ran down my back as she said the exact phrase that her sister did when she was dying. Camilla sounded exactly the same too.

"I have always been interested in flight, and for the last year I have been working on a prototype of my own to fly. The problem that I have run into again and again is weight. I have a theory that if I could make the pieces of my flyer lighter, I could and would fly. This is the only place in the world having a gathering of so many manufacturers and aviators together all at once. In my mind, it was my only chance to pick the minds of these brilliant men and solve my problem."

"Have you reached out to them before?"

She pressed her lips together. "I have written letters but got no response from anyone. I thought it was because I was signing the letters with my full name. Camilla is a woman's name, of course. To test my theory, I started signing them with my initials. C. O. Ortiz. I did receive a few responses then, but they were just blanket statements. *Thank you for your interest* and that sort of nonsense. Maybe it was foolish of me, but I really felt that this was my last chance. My belief was that if I showed up here to the fair and talked to them in person, they couldn't brush me off." She hung her head. "I have since learned that they can and will ignore me, even if I am standing in their path."

"Who did you speak with?"

"So many people. Langley from the Smithsonian, Beard

from the steel company, and more. Not one of them wanted to talk to me."

"Not Alberto Santos-Dumont?" I asked.

"I—I didn't get a chance before the incident. He had just arrived that day. I was there when he was checking the crates to make sure that everything was in place for his airship. It was late and I didn't speak to him then because I could tell he was tired. I thought it would be best to approach him after the airship was assembled. I wanted to be patient. Now, I wish I hadn't been."

"Charles Morrison said that you—or at least, who he thought was you but was actually Sylvia—was the one who stabbed the balloon," I said.

"That's ridiculous. Sylvia would never do that. She had no reason to. She knew that I wanted to see Alberto fly just as much as anyone else coming to the fair did, maybe more. I could learn about human flight by reading all the books and newspapers I could find at the library, but that wasn't the same as witnessing it in person. All I had seen in California were gliders held aloft by the ocean wind. I wanted to see the airship fly."

"Charles saw her run away from Alberto's hangar with a knife in her hand."

"That doesn't make any sense at all. Sylvia would have no reason to have a knife."

I held up my hand. "Let's just say for a second that it is true."

Her face flushed red. "My sister was the mildest person you could ever meet. We were twins and looked just the same, but that is where our similarities stopped. Our temperaments were completely different from each other."

"I'm not saying that she punctured the balloon. What if she saw whoever did it . . ."

"And that person killed her," she finished for me.

I nodded. "That is what I think."

"Do you know who that person is?"

I shook my head. "Not yet. You were around the concourse the most. Who would have been there at first light?"

She stared out at the Great Basin.

It was a bit strange to hear snippets of Italian opera being sung as the gondolas floated by our park bench. There were times that the mix of cultures at the world's fair was overwhelming. Every direction a person looked there was something different. There was so much to take in.

"The mechanics and guides like me would all be there, and Alberto's private staff would be there by then too. It has to be one of the competitors," she said. "Everyone knew that Alberto was the favorite to win the money. For the others in the contest, the only chance that they had of beating him was to damage his airship."

"Is there one in particular that you think would be capable of doing that?" I asked.

"They are all capable of it. The race to fly is one of the most hotly contested pursuits on earth. Countries are up against each other to accomplish it first. You know this from your brothers. Have they not been questioned about their success?"

"Many times," I said.

"That is because others want to claim to be first. Mark my words, people will fight over who really qualified as the first in flight for generations to come."

I clenched my jaw. It angered me that anyone would question what Wilbur and Orville accomplished. My brothers had changed the world, they were *still* in the process of changing the world, and they deserved to be recognized for it. I also knew that was the most important aspect for them. They didn't care about money or awards. They just wanted to be recognized as the first in flight. It seemed that was to be a battle we would have to continue to fight. I prayed when the patent was finally approved that it would put all the doubt to rest.

"It should have been me there that morning. Sylvia was killed because of me. If I'd never asked her to take my place, she would still be alive." Camilla buried her face in her hands.

"Where were you? Why couldn't you work that morning?"

She hung her head. "I went to one of the aviation lectures. I got there very early with the hope of sharing my ideas with these powerful men. I could not miss the chance, but at the same time I could not afford to miss my shift at the concourse. As I told you, Mr. Myers would sack whoever did not show up to work. No questions asked. I—I asked my sister to take my place. We are twins. It was nothing new for us to switch places when it was a help to one or another. In school, I excelled in mathematics and science, and Sylvia was better at literature and history. Many times, we would switch places on test days. I would take her math and science tests, and she would take my literature and history tests." Tears came into her eyes. "How I wish that I didn't switch places with her one last time. I would give anything to have her back. Anything."

My heart ached for her, and I had the urge to hold her hand, but held myself back, as it felt like too familiar a gesture to someone I didn't know. Up until an hour ago, I thought she was Sylvia Ortiz, not Camilla Ortiz. My head had difficulty grappling with that.

I cleared my throat. "But you were there so early for the lecture. It must have been hours later."

She nodded and wiped a single tear away from her cheek. "Yes, I know, but I planned to camp out near the palace until

I could speak to him. I thought maybe I could catch him going inside before his lecture and ask my questions."

"Whose lecture?" I asked.

"The one given by Beard on innovations in steel. His company was looking for ways to make it just as strong but lighter. It was exactly what I needed for my flying machine. I wanted to ask him if he would be willing to donate some of the new steel to me for my flyer. When I was successful in flight I would credit his company for their innovation in the metal."

"And did you speak to him?" I asked.

"I did. He only gave me a few minutes. He seemed interested and I had hope that I was finally going to find the help that I needed, but when I stopped speaking, he patted me on the head and called me a 'doll.'" Her face flushed bright red as she said this. "I have never been so humiliated in my life. He wasn't even taking what I said into consideration because I'm a young woman."

I wished I could tell her that Beard was the exception to these kinds of antics, but I could not. The number of times that the male teachers spoke down to me at Steele High School were countless. It would not get easier for Camilla, especially if she was determined to go into a male-dominated field like aviation, but I hoped she wouldn't give up on it, nonetheless. My opinion was that women should be in all fields of study.

We were silent for a long moment. "If you are taking Sylvia's place at the Temple of Mirth, does Zeb Dandy know that you are not your sister?"

She snorted. "He's too preoccupied with making money and with himself to take notice of me. As long as the fun house is clean, that is all he cares about. I visited my sister there many times, and know my way around it just as well as she did."

I frowned.

"And Hal?" I asked.

She spun on the bench to face me. "Why do you keep bringing him up to me?"

"Because he came into your dormitory looking for you, and he was stricken when I told him that you died."

Her face fell. "He does not have to know that it was my sister who passed, and I am still alive. I have no interest in speaking to him."

"Why?"

She turned back in her seat to face the Grand Basin again. A gondola floated by and the boat driver sang at the top of her voice. What he lacked in talent, he surely made up for in volume.

"Because I thought he was my friend, but I was wrong."

"How did you find that out?" I asked.

She sighed. "I showed him my notebook with my ideas. He showed interest in aviation, and I really didn't have anything else to talk about with him on a regular basis. Sylvia tried to listen to me prattle on about it, but I knew the conversation on the topic bored her, as her eyes would glaze over when I spoke. Hal showed genuine interest. I thought maybe we could even be a team and work on it together." She blushed.

Her blush made me wonder if there were also romantic feelings involved.

"But that wasn't to be," she added.

"Why not?" I asked.

She took a deep breath. "Because he knew where I kept my things on the concourse when I was working. At lunchtime I went to retrieve my bag to eat, and I found him there copying my plans from my notebook into a notebook of his own. I have never been so angry in my life. I ripped both notebooks from his hands and told him that I never wanted to see him again." She licked her lips. "He begged me to give his notebook back and I refused. Instead, I threw it into the street and a hansom cab ran over it, tearing it to shreds. He told me that I'd just cost him a lot of money. That was when I knew he had been stealing my ideas. It wasn't until later I realized he'd torn some of the pages from my notebook. Little did he know they weren't the most pertinent ones."

"The pages you accused me of stealing."

She nodded.

"And you knew where the notebook was hidden in the dormitory too even though you pretended you didn't because you were the one who hid it there."

"I wanted to confuse you."

And she had.

"When I first saw you at the train station, you asked me for help," I said.

She frowned. "I had gone to the station to confront Hal again and ask for my missing pages back. He grew angry with me. He frightened me with his reaction, so I ran from him. I— I didn't think he would hurt me, but I was still afraid. A woman has to follow her intuition when she doesn't feel safe."

I nodded. For a woman, her intuition is her most valuable form of defense.

"But you ran away from me at other times too when Hal was nowhere around."

"I was afraid," she said barely above a whisper. "Afraid of anyone I did not know and many I did."

"Was it fear that caused you not to stop when you saw you sister laying between the hangers that morning?"

"I wanted to. She told me to run, so I did." She hung her head. "I ran because I knew I would be next if I stayed."

I shivered. Camilla must have been truly terrified to leave her sister in such a state.

She wiped tears from her eyes. "So, you can see that I'm not well. In the last several weeks I have lost a man who I thought was my friend, and now my most beloved sister. All I have left is my flying machine, and I'm *not* going to lose that too."

CHAPTER 32

I wanted to stay longer and talk to Camilla more, but I told her I had to get back to the Ferris wheel. Because she told me so much about herself, I felt like it was only right to share an invitation to the Meachams' dinner party that night in the Ferris wheel. "Mr. Beard will be there. Mr. Meacham is hoping that he will become a client of his bank."

I watched Camilla walk away and was unsure how I felt. Was it better that she was alive and her sister was dead? I didn't believe that one life was superior to another, but after all this time believing that Camilla had been the one to be murdered, it was as if she came back to life. I also knew now why she ran away from the dormitory when Hal arrived. If he had been her good friend once upon a time, he would've known those slight differences between the twins that I, not knowing them well at all, would never see.

By the time I returned to the Ferris wheel, all the preparations for the dinner party were complete. Margaret had waited for me so we could return to the flat and dress for the party.

I was glad that we had a few hours before the party, because Margaret looked pale and needed to rest before she played hostess.

"Kate, I assume you had a good reason to run away from the Ferris wheel like that," Margaret said with a raised brow.

I smiled. "I always have a good reason, Margaret, I just don't always have the time to tell you what those reasons are before I leap into action. Shall I tell you on the ride back to the flat?"

"No, I would like to walk home, if you don't mind stopping every so often so I can rest. This humidity and heat are like a wet, hot blanket over our heads."

"Are you sure that you don't want to grab a hansom cab?" I asked.

She shook her head. "After being trapped in that Ferris wheel carriage for so long, I can't stand the idea of being in another moving vehicle so soon. Even as we stand here, I feel like I am still in motion." She pressed a hand to her forehead.

I gave her my arm. "Then lean on me as we walk. We will take it slow, and I will tell you about my latest escapade."

She unfurled her parasol and smiled. "I do love hearing about your escapades. I love hearing of them much more than I like participating in them."

I laughed.

We strolled away from the Ferris wheel along the Grand Basin and then beyond the Sunken Garden, which was a delightfully manicured garden tucked in between the palaces.

As we walked, Margaret stopped and touched a blossom on a hibiscus. "It's such a shame that in a few short months this will all be gone. It makes you wonder about the purpose of building something so temporary."

I raised my brow. I had never known Margaret to be so philosophical, but I had to agree with her. Many times while walking through the fair, I had a melancholy mood because I knew it would all be stripped away at the end. The gardens, the palaces, the displays would all be gone. Not that I believed that everything at the fair should be saved. I would be quite relieved when the Temple of Mirth was no more.

"Now, tell me about your adventure." She resumed walking.

I went on to detail my conversation with Camilla.

"Camilla is alive, and Sylvia is dead? How dreadful."

"I'm still having trouble understanding why she would take on her sister's identity like that," I said.

"Don't you see there has to be only one reason for that?"

I frowned. "What's that?"

"Camilla thinks she is still in danger, and it is very likely that whoever killed Sylvia thought it was Camilla too. It is even what the police believe, is it not? Maybe being Sylvia is the only way Camilla can stay alive."

I wondered why Camilla hadn't told me that.

CHAPTER 33

Several hours later, I let Meacham help me out of the hansom cab just steps from the Ferris wheel. When my feet were firmly on the ground, he reached inside and helped his wife.

I looked down at the lilac chiffon dress that Margaret had loaned me for the evening. It was the finest dress that I had ever worn—so much so that I felt a bit self-conscious in it. It was as if I was a little girl playing dress-up; I didn't look anything like myself.

Margaret stepped out of the cab in a lovely pink dress with gauzy puffed sleeves. She looked like a fairy princess, in my estimation, but I knew if I said that, she would hate the comparison. Meacham, for his part, looked dashing in a gray pin-striped suit. He had a matching gray bowler hat on his head.

I had gone without a hat for the occasion. The one I'd brought was beyond repair, and I didn't want to add one of Margaret's hats to the garment casualty list that I had made at the fair.

The Ferris wheel attendant pulled the carriage to a stop, and we climbed inside. The guests would arrive soon, but we would make at least one full rotation around the Ferris wheel before they got there, giving Margaret time to fret over every last detail.

As the wheel began to move again, Meacham removed his hat and handed it to one of the waiters, who hung it on a coat-tree in the corner of the carriage car. Margaret and her team had thought of everything.

Margaret clasped her hands together. "It's perfect."

And it was. The table settings were fine, the flowers perfectly arranged, and the candles lit. The last time I was at a dinner so fine, I was a student at Oberlin, and the dean had invited all of the seniors to his home to toast our upcoming graduation. Margaret had been there with me and would give me signals as to which spoon I should use for what dish. I had been so nervous that I could barely lift my glass to my mouth.

That was some years ago, and I was a different person now. Years of teaching high school students made me confident in just about any situation. I never knew what the students would throw at me, so I learned to adapt and appear calm and collected no matter what anxiety might be causing me to quiver on the inside. That was what I was trying to do that night at Margaret's dinner.

Poor Meacham, however, looked as if he was about to faint. This dinner party could make or break all of his attempts to bring new wealthy clients to his bank. He could lose his job if he was unsuccessful; that was a terrifying thought when he and Margaret were trying so hard to start a family. He started to take off his dinner jacket. There were clear signs that he was sweating through his white shirt. Thankfully, Margaret, the ever-dutiful wife, was there to intervene and make him put the jacket back on. He might be uncomfortable, but the alternative was much worse.

"Are there any final touches that need to be done?" I asked Margaret.

She shook her head. "We are ready as can be. I can't even

find a flower out of place, and I can assure you I looked." Her hostess smile was on her face.

I was about to say something more to her when I noticed one of the young women standing behind the serving table with her hands behind her back. It was Camilla Ortiz. She wore a server's uniform and stared back at me with a blank face. My heart was in my throat. I knew why she was there. She was not giving up on her plans to speak to Beard.

I grabbed Margaret's hand. "You hired Camilla to work here tonight?"

"What do you mean?" She looked around the carriage and spotted Camilla at the serving table. She paled. "I didn't hire any of the servers. The caterer here at the fair handled that."

Across the carriage, there was a determined set to Camilla's jaw. She was going to get a straight answer from Beard, no matter what.

I had no time to think on it or how to address her because the Ferris wheel came to a stop at the bottom, and the thirty-some guests entered the car.

The ladies oohed and aahed at the decorations, and the men shook hands and patted each other on the back in greeting. Outside of the Ferris wheel, the attendant held on to the brake for all he was worth.

I tried to help him the best I could and ushered people inside. When the last finely dressed guest stepped into the carriage, I gave a nod to the attendant. He released the brake, and up we went.

As the party had begun, there was nothing that I could do about Camilla being in the Ferris wheel carriage, and I was not sure I wanted to do anything at all. I took a deep breath and chatted with the women and then found my name plate at the table and sat.

As luck would have it, I was seated next to Beard.

"Good evening," he said. "It's lovely to see you again. Have you been back to admire the ancient Greek statuary that you seemed to be so fond of the night of the reception?"

I gave him a pleasant smile. "I have not. As you well know, there is so much to see at the fair, it seems a shame to go back to the same place more than once."

He nodded. "But I understand you have been to the aeronautics concourse many times."

I blinked and wondered how he would know that.

Meacham tapped his knife against his water glass to gather the tables. "Thank you all for being here tonight. On behalf of Lake Michigan Bank and Loan, I am grateful that you have accepted our invitation to learn about what the bank has to offer you and enjoy a delightful evening on this Ferris wheel." He smiled at Margaret, who was at the opposite end of the table from him. "And we all have my lovely wife Margaret to thank for arranging this party for us. I personally could not think of a better hostess." He raised his glass. "To Margaret."

All the guests lifted their glasses as well. "To Margaret."

My friend blushed, and I felt a burst of pride for her. It was quite a feat that she was able to pull off this party, especially when she had been feeling so poorly much of the week.

Beard turned and spoke to the lady on his opposite side, so I did not have an opportunity to ask him how he knew about my movements around the fair. But I found it unsettling that he knew anything at all of what I had been up to. I had had a conversation with him only twice. Once at the gala my first night at the fair, and then when he gave Margaret and me a tour of the Palace of Transportation. Neither time did I mention what I had been doing at the fair.

I looked around the room and spotted Harry at the second table. I had not seen him come into the carriage. Perhaps I had been distracted by Camilla and the overwhelmed Ferris wheel attendant. In any case, I was relieved that he was at the second table. I was still upset over the fact that he kept Charles Morrison's release from jail from me. My trust in him wavered because of it.

I was happy that my other dinner partner was Paul Laurence Dunbar.

Paul sipped his soup. "Thank you for getting this invitation for me, Katharine."

"You are a great family friend," I said. "Of course, I would ask the Meachams to invite you."

"They appear to be good people. Mrs. Meacham in particular has been so sweet and kind to me. She's introduced me to her other guests and made sure I had a drink right away."

"They are the very best," I assured him. "And there is no kinder soul on this planet than Margaret."

He smiled. "If I had enough money to stow away in a bank, I would certainly consider Mr. Meacham's financial establishment. Good, trustworthy people are difficult to find, especially here at the fair. However, with much of my family to care for, I don't have much income left over from my poems. Even so, to make a living off of my words is a true gift, and not one I take for granted."

"I will tell him that you said that. I know that he will like that very much, and Meacham is very understanding about people's finances."

On my other side, I could hear Beard speaking to another man across the table.

"I truly believe that the next step in innovation will be lighter metals," Beard said.

"If metals are lighter will they be strong enough to withstand heat and weight?" the man asked.

"That's the question," Beard agreed. "And my company is working on answering that. Of course, we won't release our new materials until they are thoroughly tested."

"Aren't you from Cleveland? Do you want to run the steel mills there into the ground?" the man across the table asked.

"Not at all. I want to diversify what we already have. Steel is not going anywhere. There are too many ways that it is essential in buildings, especially for structural integrity, but what about flight? Is that not the big event happening at the exposition? The aeronautics competition. The issue with flying, or should I say, one of the main issues with flying, is and always will be weight. Weight holds back lift. My company is working on a metal that will lighten flying machines of all types so that lifting off the ground and staying aloft is that much more successful. I am even working on a flying machine myself."

I glanced around the room and spotted Camilla refilling glasses of water. She was clearly listening to the steel man's every word.

"A flying machine?" Another man scoffed. "Aren't there enough intelligent men wasting their time and talents on such fanciful endeavors? There are enough problems on the ground that we don't need to complicate them by going into the air."

"I disagree," Beard said, and reached into his jacket pocket and pulled out a folded piece of paper. "I have the plans right here, and I am telling you, with my lighter metal it will be able to traverse the world."

The man across from him snorted in disbelief, but when Beard held the paper out to him, he opened it and looked at the plans.

Camilla stepped behind the man and made like she was refilling his glass as well, but as she looked at the plans in his hands, her face paled.

"Ladies and gentlemen, the Ferris wheel is coming to the bottom, and there may be just a bit of a lurch when it stops. I just want to tell you, so that you're not alarmed. And if anyone needs to get off this time, they are more than welcome to."

The Ferris wheel came to the rocky stop as Meacham predicted. The attendant at the bottom of the Ferris wheel opened the door. "Would anyone like to step out?"

No one moved.

"Very well," he said and closed the door. The Ferris wheel started to move again.

Camilla grabbed the plans from the man's hand and ran to the door. She threw the door open and jumped out, landing six feet below.

Everyone at the table stood up and started shouting all at once. Beard threw back his chair and ran to the door, but the Ferris wheel was too high now to jump safely. He swore. "She stole my plans!"

I went to the window. Camilla ran to the Pike.

CHAPTER 34

The minutes that the Ferris wheel was making its loop around the giant circle were tense. People whispered to each other, and Beard paced by the door. Slowly, ever so slowly, the carriage traveled up the Ferris wheel and then back down again.

When it finally came to the ground, the attendant opened the door and Beard and a few other men got off. Meacham was stricken.

I patted Margaret's arm. "I'll find out what happened." I stepped off the Ferris wheel too before she could argue with me about leaving.

Outside the Ferris wheel carriage, the air was heavy and damp. I pulled at the tight collar of my blouse, wishing I could unbutton it. However, I was far too prim and proper to do that. My skirt stuck to my sweaty legs so much, I continually had to pull the fabric from my skin to avoid tripping over myself.

In the summers, Dayton could be very hot, but it was nothing like St. Louis. I felt like I was making my way through a cloud of steam, and my face surely was as red as a crayfish that had been dropped in a boiling pot.

Despite my discomfort, I kept going. Camilla had gone to

the Pike, and I suspected that I knew exactly where she was headed. The best place she could hide: the Temple of Mirth.

I had to reach her before Beard did. I was almost certain those flying machine plans Beard was showing at the table were Camilla's, and they might be the very reason her sister was killed. Sylvia had said *aeronautics competition* with her dying breath. She was telling me why she had been stabbed.

I didn't know if it meant that Beard was the killer. How could he be, if he was about to give a lecture on the other side of the fair when Sylvia was stabbed?

As I entered the Pike, laughter and shouts filled the air from the rides and games throughout the fair. Even at night, the Louisiana Purchase Exposition vibrated with energy.

I looked every which way. I was an early to bed, early to rise woman. I certainly wasn't a person that would find amusement after dark at the fair. Typically, by this time of night I was tucked into bed with a book, or maybe two, depending on how good the first one was.

To my surprise, Zeb Dandy was not in front of the Temple of Mirth. In fact, there was no one there to sell tickets. A group of young people appeared to be disappointed that they could not enter the amusement, but their female companions appeared more than relieved.

I stood a few feet away and waited for them to leave. When they did, I walked casually toward the door and prayed it was unlocked.

I had just reached the door when I heard a whooshing sound, and Achilles landed on my shoulder.

I looked over at the large blue bird. "Are you going to help me with this?"

He bobbed his head up and down.

I stepped into the fun house.

To my relief, the jack-in-the-box was already deployed and hung limply out of the side of his box. Perhaps he never really recovered from the wallop I had given him with Margaret's parasol.

"Do you know your way around here?" I asked the parrot.

He hopped from my shoulder and knocked his beak on a plain black wall. The next thing I knew the door opened and we were in the hall of mirrors.

All I could see in all directions around me was Achilles's and my reflections, but I could hear arguing.

"You're the reason my sister is dead. I thought it was you," I heard Camilla shout. "I kept talking myself out of the fact that it was you, but I knew it in my heart, Hal. You have wanted these plans to sell to Beard for weeks. You had already ripped them from my notebook. Why keep trying to take the notebook again, when you already had the most valuable part?"

"Because I needed more. I was told there had to be more. You have to give the plans to me. We can split the money, I promise," Hal said.

My breath caught. Even though I couldn't see Camilla and Hal, I didn't know if, in this unpredictable place, they could see me.

I ducked down low.

Achilles cocked his head at me and then hopped across the room. He tapped his beak three times on one of the mirrors, and a space just big enough for me to pass through opened. The parrot went into the void, and I didn't have much choice but to follow him. I was trusting that he knew what he was doing. It seemed to me that he had been trained to guide people through the fun house.

We were at one end of the barrel of love and Camilla and Hal were at the other. The barrel was off, but I didn't trust it would stay that way. I kept my distance from it.

Camilla stood poised on the balls of her feet as if she was about to bolt.

Hal stood across from her in tears. "It wasn't me."

"You were there. Charles saw you there. He told me," she snapped.

"I was there, yes, but I wasn't alone.

Achilles grabbed the edge of my skirt and pulled me away from the barrel.

"What?" I whispered as I followed him behind a partition.

A moment later the door that Achilles and I had come through opened, and Zeb Dandy stepped through.

I stifled a gasp. In the garish yellow electric light, his clown makeup looked even more frightening.

He stepped into the barrel and began to walk toward Hal and Camilla. "Hal, my boy, it seems that you have been found out. This is most inconvenient for us."

"I found him out," she snapped. "He killed my sister."

"Now, Sylvia, or should I say, *Camilla*," Zeb said, "don't put that on Hal, when I was the one who did it. She saw Hal stab the balloon. The silly girl even tried to stop him. She kicked the ladder out from under his feet and stole his knife. We couldn't have that. Thankfully, I was able to catch up with her and remedy the situation."

Camilla lunged at him, but Hal caught her and pulled her back.

"You monster," she spat.

Zeb laughed. "I have been called worse."

"You did all of this because you wanted what?"

"My girl, what do you think a man like me wants?" He looked at his white-painted nails like he was bored. "It was money, of course. Hal and I were being paid a nice tidy sum to do a job. Our benefactor didn't want Santos-Dumont to be successful in flight. He needed the one-hundred-thousand-dollar prize to be there when his flying machine was ready in a few months' time."

She shook Hal away from her. He did not fight to keep

hold of her when it was clear that he could have over-powered her if he wished. He was twice her size.

"It was for Beard, wasn't it?" Camilla said and turned to Hal. "And you stole *my* plans for *my* flying machine to sell to him, so he could build it and win the competition."

"He certainly can pay a pretty penny," Zeb said.

Achilles hopped over to the lever, and I knew what he was telling me to do. Zeb was still inside the barrel of love while talking to Hal and Camilla.

I pulled down on the lever with all my strength and the machine came to life. Zeb cried out as he lost his footing and flew into the air.

Achilles flew through the spinning barrel, but I couldn't do that, and I knew the only way out was through the barrel.

My only choice was to run through while Zeb tumbled about.

I lifted my skirt and counted out the spin, and then I made a dash for it. I leapt over Zeb who was being flipped head over heels. How I wished I had Margaret's parasol to smack him with as I ran by.

When I was on the other side, Camilla and Hal stared at me as if they had never seen a person like me in their lives, and maybe they hadn't.

"Camilla, let's go," I said to the girl.

Achilles already perched near the open exit door.

She turned to Hal. "I trusted you. You were my friend, but now I know that money is more important to you than friendship."

"I didn't kill Sylvia. You have to believe me."

"I do. I know it was Zeb," she said, looking him in the eye. "But it's still as much your fault as his that she is dead." With that, Camilla walked out the door.

I was right behind her, and as we came out into the light, I ran into her back. Why had she stopped?

It only took a second for the answer to my question to be clear. Beard stood at the exit, holding a small pistol pointed at Camilla's chest.

I heard the barrel of love behind me come to a halt, and Zeb's moaning. He shouted curses at Hal. Camilla and I couldn't go back inside. We were stuck between a rock and a hard place.

Just when I believed that we were done for, Achilles flew over my head. His talons were out, and they were aimed right at Beard. The steel man screamed as the parrot scratched his face. The gun flew from his hand. I ran to it and scooped it up.

"Secure the door," I yelled at Camilla.

She picked up a scrap of wood from the pile behind the building and shoved it into the door handle so that it could not open.

I pointed the pistol at Beard. "Don't move." Over my shoulder, I told Camilla, "Go find the police."

EPILOGUE

Two weeks later, I was at the train station saying good-bye to my old and new friends. I had spent longer than I expected to in St. Louis, as Margaret's illness had come back with a vengeance. She told me not to worry, but I could not help but fear for Margaret. She was my greatest friend.

Meacham held her about the waist as they stood on the platform with me as I was about to board the train. He looked more relaxed than I had ever seen him, and that was because he had been able to secure two large accounts from the ill-fated dinner party on the Ferris wheel. They were both from foreign investors who thought Camilla's and my antics of running from the Ferris wheel were an American version of dinner theater for their entertainment, and Meacham and Margaret had the good sense to play that up.

I held Meacham's hand. "Please take care of her. She's precious."

He squeezed my hand. "I know she is, and I promise you I will."

Margaret was pale, but she was not too sick to abstain from making a comment on our melodrama. "Good heavens, the two of you. I will be fine. Meacham and I head back to Chicago in a week's time, and the doctors there will know what to do." She looked up at her husband. "As long as we are together, all will be well."

Meacham beamed at his wife.

I gave her a big hug. "I love you, my dearest."

"And I love you," she said in return.

Harry Haskell stepped forward. "I can't thank you enough for giving me the scoop on your detective work here at the fair. My editor is quite pleased and said that I might even be up for a promotion." He grinned. "I have you to thank for that. I always admired you, Katharine. You are one of the most intelligent people that I know."

I arched my brow at him. "Not one of the most intelligent *women*?"

"People," he said. "I was just telling Isabella in a letter how you unraveled this entire scheme. She was mighty impressed too."

"Please give her my regards," I said.

The train whistled.

"That's my cue," I said.

And just as I was about to climb onto the train, a slight figure with black hair ran through the steam pouring out of the engines, just as she had the day that I arrived.

Behind her, a large blue bird flew through the air.

"Katharine! Wait!" Camilla yelled.

This time, instead of pushing me aside, she was looking for me.

She reached me and crushed me in an embrace. "Thank you."

Achilles landed on her shoulder as she pulled away and squawked his own version of thanks. Or at least, I thought that was what he was trying to say.

"Don't give up on your flying machine," I said.

"I won't. And over the last few weeks my attention has been on the loss of my sister. Sylvia is now laid to rest. She would want me to carry on."

"She would," I said.

She hung her head. "I wish I could have done more for Sylvia. She didn't deserve what happened to her. And what happened to her was because of me. I should have been the one there. It's something I will have to live with. Right now, I don't know if I can."

"You can, because that is what she would have wanted for you. Sylvia would want you to go on."

She nodded. "I will remind myself of that every day."

The train whistled. "Eastbound train for all aboard," the conductor yelled.

She gave me one last hug. "I admire what your brothers have done. They are geniuses and will change the world, but I believe you are and will too. The way that women change the world is with one dogged step forward at a time, and with compassion. That is just as powerful as anything your brothers ever do."

Tears came to my eyes, and I couldn't speak.

"Last call!" the conductor bellowed behind me.

"Katharine, you should get on or you will miss the train." Margaret wrung her hands.

I nodded and hopped on the train. As it began to roll away, Achilles took off and followed me to the very end of the station, where he finally turned around and flew back to Camilla for good.

AUTHOR NOTE

The Louisiana Purchase Exposition, more commonly known as the 1904 World's Fair, showcased the very best and the very worst of life at the turn of the twentieth century. It had great displays of human invention and ingenuity. For the first time people from all over the world saw flying machines, motorcars, and machinery of all types. Also, the 1904 Olympics were held at the fair.

In June 1904, Katharine Wright traveled to the 1904 World's Fair alone to be with her closest friend from Oberlin College, Margaret Meacham. Katharine was to keep Margaret company seeing the sights, while Margaret's husband, W. C. Meacham, conducted business at the fair. While at the fair, Margaret became very ill with a digestive issue. Although it was never proven, it is believed she became sick from something she ate at the fair. Because of this, she had stomach ailments the rest of her life and never truly recovered. She eventually died from her condition a few short years later. Katharine was heartbroken and endowed a scholarship for literature students at Oberlin College in her friend's name.

Paul Laurence Dunbar was one of the first influential Black poets in American literature and grew up with the Wrights.

He and Orville went to high school together and remained friends. In fact, when Wilbur and Orville had a printing press, they published Dunbar's newspaper for the Black community in Dayton, Ohio. In truth, Dunbar was not at the fair at the same time that Katharine was, but as he was such an influential writer and person in the Wrights' lives, I took the liberty to add him to this novel and share his valuable perspective on the fair with Katharine.

However, Brazilian aviator Alberto Santos-Dumont, who arrived to much fanfare because it was believed that he would win the aeronautics competition at the fair, was there at the same time Katharine was. The cash prize for success in the competition was one hundred thousand dollars.

His first morning at the fair, Santos-Dumont found that the balloon of his airship had been stabbed a total of eight times with so much force that it made forty-eight slashes into the balloon. The crime was blamed on a man, Charles F. Morrison, who loitered around the hangars on the concourse, but Morrison was later cleared and released. The crime was never solved, and Santos-Dumont refused to allow the fair officials to have the balloon mended. He returned to his adopted home of Paris without taking flight, much to the frustration of the fair officials and the public.

Sadly, the amusements that Katharine and Margaret enjoyed were in stark contrast to what else was happening at the fair.

The organizers wanted to focus on cultures of the world, and many countries sponsored their own exhibits and showed their culture as they wished. Unfortunately for developing countries and regions of the world, the fair made the decisions on how they would be exhibited. Native Americans, other indigenous groups, Filipinos, and Africans were all on display as curiosities for the predominately white audiences to view.

The "human zoo" at the 1904 World's Fair is not the focus of this novel, as the focus of the mystery is aviation. However, I felt it would be irresponsible to not include this atrocity in some capacity. If I made any mistakes along the way, those are mine and mine alone.